TOUCHY AND FEELY

Recent Titles by Graham Masterton available from Severn House

The Sissy Sawyer Series

TOUCHY AND FEELY

The Jim Rook Series

ROOK

THE TERROR

TOOTH AND CLAW

SNOWMAN

SWIMMER

DARKROOM

Anthologies

FACES OF FEAR

FEELINGS OF FEAR

FORTNIGHT OF FEAR

FLIGHTS OF FEAR

Novels

DOORKEEPERS

GENIUS

HIDDEN WORLD

HOLY TERROR

MANITOU BLOOD

TOUCHY AND FEELY

Graham Masterton

This first world edition published in Great Britain 2006 by
SEVERN HOUSE PUBLISHERS LTD of
9–15 High Street, Sutton, Surrey SM1 1DF.
This first world edition published in the USA 2006 by
SEVERN HOUSE PUBLISHERS INC of
595 Madison Avenue, New York, N.Y. 10022.

British Library Cataloguing in Publication Data

Masterton,   Graham
    Touchy and feely
    1.   Psychics - Connecticut - Fiction
    2.   Occultism and criminal investigation - Fiction
    3.   Detective and mystery stories
    I.   Title
    823.9'14 [F]

    ISBN-10: 0-7278-6332-0   (cased)
                    0-7278-9160-X   (trade paper)

Typeset by Palimpsest Book Production Ltd.,
Polmont, Stirlingshire, Scotland.
Printed and bound in Great Britain by
MPG Books Ltd., Bodmin, Cornwall.

'And the way up is the way down, the way forward is the way back.'

T.S. Eliot, 'The Dry Salvages'

Two Storms Coming

Sissy stepped out into the yard and lit her first cigarette for two days. She was trying to quit, but while she was waiting for Mina Jessop to show up she had read her own fortune and the cards had given her a warning that she had never seen before.

Two storms coming, both at once.

Mr Boots her black Labrador jostled past her and bounded out onto the grass. He lifted his leg against the leafless cherry tree, and shook himself, and then he stood still, listening, looking around. Occasionally he glanced toward Sissy, as if he expected her to explain what was happening.

Her yard was sheltered by a steep slope and a stand of tall fir trees, but all around her she could hear the wind getting up, and the first few flakes of snow came whirling down and settled on her shawl. The wind was whispering and rustling everywhere, like ghosts in other rooms. She couldn't hear any traffic, or dogs barking. She felt as if she were the only person in Litchfield County left alive.

She drew deeply at her cigarette and blew out smoke through her nose. She didn't really enjoy smoking outside, but she was expecting Trevor to come around at four o'clock and she couldn't stand his disapproving sniffing.

Trevor disapproved of everything about her. He disapproved of her wild white hair, and the odd collection of art-nouveau pins she used to fasten it into a bun. He disapproved of her long black dresses and her lace-up boots and her layers of multicolored hand-knitted sweaters. He disapproved of her dangly silver earrings and all the silver necklaces she wore.

'You look like a fortune-teller, momma, from a traveling carnival,' he told her.

And yes, she supposed she did. But she *was* a fortune-teller.

1

She could read people's tea-leaves and see at once if they were going to be happy. She could look at the palms of their hands, and see how well they were loved. She could sometimes coax a ouija board into giving her a garbled message from beyond, A JNE WEDNIG. Her specialty, though, was the DeVane cards, a rare pack printed in France in the eighteenth century, almost twice the size of the Tarot, more like table mats than playing cards. They were called 'The Cards of Love,' and when she was laying them out, Sissy could almost *taste* the various sweetnesses of human affection. As sickly as syrup, sometimes; or tinged with bitterness, like blood.

Occasionally, however, the DeVane cards predicted that something bad was going to happen. They could warn you if your illicit love affair was about to be blighted by an unexpected diagnosis of cancer; or if you might be paralyzed in a car-wreck, or ski slap-bang into a tree. They could tell you if your friends were saying vicious things about you, behind your back, or if your husband was making love to a girl who was barely out of orthodontic braces.

This afternoon, when she had laid out her cards on the coffee table, Sissy had turned up two Predictor cards. On the first card, two men in gray topcoats were sheltering from a downpour under a monstrous black umbrella. On the second, a man and a boy were walking hand-in-hand across a snowy cemetery, with the snow still falling on the headstones. The boy's face was as pale as a moonlit window.

The right-hand Predictor was supposed to foretell the *worst* that could happen, while the left-hand Predictor was supposed to foretell the *best*. Usually, when a storm card came up, a sunny card came up, too; or at least a promise of settled weather.

Sissy had never turned up two storm cards together, not like this, and she couldn't tell exactly what this meant, except that there was serious trouble coming, of one kind or another, and that there was no escaping it.

'What's happening, Mr Boots?' she asked, out loud. Mr Boots made a curdled noise, deep in his throat. 'The cards said two storms coming, both at once. What do you make of that?'

2

She finished her Marlboro, right down to the tip, and then she crushed it out in the geranium pot next to the back door, pushing it right below the surface of the soil so that Trevor wouldn't see it.

'Come on, Mister,' she said, and went back into the kitchen, where it was warm, and filled up the kettle.

A Potential Catastrophe

As they passed Cannondale, Howard glanced down at the gas gauge and saw that the needle had crept below half full. 'Shit. I'll have to stop for gas.'

Sylvia was frowning at her roots in the illuminated vanity mirror. 'For God's sake, Howard. Can't you fill up on your way to the office tomorrow?'

'It won't take long. There's a gas station right up ahead.'

'Howard, I need to get home. My chicken is going to be pot-roasted to rags.'

But through the grayish-green three o'clock gloom, Howard had already fixed his eyes on the yellow Sunoco sign in the middle distance. 'If you're worried about your chicken, call Lisa and have her switch the oven off.'

'Just because your father had a fetish about never letting your gas tank go below half.'

'It's not a *fetish*, Sylvia. It's common sense. Look at that sky, for Pete's sake! Is that impending snow or is that impending snow? Supposing we get stranded all night. How do you think we're going to stay warm?'

'Howard, it's less than forty minutes home. There isn't going to be a blizzard between then and now.'

Howard went deaf. That was Howard's response to anything he didn't agree with. He wasn't an argumentative man, but things had to be done a certain way. Life was a series of potential catastrophes and if you didn't take sensible precautions then one or more of those catastrophes would happen to you. He never tired of coming into the kitchen when Sylvia was cooking and reading out loud from the *News-Times* about avoidable accidents.

'A 53-year-old Sherman man broke his back when he fell off the roof of his house while clearing leaves from the gutter.

George Goodman will be confined to a wheelchair for the rest of his life. His wife Mrs Martha Goodman blamed an unsecured ladder.'

Howard had let out a '*Hah!*' of incredulity. 'She blames the *ladder*? A ladder is an inanimate object. A ladder can't see that an accident is waiting to happen. Why doesn't she blame the idiot who climbed up it without making sure that he asked a friend to hold it for him?'

Sylvia, cutting out pastry rose petals for the top of her apple pie, had said, 'Don't you think the poor man has been punished enough?'

Howard checked his rear-view mirror, flicked his right-turn signal and slowed down. A red Datsun had been following them all the way from Norwalk, much too close for Howard's liking, considering the slippery road conditions, and Howard wanted to make sure that the Datsun's driver was fully aware that he (Howard Stanton) was pulling off the highway.

'I don't know why that A-hole didn't ask me for a tow.' This was Howard's response to anyone whom he considered to be tailgating.

He pulled into the gas station, stopped, and switched off the engine. Sylvia twisted herself around to look at the wicker basket on the back seat. 'It sounds like he's asleep,' she smiled.

'Well, don't wake him up. I couldn't stand any more of that pathetic whining.'

'Let me just check that he's OK.'

'Of course he's OK.' Howard opened the storage box in the center arm-rest and took out a brown wooly bobble-hat and a pair of brown wooly gloves. He pulled the hat on and tugged it down low. He always thought it made him look like Richard Dreyfuss in *Jaws*. Sylvia secretly thought that it made him look like Bert, from *Sesame Street*.

While Howard was fastidiously tugging on his gloves, finger by finger, she unfastened the basket, lifted the lid and peeked inside. There, fast asleep on a folded-up tartan shawl, was a glossy black Labrador puppy, only just old enough to be separated from his mother.

'Suzie's going to love him to pieces.'

'I don't know. He's a little snappy, don't you think? I just

5

hope he doesn't have behavioral problems. I'm not sure we shouldn't have gone for the bitch.'

'Oh, Howard, he's adorable.'

Howard opened the Explorer's door and climbed out. It was breathtakingly cold outside, and there was a ragged crosswind blowing from the north-north-west. He unscrewed the gas cap and started to fill up the tank.

The A & J Gas Station was situated on Route 7 at the Branchville intersection. Now that it was growing dark, the road was almost empty, except for an occasional thundering truck laden with Christmas trees. On the opposite side of the road stood a boarded-up hut that looked as if it had once been a grill and diner, with a rusty old pickup outside it, supported on bricks, and a dirty bronze Chevy Caprice parked at the side. Beyond the hut there was nothing but woods.

The gas station was brightly lit and Howard could see the cashier behind the counter, his chair tilted back, his sneakers on the counter, watching television. Howard deplored self-service. Why should the cashier sit in the warm, doing nothing at all, while the customer had to shiver out here in the wind, and end up with his hands reeking of gas? The pump was slow, too, which irritated him even more.

Sylvia knocked on her window, and waved to him. He gave her a quick grimace but didn't wave back. There was a fine rain flying in the wind and he was sure that it was cold enough to snow.

The Garden of Love

'He loves you,' said Sissy, holding up the Garden card. 'No question about it, the fellow's besotted.'

'Are you sure?' asked Mina. 'I'm so worried that I'm going to make a fool of myself.'

Sissy shook her head. 'My dear, I can feel the radiance of genuine love through a foot-thick cinderblock wall. It's my talent. It may be my *only* talent, but I've never been wrong yet.'

'You make delicious cookies,' said Mina, who had eaten five of them, and kept glancing at the remaining two, as if they were going to try to make a run for it. '*That's* a talent.'

'Store-bought. I can't bake. Gerry used to say that my cooking timer was the smoke alarm.'

Mina sat back on the worn brown velvet couch. She was small, but her head looked too big for her body, and her hips said 'consolation eating.' 'I never thought that Merritt would ever *notice* me, let alone love me.'

'You should give yourself more credit. Look at you, you're only thirty-one years old, you're petite, you're pretty. Your hair's a mess but that won't take much sorting.'

Mina tugged at her choppy blonde hair. 'I saw it in *Complete Woman*.'

'Don't ever try to copy anything from a women's magazine, my dear, especially hairstyles and sexual positions. The people who produce women's magazines are only trying to make you feel inadequate. That's their job. Would you ever buy a women's magazine if you didn't feel inadequate? Of course not.'

'I've known Merritt ever since junior high,' said Mina. 'I used to see him standing by the running-track, you know. His hair was so curly and the sun used to shine in his curls, and I used to think that he was a *god*.'

'He's a man, Mina, just like any other. He makes mistakes,

7

he tells lies, he scratches his ass. But for all of that, he loves you.'

'And that's definitely what this card means?'

Sissy handed Mina the card so that she could examine it more closely. It showed a formal garden, under a cloudless sky, where roses bloomed, and pears ripened on espaliers. In the center of this garden sat a woman in a powdered wig and a crinoline and a tight lace bodice; yet bare-breasted. Close beside her sat a young man, completely naked except for a tricorn hat. Butterflies formed a cloud around their heads.

'Le Jardin d'Amour,' said Sissy. 'This card never comes up unless you're in love, and the person you love loves you.'

Mina kept chewing at her lower lip. She seemed reluctant to believe that the cards weren't playing a trick on her.

Suddenly she blurted out, 'It was such a chance meeting, you know. We hadn't seen each other in maybe ten years. But there he was, walking across the square, and I recognized him right away, even if he didn't recognize me. If our dogs hadn't stopped to have a sniff at each other, and their leads hadn't gotten tangled up—well, he would have walked right past me and not even known it was me.'

'Well, funnier things have happened.'

Mina lowered her eyes. 'Last night he took me to dinner at Oakwood's. He bought me strawberries and he said that I was special.'

'He didn't actually say, "I love you"?'

'No,' said Mina. 'Not those actual words.'

'That doesn't matter,' Sissy told her, slowly reshuffling the cards. It was early afternoon but her living room was so gloomy that she could hardly see Mina's face; only two reflected ovals from her glasses. 'The cards know when a man desires you, even if he won't admit it. And when the cards know, believe me, then *I* know.'

There was a very long silence between them. Mina took out her purse and frowned into it as if she couldn't remember what she was supposed to do next.

After another long silence, Sissy said, 'Twenty-five dollars should cover it, my dear.'

The Fatal Moment

At last the tank was full and Howard snapped shut the filler-cap cover and went inside to pay. On his way to the counter he picked up two Reese Sticks, a snack pack of Oreos and some peanut-flavored Cookie Dough. Sylvia had him on a diet but he always craved candy to eat while he was driving to work. How was he expected to face a stressful day at the office on nothing but two cups of milkless tea and a bowl of horse food?

'Pump number?' asked the cashier, without taking his eyes off the television.

'I didn't look, I'm sorry. But I'm your only customer. Maybe you could *guess*?'

The cashier was about eighteen years old. He had a large mooselike nose and greasy brown curls and a cluster of raging red spots on his face. He was gnawing a yellow-and-blue Sunoco ballpen. With his eyes still fixed on the television, he swiped Howard's card, tore off the paper receipt, and tossed the pen across the counter.

'Wanna sign that?' he said.

Howard stared at the pen and didn't move. After more than ten seconds had elapsed, the cashier turned at last to look at him. 'You wanna—?' he repeated, making a signing gesture, as if Howard were retarded.

'No,' said Howard. 'Not with that pen, anyhow.'

The cashier blinked at him. 'What's the matter, man? That one writes good.'

'I don't care. It's been in your mouth and I don't want to touch it.'

The cashier abruptly jolted his chair into the upright position. 'You're trying to say *what*, man? I have anthrax or something?'

'I want a clean pen, that's all, without any of your saliva on it.'

'Oh, excuse *me*.'

'Apology accepted. But if you want my John Hancock, you'll have to find me a clean pen to write it with.'

The cashier pulled open a drawer and rummaged through an assortment of string and screwdrivers and Doublemint wrappers and cash-register rolls. Eventually he had to climb off his chair, walk to the back of the store, and come back with a new pen from the stationery display. Howard signed the check and handed the pen back.

'Freak,' said the cashier, boldly. He had disturbingly near-together eyes, as if he was three generations inbred.

Howard said nothing. He stowed his candy bars into the pockets of his red weatherproof squall and carefully fastened the studs.

Silence always gives you the edge, that's what Howard believed, especially when you're dealing with people of limited intelligence. Make them feel that you know far more about the world than they do. That will cut the turf from under their feet, far more effectively than anything you could say to them. And silence can never be misquoted.

He pushed his way through the door and out into the wind. He had been right about the snow: it was starting to tumble across the highway thicker and faster. Halfway back to his car, he looked back. The cashier was still standing at the window, staring at him with such beady-eyed hostility that he couldn't help smiling in private triumph. *Silence, that's the answer. Don't give the bastards a chance to talk back.*

It was then that he was hit in the right side of the forehead with a .308 bullet traveling at more than 2,500 feet per second. His brains geysered out of his brown wooly hat and he was thrown sideways and backward, hitting his left shoulder against the concrete. His legs and his right arm flew up into the air and then he lay still.

There was a very long silence. The snow prickled onto his coat, and immediately melted. His blood, made more gelid by the cold, crept along the cracks between the concrete forms, southward, and then began to slide westward.

The Explorer's passenger door opened, and Sylvia screamed out, 'Howard! *Howard!*'

Feely Heads North

Feely had only $21.76 left which meant that his options were now limited to three.

1) Buy a bus ticket home.

2) Buy something to eat and try to hitch a ride home.

3) Save his money and stand on this corner until he froze into a municipal statue.

It was snowing so furiously that he could hardly see the other side of the street. He was sheltering under the awning of Billy Bean's Diner in his thin brown windbreaker, his hands thrust deep into his pockets. It was 3:47 in the afternoon but it could just as well have been the middle of the night. Snow-covered automobiles rolled past like traveling igloos.

Feely was three days past his nineteenth birthday—a thin, sallow-skinned boy with the big liquid eyes of a Latin romeo, with lashes to match, and a broken nose. His curly black hair was covered by a purple knitted cap, with ear-flaps, the kind worn by Peruvian peasants. He had no travel-bag with him, only a battered green cardboard folder tucked under his arm, and no gloves.

Without him hearing it, a police car drew into the slush-filled gutter beside him. As soon as he saw it, he did a little defensive dance sideways. But the police car's window came down and he heard a penetrating whistle.

'Hey, you! Yes, you! Baron von Richthofen!'

Feely looked around but of course there was nobody else standing outside the diner, only him.

'Me?'

'C'mere, kid.'

Feely approached the squad car and bent down, shivering. He could feel the warmth pouring out of the window. In the passenger seat sat a bulky police sergeant with prickly white

11

hair and a bright pink face like a canned ham. Next to him, the driver looked creepy and boggle-eyed and smirky, a distant cousin of the Addams family.

'What you doing, kid?' the sergeant demanded.

'I was, like, reading the menu.'

'No, you weren't, kid. Not unless you have eyes in the back of that stupid hat.'

'What I mean is I read it already, and I was cogitating.'

'Cogitating, huh? You hear that, Dean? He was *cogitating.* Didn't you know that cogitating in public is a misdemeanor here, in Danbury?'

'No, sir, I wasn't aware of that.' Feely knew better than to get smart with cops.

'Let me see some ID.'

Feely reached into the back pocket of his jeans and produced his library card. The sergeant took it and turned it over and even, for some reason, sniffed it, as if it might have traces of cocaine on it.

'This all the ID you got?'

'Yes, sir.'

'Thirteen-thirteen, East 111th Street, New York City. You're a long way from home, kid.'

'Yes, sir.'

'Mind telling me what you're doing here?'

Feely's eyes darted from side to side. The sergeant had asked him a legitimate question, no doubt about that, but he couldn't immediately think of an answer that wouldn't sound either insolent or weird. He was here because it was anyplace but home, but he could just as easily have taken the bus to Jersey, or upstate New York, so there was no easy response, and he didn't want to say anything provocative like 'serendipity.' So he shrugged, and sniffed, and said, 'I guess I'm chilling out, that's all.'

'Got any money?' the sergeant asked him.

Feely reached into his pocket and pulled out three crumpled fives and change. The sergeant counted it with his eyes and then looked up at Feely with an expression that was part pity and part irritation.

'Seeing how it's Christmas, and I'm full of seasonal bonhommy, I'm going to let you go about your business. But if I see you hanging around here again, I'm going to haul you in on suspicion of being a waste of space.'

'Yes, sir.'

'And quit that cogitating.'

'Yes, sir.'

The sergeant closed his window and the police car drove off. Feely was left on the sidewalk feeling even more isolated than ever. He wondered what Captain Lingo would have replied. *'A waste of space? Space, my friend, is a limitless extent and therefore cannot by definition be wasted.'* But Captain Lingo would have come out with it there and then, right to the sergeant's ham-pink face, not when the squad car was two-and-a-half blocks away, and its brake lights were barely visible through the snow.

All the same, the sergeant had made a decision for him. He couldn't stay out on the sidewalk without being collared, so he would have to go inside; and if he went inside, he would have to order something to eat.

Hold the Beans

Feely pushed his way in through the door of Billy Bean's Diner. It was warm inside, paneled with light-varnished oak, and the tables were covered with red-and-white checkered cloths. He sat down at a table in the corner, by the coatrack, the most inconspicuous seat he could find, and picked up the plastic-laminated menu. The ceiling was hung with twinkling fairy-lights and a tape was playing 'Santa Claus is Coming To Town.'

A middle-aged waitress came bustling up to him. She had frizzy black hair knotted in a red gingham ribbon, and a large brown mole on her upper lip, although she must have been reasonably cute in another life. 'How are you doing, sugar?'

'I'm glacified.'

'You're what?'

Feely pointed to the menu. 'I'll have a cup of hot chocolate, please. And a cheeseburger.'

'Well, I can do you Billy Bean's Beanfeast Burger for seven seventy-five. That includes two quarter-pound burger patties, with cheese, bacon, tomato and beans as well as a double portion of freedom fries and unlimited relish.'

'OK, that sounds like a shrewd choice. But can you hold the beans, please.'

She blinked at him. 'It's Billy Bean's Beanfeast Burger, honey. It *comes* with beans.'

Feely didn't know what to say. He had always suspected that there was a conspiracy against him—that everybody was working together to confuse him, and to make him feel that he was unhinged. But he hadn't realized that the conspiracy had reached as far as Connecticut.

You ask for something. They tempt you with a better deal, like Billy Bean's Beanfeast Burger at only $7.75. But that's

14

how they trick you into accepting something that you seriously don't want, and Feely seriously didn't want beans.

Feely seriously didn't want beans because beans reminded him of his older brother Jesus, in the weeks before he OD'd. Jesus had lived off nothing but beans and smack, and every time he shot up he puked fountains of beans all over the apartment. *Fountains.* Two months after Jesus's funeral, they were still finding dried beans down the back of the couch-cushions.

'I'll just have the cheeseburger, thanks.'

'You know that comes with complimentary beans?'

While he was eating, the waitress came up to him and asked if he wanted another cup of hot chocolate. He swallowed before he was ready, and he had to smack his chest before he could speak.

'It's our winter special,' she encouraged him. 'Buy one hot chocolate, you get a second hot chocolate free.'

'OK, then. Thanks.'

Instead of bringing it, though, she stood by his table watching him, and after a while she said, 'You're running away, aren't you?'

'Me? No, ma'am.'

'You don't have any bags with you, do you? And your coat's so thin.'

Feely wiped his mouth with the back of his hand. 'I'm running, yes. You've assessed that correctly. But I'm not like running *away* from anything. I'm like running *toward* something, you know? I'm trying to catch up with my future.'

The waitress smiled sympathetically but it was obvious that she didn't understand; or that she simply didn't want to.

Feely used his finger to describe an endless circle on the tablecloth. 'I was like trapped in orbit. I was circling around and around and I was never getting anyplace. I broke free, that's all. I managed to reach escape velocity.'

'You ran away.'

Feely didn't try to correct her a second time. People who were involved in the conspiracy often tried to rationalize his behavior, and it wasn't worth the effort of contradicting them. They accused him of using complicated words to hide his real feelings, but that wasn't true either. He was seeking ways to express himself more precisely, so that he would have power over other people.

Language is power, that's what Father Arcimboldo had told him, in the sixth grade. Forget about fists. The right word can stop a man in his tracks. The right sentence can bring him down to his knees. What do you think has changed the world more, Fidelio? The atomic bomb, or the Bible?

And poor young bullied Feely, with his nose still bleeding and tears still drying on his cheeks, had nodded, and understood, and the following day he had stolen a dictionary from Book Mart and the day after that he had gone back and liberated a thesaurus.

Feely stayed in Billy Bean's Diner until the waitress came over and said, 'Kenny says you have to buy at least a muffin or else you'll have to leave.'

It was six minutes past five. Feely knew that he didn't have enough money to stay here any longer, buying muffins.

'Listen, there's the Dorothy Day Hospitality House on Main Street, if you really have noplace to go. They'll give you a bed for the night.'

'That's OK,' said Feely. 'I appreciate your concern but I mustn't lose my momentum.'

'No,' the waitress agreed. She studied him dubiously, as if she expected to see his momentum hanging around his neck on a string.

'How much do I owe you?'

The waitress glanced behind her, toward the counter, and then gave him a quick shake of her head.

'I have money,' said Feely. 'I don't expect charity.'

'It's Christmas. Well, it's nearly Christmas. One cheeseburger won't make Kenny go bankrupt.'

Feely stood up, and zipped up his windbreaker. 'Thanks,' he said. 'I hope one day that I can repay your abundant generosity a hundredfold.'

Unexpectedly, the waitress leaned over and kissed his cheek. 'Just onefold will do, sugar. Good luck.'

Tender is the North

Twenty-five minutes later he was standing out on Route 6, at the intersection with Tamarack Avenue, with his right thumb extended and his left hand lifted to shield his face from the wind. Behind him, the Wooster Cemetery was covered in whirling snow, so that the dead were buried even deeper, and the angels stood around in bizarre white party hats.

He felt warmer and a little more together for having eaten, and he believed that his encounter with the waitress had been a sign that he was doing the right thing, even though she had tried to cajole him into ordering beans. He still had his $21.76, and his destiny lay northward, although he didn't really know why. Bright and fierce and fickle is the South. Dark and true and tender is the North.

Trucks and SUVs sped past him, their headlights gleaming dimly through the snow, but none of them stopped. Maybe they couldn't see him, but he couldn't stand too close to the highway because every vehicle was spurting out filthy gray slush and he was soaked already. His flappy hat was sodden and there was melted snow leaking down the back of his neck. He tried his best to protect his folder but even that was getting buckled.

Mind telling me what you're doing here, kid? he asked himself. *You could be back home, where at least it's warm.*

But he could see the second-story apartment on 111th Street as clearly as if he had a miniature TV set in his head. The Christmas tree would be propped up, wrecked, in one corner, where his stepfather Bruno had pushed his mother into it. Bruno would be sprawled in his tilted three-legged armchair, already drunk, his greasy gray pompadour sticking up like a spavined cockatoo. His mother Rita would be lying in bed sobbing and praying and nursing her broken ribs, so there wouldn't be anything to eat, and the kitchen sink would be heaped with *estofada*-encrusted dishes from two days ago. There wouldn't be any sign of his younger brother Michael except for a dirty unmade bed with a sheet like the Indian rope-trick: Michael would be out with his crackhead friends in some derelict building smoking anything that could be made to smolder and drinking stolen tequila. His sister Rosa would be lying on her bed with one heavy leg raised in the air so that her crimson satin crotch was exposed, polishing her toenails purple and complaining loudly about her boyfriend Carlos he's such a dumb vomiticious dumbass. Rosa only knew three adjectives: dumb, vomiticious, and cool. Feely knew four thousand, seven hundred and eighty-three adjectives.

You didn't need travel-bags when you knew four thousand, seven hundred and eighty-three adjectives. But a warm pair of gloves would have been welcome.

Another semi bellowed past, with *Coca-Cola* emblazoned on the side of it, like the TV ads. Happy Christmas, thought Feely. What had happened to Santa and the shiny lights and the rosy-cheeked children? The snow was falling so furiously now that he couldn't see more than thirty yards down the highway.

Feely's favorite adjective was 'gregarious.' It brought to mind friendly people clustering around to give each other cheer. He said 'gregarious,' over and over, and out here on Route 6 it made him feel as if he wasn't entirely alone.

A Warning From Beyond

Trevor stepped into the hallway and sniffed twice. 'You've been *smoking!*'

'Have I?' said Sissy, in mock surprise. 'I can't smell anything.'

'Momma . . . really. I brought you some Chase's Cherry Mashes, too.'

'What? As a reward? I'm not a *dog*, Trevor, and if I want to smoke, I will.'

'Well, you shouldn't. You know darn well you shouldn't.' He handed her the bag of Cherry Mashes and took off his coat.

Sissy peered into the bag. 'These are just as bad for me as cigarettes. You should bring me fresh fruit if you're worried about my heart.'

Trevor followed her into the living room. He looked so much like his father, sloping-shouldered and plumpish, with chipmunk cheeks, but for some reason he hadn't inherited his father's geniality. When Gerry walked into a room, people used to smile, even before he had said hallo. But Trevor had a way of blinking at people that immediately made them feel uneasy, as if they had a fleck of spinach on their front tooth, or there was a drip swinging from the end of their nose.

He had never dressed as smartly as his father, either. Today he was wearing a sagging Hershey-brown cardigan with wooden buttons, and baggy tan corduroy pants. Gerry would have told him that he looked like a feedbag.

'How about some tea?' asked Sissy.

Trevor was blinking at the cards on the coffee table. 'You've been telling fortunes, too.'

'Don't worry, darling. You can't be affected by passive soothsaying.'

'All the same, Momma, it's not *healthy*, is it? Living out

here all on your own, smoking and fortune-telling and having conversations with dead people.'

Sissy gave a dismissive *pfff!* 'My cards are my *friends*. They talk to me, they tell me what's going to happen to me next. They're very comforting. Well, most of the time, anyway. At the moment, they're—' She paused. 'Well, I'm sure you're not at all interested. How's little Jake?'

'Jake? He's great. You'd hardly recognize him. He's cut two new teeth. Top ones.'

'I can't wait to see him again.'

'Yes,' said Trevor. He stood over the coffee table, looking down at the cards. 'As a matter of fact, that's the reason I've come up here to see you. I, ah—that is, Jean and me—we were wondering if you'd like to spend the holidays with us.'

'In New York, darling? I really don't think so.'

'Well, no, not New York. We've rented a house in Florida, just outside of St. Pete. It has three bedrooms, so there's plenty of space; and a pool, of course. The warm weather would do you so much good . . . and you could get to know Jake so much better.'

'You mean I could babysit, free of charge.'

Trevor vehemently shook his head. 'That's not it, Momma. I mean, of course you could babysit, if you wanted to. We'd *pay* you, for Christ's sake. But that's not the point. It's so frigging cold up here during the winter, and you're not getting any younger, and we worry about you.'

Sissy went through to the kitchen and lit the gas under the kettle. Trevor followed her and stood in the doorway, watching her.

'What?' said Sissy. 'I've celebrated Christmas in this house every year since 1969. And your father would have sent you to your room, if he had heard you say frigging.'

'I'm sorry, Momma, but you have to admit that you can't really manage any more. I mean, look at this place.'

'It's a little dusty, I'll admit. But what's a little dust?'

'Momma, it looks like nine-eleven.'

Sissy pursed her lips. 'Would you like some tea, or are you afraid that I might not have washed my cups properly?'

'Momma, it's time you thought about living someplace comfortable, where you wouldn't have to cook or do your own chores. Not only that—someplace where you wouldn't be alone, and you could have meaningful daily interaction with other people of your own generation.'

'Don't use that human-resource jargon on me, Trevor. You want me to move down to Florida and live in an old folks' home.'

'It's not an old folks' home at all. It's supervised accommodation for your dignity years.'

The kettle gargled, and belched, and then set up an ear-splitting whistle.

'My dignity years!' Sissy protested. 'What's dignified about sitting in a lounge all day with twenty other old relics in pale-blue leisure-suits, watching *Rugrats*?'

Trevor took the kettle off the hob. 'Momma, Jean and I are both deeply concerned. Anything could happen to you here, especially in winter. Supposing you fell and broke your hip, and you couldn't get in touch with anybody?'

'Mr Boots would go for help.'

'Mr Boots is as old as you are. You have to admit it, Momma, the time has come for you to leave New Preston behind.'

Sissy opened the tea caddy but when she tried to spoon the tea into the teapot, she found that her hand was shaking. She stopped, and took two deep breaths. This was the last thing she had expected this Christmas, but maybe Trevor was right. Maybe the year had come around at last.

'I'll, ah—I'll have to consider it,' she said.

'You don't have too long, Momma. We're leaving on the nineteenth.'

She put down the spoon. 'It's not just a question of what *I* want, Trevor. The cards have predicted that something very bad is going to happen.'

'The what? The *cards*?'

'Yes. I know you think that I'm nine parts doolally, but they've never been wrong yet. They told me six months before you proposed to Jean that you were going to meet an auburn-haired girl and marry her, and they told me that she really loves you. They also told me that your father was going to pass over, and *when*, almost to the day, even though I never told him, God rest his soul.'

'Momma, you can't let a pack of cards decide how you're going to live your life! It's insane!'

'You make your living out of insurance, don't you, and that's all odds and predictions.'

'The difference is that I use *statistics*, not magic.'

'Oh, yes? And *Exxon Valdez* to you, too.' Sissy took hold of his sleeve and pulled him back into the living room. 'Take a look at these two Predictor cards. Go on, look. I turned them up this afternoon.'

When Trevor wouldn't look, she picked up the card with the two men huddled under a large umbrella, and held it up to his nose. 'Les Deux Noyés,' she said. 'The Two Drowning Men. This card predicts sudden and unexpected death. The men are trying to shelter from the downpour, but it will do them no good.'

She held up the other card, of the man and the boy in the graveyard, in the snow. 'Les Visages Endeuillés. The Faces of Mourning. This card predicts that dozens of people are going to die. Dozens! As many people as snowflakes.'

Trevor gently took the cards from her and laid them back down on the coffee table. 'Momma, this is nothing but hocus-pocus.'

'You can say whatever you like, Trevor. But you mark what I'm telling you. Something terrible is going to happen round about here, very close by, and I could be the only one who's aware of it. How do you think I'd feel, if I was sunning myself in Florida, and I heard that people in Litchfield County were dying like flies?'

Trevor opened his mouth and then he closed it again without saying anything.

'You do understand, don't you?' said Sissy. 'My talent . . . it gives me a great responsibility, too.'

'So what exactly is going to happen?' Trevor demanded. 'An earthquake? A plane crash? A SARS epidemic?'

'I can't tell you, Trevor. Not yet. I'll have to read the cards again; and then *again*, probably. As this terrible thing comes closer—whatever it is—the cards will be able to give me much more detail.'

'Momma—even if you're right—what can you do about it? You're a sixty-seven-year-old woman with angina.'

'I don't suppose I can do anything much, my darling. But at least I won't have run away.'

22

The Ghost of Christmas Yet-to-Come

Steve walked across the filling-station forecourt with an awkward hobble. He had pulled on his boots too quickly and his right sock had bunched up under his instep. Doreen followed him, zipping up her coat. Two patrol troopers were already here, red-nosed and nervous, as well as four or five people who looked like passing motorists, and a pair of truckers, and a boy with a moose-like nose wearing a shiny blue Sunoco windbreaker.

The victim was lying on his back with his blood frozen in a zig-zag pattern aross the concrete. A light fleece of snow covered his chest, and snowflakes clung to his eyebrows. His eyes were still open and he looked vaguely mystified, as if he couldn't understand why he was unable to get up.

Steve looked down at him, and then circled around him, tilting his head one way, and then the other. He was a big man, six foot four, with wiry black hair and a rough-cast face, with deep-set eyes and a nose like a pug, but he moved with considerable delicacy, as if he were following waltz steps painted on the ground.

One of the troopers approached him, wiping his nose with the back of his glove. Steve took out his badge and held it in front of the trooper's face, too close for him to focus. 'I'm Detective Steven Wintergreen, in case you were wondering. This is Detective Doreen Rycerska.'

'Oh. Sure. I'm Trooper Baxter Patrick. And that's Trooper Willy Jones.' Both troopers looked about seventeen years old, with creamy boys' complexions and rosy cheeks. Baxter Patrick had gingery hair and Willy Jones had a little black mustache that must have taken him about six months of hard straining.

'Do we know exactly when this happened, Trooper?'

'Three-oh-seven. Willy and me was out looking for a stolen quad bike. We was less than five minutes away, at Allen's Corners.'

'Talked to any of these people yet?' Steve asked him. 'Which of them were eyewitnesses and which weren't?'

'Only the cashier saw it actually happen. The victim's spouse was in the vehicle at the time, but she happened to be looking the other way.'

'And these others?'

'Stopped to help, when they saw that there was something wrong.'

'Nobody touched anything?'

'The victim's wife gave him CPR, that's all.'

'Some people watch too much TV,' said Doreen. Doreen was small and pasty-faced and sharp-featured, with unusually pale eyes. 'CPR's not much help for missing brains.'

Steve looked around the gas station, and across the highway, to the abandoned diner, and the woods. 'Anybody see anything? Anybody hear a shot?'

Trooper Patrick shook his head. 'According to the cashier, the guy just dropped.' He opened his notebook and said, 'Howard Stanton, aged forty-seven years old, realtor, 1441 Pine Vista, Sherman.'

They heard a siren approaching. An ambulance pulled into the filling station, followed by a Jeep from the coroner's department. Steve walked over to the Ford Explorer where Sylvia Stanton was sitting in the passenger seat, with a plaid blanket wrapped around her. She was being comforted by a plain-looking woman with greasy blonde hair. Sylvia's eyes were wild and she was shaking as uncontrollably as if she had Parkinson's disease.

'Mrs Stanton? My name's Detective Steven Wintergreen, Connecticut State Police. This is Detective Doreen Rycerska. We're deeply sorry for your loss, Mrs Stanton.'

'I could take her home,' said the plain-looking woman.

'That won't be necessary, thank you. She's in shock. We'll take her to the hospital and have her checked out.'

'She needs warm milk with a shot of brandy in it,' the woman persisted. 'My mother gave my father warm milk with a shot of brandy in it, when he sawed all his fingers off.'

'I'll remember that,' said Doreen. 'You know, if ever I—' and she loosely flapped her wrist.

'You've been very helpful,' Steve told the woman, and smiled. The woman nodded, and then scowled at Doreen. Doreen took no notice. Doreen was used to being scowled at. Her husband Newton had walked out on her the Wednesday before Thanksgiving and taken the children, and the dog, and the First Connecticut savings book. She badly missed the savings book.

Steve took hold of Sylvia's hands. 'Mrs Stanton, we're going to get you to the hospital, but first I have to ask you a couple of questions.'

Sylvia stared at him, still shaking. 'I didn't see anything. I was trying to tune the radio. I didn't even see him fall down.'

'You didn't notice anybody lurking around the filling station?'

'Nobody. No.'

'You didn't see any passing vehicles on the highway, moving very slowly, maybe?'

Sylvia shook her head.

'How about stationary vehicles?'

'There was nobody else here. We were the only customers.'

'Did you hear anything? Like a car backfire?'

'I didn't see anything and I didn't hear anything. I only looked around because Howard seemed to be taking such a long time to pay for the gas. That's when I saw him, lying on the ground. I thought . . . he's fallen over, why doesn't he get up?'

'And you didn't see anybody else in the vicinity? Or any vehicles?'

'Not that I can recall, no.'

Doreen said, 'Mrs Stanton, do you know of anybody who might have wanted your husband dead?'

Sylvia blinked at her. 'What are you suggesting?'

'I'm asking you if anybody bears your husband any kind of grudge. Somebody he's been doing business with, maybe.'

'Of course not! Howard's a Rotarian!'

Doreen was about to say something, but suddenly there was a whining noise from the back of the Explorer.

'Oh, the poor little thing's woken up,' said Sylvia. She

25

reached over and lifted the Labrador puppy into her lap. 'My daughter's Christmas present. We just drove down to Norwalk to collect it.'

Steve said, 'OK, Mrs Stanton. We get the picture.' He beckoned a young woman paramedic to take care of Sylvia, and led Doreen away.

Doreen hissed, 'He was a Rotarian and so he didn't have enemies?'

'We'll talk to her again, don't worry. She's too shocked right now to make any sense.'

'Well, I believe in striking while the iron's hot.'

'I know you do. But *I* believe in finding out more about the guy's background before I start asking questions like that. She might tell us that somebody at work was out to get him, but we have no way of validating it, not yet.'

He walked around the back of the Explorer and Doreen reluctantly followed him. The cashier was shuffling from one foot to the other, as if he needed to pee. He was so edgy that Steve could almost have believed that *he* had shot Howard Stanton.

'What's your name, son?'

'Willis Broward. Willis like in Bruce Willis.'

Steve wrote that down. 'Well then, Willis. You actually witnessed Mr Stanton falling down?'

'That's right. He pays for his gas, OK, and he's walking back to his car. He turns around to look back at me and then he just pitches over. It's like somebody hits him with this invisible baseball bat. Whop.'

'Which way did he fall?'

'This way. Same way he's lying now. Only he drops onto his side. His wife jumps out of her vehicle and she's screaming and she turns him over and starts hitting him in the chest.'

'What did you do?'

'I come out here to see what's happening but when I see the guy's brains is spread all over the floor I go right back in and call 911.'

'Did you see anybody hanging around here? Like, *before* this happened?'

The cashier sniffed and shook his head. 'I was watching TV.'

26

'You didn't see anybody running away? Or a vehicle, maybe, driving off at speed?'

'There was nobody, man. The guy just dropped. Maybe there was a sniper or something, out in the woods.'

'OK,' said Steve. 'We'll need to talk to you later.'

The cashier hesitated for a moment, and then he said, 'I'm real sorry he's dead and all, but the guy was a jerk.'

'Oh, yes? What makes you say that?'

'He won't use my pen to sign his credit-card slip. He says I might be carrying some kind of disease.'

'And *do* you?' asked Doreen.

Feely Gets a Ride

Feely stood by the highway for over two hours but nobody stopped for him. Nobody even slowed down. His chin was so rigid with cold that he couldn't unclench his teeth, and his sneakers contained nothing but ice-sculptures of human feet. He would have to give it up, and make his way back to the center of town.

He closed his eyes. 'Oh Mary Wonderful Mother of God please help me to go North and fulfil my destiny. But, if you would prefer me to do otherwise, I will acquiesce and go to wherever your diamantine wisdom directs me. Amen.'

He was already struggling back up the bank when a dark-colored Chevy appeared out of the snow and slithered to a stop in the layby where he had been standing. It took almost twenty-five yards to come to a halt, and when it had stopped it stayed at an angle, its exhaust smoking scarlet, as if it were a vehicle from hell, and Jack Nicholson was driving it.

Feely hesitated. He wasn't sure if the car had stopped for him or not. But it stayed by the side of the highway, with its engine running, and after fifteen seconds had gone by, it gave him an impatient blast on its horn. He slithered back down the bank, and approached the passenger door.

The window was rolled down. Feely smelled cigarette smoke and alcohol. 'You looking for a ride?' asked a dry, scraping voice.

'Yes, sir. I've been standing here forever and I'm glacified. I'd almost surrendered all hope.'

'Where are you headed?'

'I don't have any special destination in particular.' Feely shielded his eyes with his hand but the driver remained in silhouette.

'No special destination in particular? I like the sound of

that. Why don't you climb in, and we'll go there together.'

Feely cupped his hand under the door-handle, but as he did so, the central-locking system clicked shut.

'One thing, before I let you in,' said the driver. 'I want your assurance that you don't suffer from any unusual personal odors.'

Feely tugged open the neck of his windbreaker and sniffed. He smelled of damp sweatshirt, and cooking fat from Billy Bean's Diner, but that was all. 'No, sir, I don't think so.'

The door clicked open. 'Welcome aboard, in that case. Do you like Jack Daniel's? Shot of Jack Daniel's, that'll make your bells jingle.'

The Chevy snaked away from the roadside in a shower of slush, and the man put his foot down until the speedometer needle was hovering at sixty.

'Hell of a day to be going anyplace,' he remarked, cheerfully. 'Let alone noplace at all.'

They sped due northward with the snow battering the windshield like a swarm of locusts. Feely glimpsed a sign saying Boardman's Bridge, but the only signs of human life were a few unlit farmhouses, and snow-covered cars, and fields, and then they were gone.

The man drove so fast that he couldn't possibly have seen anything before he hit it. A cow, a parked truck, a fallen tree: it made Feely's forehead tingle to think about it. He tried to fasten his seat-belt, but he couldn't find the buckle, so he twisted the belt around both hands like a bellringer and prayed to the Holy Virgin that the road was clear up ahead of them.

'Am I *scaring* you?' the man asked him, in that glasspaper rasp.

Feely said, 'No.'

'You don't have to lie to me, son. If you're scared you should say so. But let me tell you that there's nothing to be scared about. Once they've taken everything away from you, what's death?'

'I'm not nervous,' said Feely. 'I'm just speculating.'

'You're what?'

'Thinking. Like, if *I'm* not going to any destination in particular, and *you're* not going to any destination in particular,

29

and the weather's so inclement—why are we in such a hurry?'

'Hah! Because we have to make tracks, my friend, that's why. We have miles to go before we sleep; and we have a whole lot of very necessary things to do.'

Feely hung onto the seat-belt as the man steered the Chevy round a long left-hand curve. He could feel the tires losing their grip on the road, and the tail-end of the car starting to slide away. The man frantically spun the steering wheel clockwise, and then counter-clockwise, and the car swayed and dipped and eventually straightened up.

'*Hakamundo!*' said the man, with satisfaction.

Feely said nothing. He *was* scared, but not in the same way that Bruno scared him, after a bottle-and-a-half of tequila. One minute Bruno was laughing and cracking jokes and telling you what great buddies you were. The next he was screaming in fury and smashing the dinner plates.

The fear that Feely felt in this car was much more abstract. It was like a dream, as if he wasn't really sitting here at all. It wasn't the fear of pain; but the fear of not being there any more, of the world going on without him.

'You eaten?' the man asked him.

'I had a cheeseburger. They gave me beans with it but I have a disrelish for beans.'

'They gave you *beans* with it, hunh?' By the dim green light from the instrument panel, Feely could see that the man wasn't as old as his voice. Late thirties, maybe. He seemed to be fit and well-built, although he was wearing a thick sheepskin coat and so it wasn't easy to tell. His hair was cut short, almost military, and a few silver hairs sparkled around his temples. His face was round, although his nose was sharp and triangular, like the pointer on a sundial. Feely knew that the pointer on a sundial was called a gnomon.

There was very little in the car to tell Feely what kind of a man he was. A bottle of Jack Daniel's tucked neatly into the armrest niche, beside his seat. An open ashtray crowded with cigarette butts, most of them less than a quarter smoked, as if he kept lighting them and crushing them out after two or three puffs. A photograph of two small children on a swing-set, stuck to the glove-box with yellowing Scotch tape.

An empty Mr Pibb bottle, which kept rolling around the foot-well.

Feely noticed that the man wore a wedding band and a heavy gold chain on his wrist, but it was obvious that he wasn't wealthy. The Caprice was more than fifteen years old, before they brought in the curvier 1990 model. It smelled of pine air-freshener and something in the bodywork kept knocking, sometimes loud and sometimes soft, like a nagging reminder that everything gets older, and everything wears out.

All the same, there was something about the man that Feely instinctively liked. In spite of the reckless way that he was driving, Feely felt that he was the kind of man who wouldn't lie to you, and would never let you down. If he promised to show up, he would show up, even if he didn't really feel like it. And he wouldn't suddenly go berserk, and tip over the supper table with everybody's food on it, and punch you on the bridge of the nose with his signet ring.

'I didn't personally eat yet,' the man said, as they sped past the sign that said Cornwall Bridge. They were deep in the Litchfield Hills now, and on his right, Feely could just make out the dark serrated tree-line that followed the course of the Housatonic River. He thought it looked like the forest in fairy stories, where wolves lived.

The man continued, 'It didn't occur to me that I was going to be hungry, you know, but I am. I could eat a horse. I could eat two horses, and a pig, and a side-order of ducks. I guess the adrenaline's worn off.'

Feely still wanted to make sure that the man understood about the beans. 'My brother was always eating beans, before he died. That's why I disrelish beans.'

'Sure. I understand. The funniest things can put you off certain food, don't you think? I can't eat corned beef. I was eating some corned beef once and I found a human ear in it. Well, it probably wasn't a human ear but it looked like a human ear. I mean I had it in my mouth and it was all squeaky and gristly like a human ear.'

Feely nodded. 'In the diner, the waitress kept cajoling me to eat these beans. I think she was cajoling me intentionally, you know, to make me deny my brother. Like Peter denied Our Lord.'

'She kept cajoling you, huh? What a Jezebel.'

They drove in silence for another ten minutes. The man looked over at Feely from time to time but he didn't say anything until they passed through West Cornwall. Then he suddenly said, 'What do you think? Do you think there's any escape?'

'I don't know what you mean, sir. Escape from what?'

'*Escape*, that's all. Or do we *have* to wake up every morning, and finish what we started the day before?'

'Oh, I think there's escape, very much,' said Feely. 'I think that fate is always showing us ways to unburden ourselves of our problems and begin a refreshed existence.' Just at this moment, he was supremely confident about it. After all, he still had $21.76, didn't he? And he was still heading north.

'You really believe that?' the man asked him.

'I think I have achieved it myself. Or at least, I am on the verge of achieving it.'

The man sniffed in one nostril. 'What are you, Puerto Rican? Dominican?'

'Cuban. My grandparents came from Ciego de Avila.'

'Cuban, hunh? You don't come across too many Cubans in Connecticut. Cuban, how about that. What should I call you?'

'I don't know, whatever you choose.'

'You don't have to tell me your real name, but I can't go on calling you "you," can I?'

'Well, it's Fidelio Valoy Amado Valentin Valdes.'

'Jesus.'

'No, sir, my brother was called Jesus. For convenience most people abbreviate my name to Feely.'

The man shook Feely's hand. 'Good to know you, Feely. My name's Robert.'

'It's very gratifying to know you, sir,' said Feely. 'I want to reiterate my appreciation that you stopped for me. I realize that my appearance must be disreputable. I left New York with some expedition.'

'Oh, yeah? What expedition was that?'

'By expedition I mean speed.'

'Oh. I thought you meant Exiled Cubans in Search of Santa's Workshop, something like that. I'm sorry, you'll have to forgive me, I'm a little drunk.'

32

The car slewed again, and its nearside wheel banged into a pothole.

'Shit,' said Robert. 'This damned road's all over the place. You'd think they'd have the freaking intelligence to build it straight.'

'Maybe we should stop someplace,' Feely suggested.

'Stop? We have miles to go before we sleep, my good fellow. Miles to go and very necessary things to do.'

'Maybe if we stopped for a while—well, maybe the snow would ease off.'

'Ah, yes, but if we stopped for a while, then I'd sober up, and I always drive better when I've been drinking. Especially in crap like this.'

He took the next left-hand bend on the wrong side of the road, and without warning there was a truck coming straight toward them, with about a million candlewatt of headlights blazing and its klaxon blaring in nine different keys of terror.

Robert twisted the wheel and the Chevrolet slewed sideways, clipping the truck's offside fender. It spun around and around, so that Feely saw a blurred carousel of snow-lights-darkness until *wham* they collided backward with a tree beside the road.

The engine stopped. They sat in silence while the snow softly settled on the windshield. At last, Robert turned to Feely and said, 'Did I ask you before if you were scared?'

'Yes, sir, you did.'

'What did you say? I'm not sure that I remember.'

'I said I wasn't.'

Robert tried the ignition key and the Chevrolet's engine whistled into life. 'Good,' he said. 'Because God hasn't finished punishing me yet, and until He does, He's going to keep me good and safe. You want to lead a charmed life, kid, you stick with me.'

He sat nodding for a while, agreeing with himself. Then he said, 'What did you say your name was?'

'Feely.'

'Feely,' Robert repeated. He switched on the interior light and fumbled in his coat pocket. Eventually he produced a business card. It said, *Transparent Rulers Inc. Robert E. Touche, Divisional Sales Director.*

'See that?' he said, leaning over and breathing whiskey into Feely's face. 'Touche, pronounced "toosh." But a whole lot of my customers get it wrong, you know, and they pronounce it "touchy."'

'Oh, yes?' said Feely. He wondered if he ought to get out of the car and try walking. Compared to being a passenger in Robert's car, falling into a snowdrift and dying of hypothermia seemed positively alluring.

'Don't you get it?' Robert persisted. 'That's *fate*. That is one hundred and ten percent *fate*. What are the chances of two people meeting in the middle of a blizzard in Connecticut, one called Feely and the other called Touchy?'

Feely leaned away from Robert's breath, but tried not to do it too obviously, in case Robert was offended. 'Slender,' he said.

Robert stared at him as if he had never seen him before. Then he said, '*What?*'

'You asked me what are the chances, and I said slender.'

'Slender. *Slender.*' He repeated it several times, pronouncing it '*sur*-lender.' Then he turned back to Feely and said, 'Are you sure you're from Cuba? For a Cuban, you know, you talk almost perfect Martian.'

Another Warning

Sissy promised Trevor that she would call him no later than tomorrow afternoon. Trevor said '*Promise*, Momma?' and Sissy said 'Cross my heart and hope to spontaneously combust.' She stood on the doorstep with the snow whirling all around her and waved him goodbye.

'Get inside, Momma!' he called back at her. 'You'll catch your death!'

She blew him a kiss and then she closed the door. As she returned to the living room, she jolted with shock. She thought she saw Gerry disappearing into his study, just a glimpse of him. She stopped, with one hand on her chest, and took two or three deep breaths. She didn't see Gerry very often, but when she did it gave her that unbalanced feeling like stepping off a fairground ride and the world was still moving under her feet. But of course Gerry had died nearly three years ago, in February, on one of the darkest days that she could ever remember. The day that Gerry had died, she had had to keep the lights on from morning till night.

Mr Boots was watching her from his basket, one ear folded awkwardly back. Mr Boots knew when there were ghosts around.

'What do you think, Mister?' she asked him. 'Do you think I should spend Christmas in sunny St. Pete?'

She waited, but Mr Boots said nothing; so she turned toward the study door. 'More important, what do *you* think, Gerry? Do you think you'd be lonely, if I left you here, all on your own?'

Of course there was no answer. She knew that Gerry would have encouraged her to go, if he were still alive. 'I'll be OK on my own, you silly woman. I can cook ten times better than you. And I can finish sorting out my stamp collection.'

But he was dead now, and he couldn't cook, or sort out his

35

stamp collection, and she was worried that he might spend the winter wandering disconsolately from one chilly room to another. Worse than that—she, in Florida, would miss him so much that she couldn't bear it. She poured herself another cup of tea, but it was cold now, and she couldn't be bothered to brew a fresh pot.

Trevor and Jean always took wonderful care of her. In fact they looked after her *too* well, which made her suspect that they didn't really like having her at all. Not *her*, as she actually was. Jean bought her flowery lilac dresses to wear, with pie-crust collars, and matching cardigans, so that she looked like a granny out of a child's picture-book. Not only that, they gave her organic food and they always made sure that she washed her hair every day and they wouldn't let her smoke. They allowed her two glasses of red wine with her evening meal ('the Surgeon-General says it's good for the heart'), but vodka was a no-no. Young Jake couldn't have a grannie who dressed like a gypsy, breathed smoke out of her nostrils, talked to dead people, and drank Stolichnaya straight up. 'I mean, what kind of an example is that, Momma?'

It's probably an example of somebody who was brought up in an age when smoking and drinking weren't dangerous, and people said exactly what they meant, whether it offended anybody or not. The good old days (although we didn't know it at the time).

But Trevor was Gerry's son and she couldn't help loving him (for all that he dressed like a feedbag) and she adored little Jake and she could just about tolerate Jean if she didn't start talking about *feng-shui* or colonic irrigation. 'It makes you feel so *clean*, inside and out.' Sissy couldn't even tell Jean that she was full of shit, because she simply wasn't, and she had the receipts to prove it.

Let the cards decide, Sissy decided. *They* can tell me if going to Florida is a wise idea. She opened up the bag that Trevor had brought with him, picked out a Cherry Mash, unwrapped it, and took a large bite. Then she went into the kitchen, opened the freezer and wrenched out the frosted bottle of Stolichnaya. She poured herself a generous glassful and took it back into the living room. She poked the fire a little, so that the logs lurched, and a shower of sparks flew up. She could hear the wind moaning across the chimney. It was going to be bitter out tonight.

She sat down again and opened up the large cardboard box that contained the DeVane cards. It was worn at the edges, and the lid had been repaired with Scotch tape.

'Pictures of the world to be . . . I beg you now to speak to me.'

She always said these words when she took the cards out, even if she murmured them under her breath. The cards were so potent, so full of meaning, so characterful, she felt that they had to be asked for their co-operation. You had to give them *respect*. After all, you wouldn't just walk into a roomful of clairvoyants and shout 'Listen up! What's going to happen to me tomorrow?'

She put the rest of the Cherry Mash in her mouth and then she turned up the first five cards and laid them in a diamond shape. These were called the Ambience cards and they explained the background to what was going to happen in the near future. Two of the cards were the Drowning Men and the Faces of Mourning. She had expected this. Everything that happened in the next few days would be affected by the simultaneous arrival of the two storms.

The other three cards showed a widow sitting in a room carpeted with hundreds of live green frogs; and a small boy on a bridge, trying to catch a skeptical-looking carp; and a blindfolded man standing amid sand dunes, his face raised toward the sun.

The widow was Sissy herself, and the live frogs were undecided questions: which way were they all going to jump? The small boy was Trevor, trying to persuade her to go to Florida for the winter; and the message of the blindfolded man was obvious. *Those who look for meaning in the sun will lose sight of everything.*

She laid out seven more cards, on top of the five. These were the Imminence cards, which told her what signs to look out for. She must be wary of a childless woman; and a boy from a tropical country; and two men sawing wood. She must be careful when the wind changed; and watch for some kind of unexpected trap. This card showed a red-breasted bird caught up in brambles, and bleeding. She must also keep her eyes open for footprints that led into a lake; and a man

37

concealed in a brass-bound chest. This last card took the center position, which meant that it was especially significant.

Sissy sat back and looked over the Imminence cards, tapping her fingers on the table top. It was difficult to work out exactly what they were trying to tell her, but she knew that even when they spoke in riddles, they were always very specific. She couldn't understand why the man in the brass-bound chest was so important. Maybe it was Gerry, and he had left something hidden in a box for her to find. Maybe she was going to meet a new man, in an unexpected place.

So far, however, there was nothing to suggest that she ought to go to Florida.

'What do you think, Mr Boots?' she asked him. Mr Boots tilted his head on one side but said nothing.

She took a large swallow of vodka and then she turned up the two Predictor cards, laying them on top of the Imminence cards. The first Predictor was La Poupée Sans Tête, the Headless Doll. This depicted a young mother in a yellow dress trying to replace the idiotically smiling head of a little girl's doll, while the little girl herself stood beside her, weeping. The other was La Faucille Terrible, which showed a man with a reaping-hook, trying to cut a path through overgrown weeds. The hook had slipped and he had stuck it into his own eye. On the other side of the field, another man was hysterically laughing.

Two more bad Predictor cards. And neither of them gave her any advice about leaving New Preston to spend the winter in Florida. La Poupée Sans Tête meant that a child or children were going to be tragically orphaned; and La Faucille Terrible warned that somebody was going to be injured while performing a mundane, everyday task.

All of the Ambience cards said that these events were going to happen here, and that she (the widow) was going to be part of them. If she were going to Florida, the Imminence cards wouldn't have warned her about traps, and childless women, and the wind changing. This was her future, and she knew from experience that she couldn't avoid it. One morning four years ago she had turned up Le Pêcheur Perdu, the Doomed Fisherman, which showed a man on a desolate beach, surrounded on all sides by crabs. She had known then that Gerry's prostate cancer was going to kill him.

38

Breakfast in Canaan

Feely opened his eyes. He had never felt so cold in his life. In fact he was so cold that he thought he must be dead. The car windows were covered in plumes and feathers of frost, and the interior was filled with brilliant white sunlight. All that was missing was a heavenly choir.

It was only when he tried to move that he realized he was still alive. Every joint in his body had seized up. He had wedged himself sideways in the Chevrolet's front passenger seat, with his head resting against the window. His hat was actually frozen to the glass.

'Urrghh,' he said. He managed to sit up straight, and look around. At first he thought he must be alone, but then he heard a catarrhal snort from the Chevy's rear seat. He peered over and saw Robert lying under several spread-out sheets of newspaper, his stubble sparkling with ice. For the first time, Feely saw that he had a large BandAid stuck to his left temple.

Robert opened one eye. 'What time is it?'

'I don't know. Hold up. Five after eight.'

'Jesus,' said Robert, pushing the newspaper onto the floor. 'The dreams I've been having.'

'Me too,' said Feely. 'I dreamed I was back in school, and my teacher was throwing broccoli at me.'

Robert sat up straight and rubbed the window with his sleeve, but the ice was on the outside. 'God it's cold. Let's get the engine started up.'

The rear door was stuck fast with frost, and he had to throw his whole weight against it to get it open. He eased himself into the driver's seat and turned the key. The engine made a groaning noise, but at first it didn't fire up.

'Come on, you bastard,' he snarled at it, and tried the key again. This time the engine burst into life. 'You see?' he told

39

Feely. 'You don't have to take any crap from anything; or anyone. Your life is your own. You have inalienable rights.'

They waited while the interior of the car warmed up and the ice gradually slid from the windows. When it did, they discovered that they were alone in the middle of a disused railroad yard. The sky was golden, and the sun sparkled on the snow.

'Can you feel your feet yet?' asked Robert.

Feely nodded. His feet were beginning to itch, as if his boots were crawling with fire-ants.

Robert said, 'This is when you have to respect guys like Peary.'

Feely said nothing, but blew on his gloveless hands.

'You know who I'm talking about?' Robert asked him.

Feely shook his head.

'You never heard of Robert Edwin Peary, the first man to reach the North Pole? April 6, 1909.'

'I never heard of him,' Feely admitted.

'Schools today,' said Robert. 'Just because Peary was white, and male. I'll bet you've heard of Malcolm X.'

'Malcolm X? Sure.'

'There you are, see. But Malcolm X never went to the North Pole, did he? Malcolm X never went within a thousand miles of the North Pole. Just as well for him. He probably would have been eaten by a polar bear, mistook him for a giant penguin.'

'I don't think so,' said Feely. 'Penguins aren't indigenous to the North Pole. Only the South Pole.'

'Indigenous,' Robert repeated.

'That means naturally living there.'

'I know what it means. I just can't get over the fact that you can say it at eight o'clock in the morning. Let's go get some breakfast.'

He drove out of the railroad yard, past boarded-up sheds and rusted bogies. They had stopped here late last night after they had managed to get themselves hopelessly lost. Robert had tried to take a cutoff at West Cornwall, but they had ended up driving for three-and-a-half hours around Red Mountain and Lake Wononpakook with the snow falling so thickly that they felt they were being buried alive. Eventually they had found their way back to Route 7, only five miles north of where they had left it. Robert had sent Feely into a roadside store outside Falls Village for bread and Kraft cheese slices and Twinkies, and they had eaten a picnic in the car, with the engine running to keep them warm.

As they drove into the center of Canaan, Robert said, 'Let me give you some advice, Feely. You can use all the twenty-dollar words you like, but these days nobody listens, and even if they *did* listen they wouldn't understand half of what you're talking about. So you should save your breath to cool your chowder.'

Feely said nothing, so Robert gave him a nudge with his elbow. 'If you want people to respect you, Feely, you have to *do* something. And I don't mean something pissant. I mean something cataclysmic. Now that's a twenty-dollar word for you. Cata-freaking-clysmic.'

Feely looked out at the snow-covered houses. 'Are we still talking about Peary?'

'No, we're talking about anybody. We're talking about you and me and that old geezer standing on the corner over there. If you don't do something cataclysmic, people will never take any notice of you, and they'll never remember you after you're gone, like your father's sperm never even wriggled as far as your mother's egg, and how tragic is that? Or if they *do* remember you, they won't remember the good things you did, the little acts of kindness that you never asked for any credit for. Oh, they'll remember the times you screwed up, or the offensive things you said after fifteen Jack Daniel's. But if you want to make any kind of impression in this world, my friend, it's no good trying to be persuasive. You have to do something that pulls the rug right out from under people's feet. Something that makes them go *ho-o-oly shit.*'

As they neared the town center, they passed a small yellow house on a hill. It had a snow-filled yard that sloped steeply down to the road. Although it was so early, a small girl in a bright red coat was building a snowman, with twigs for arms and a carrot for a nose. Her mother was watching her from the kitchen window.

Robert slowed down. 'What do you think *that* is?' he said. But before Feely could answer, he said, 'Happiness, that's what that is. Completeness. The mother. The child. Beautiful.'

He drove on. Where the sun was falling across it, the snow was already melting, and the streets were thick with slush. Feely still hadn't stopped shaking with cold and he urgently needed to go to the bathroom. After a few minutes, however, they reached a large Victorian railroad station on the right-hand side of the road, its rooftops covered in snow, and Robert slowed down again.

'Union Station,' said Robert. 'This is where the Housatonic Railroad used to meet up with the Connecticut Western line. It used to be really something, this station, a grand historical monument. But there was a fire, four or five years ago, and all the timbers were soaked in oil, as a preservative. That was good thinking, wasn't it? They were damned lucky to save anything at all.'

Feely could see that the building had once been L-shaped, but the southern wing had been burned down almost to the ground. A tower that stood at the corner of the L had been charred black, but restoration work was already well advanced, with scaffolding and freshly re-boarded walls.

On the left side of the station parking lot stood a diner made of converted railroad cars, painted red-and-cream, with a neon sign on top saying Chesney's Diner. 'This'll do us,' said Robert. 'I think we could both use a cup of strong coffee and a shit.'

He parked around the side of the building so that the Chevy couldn't be seen from the road. As Feely climbed out, the cold air cut into his nostrils like a craft knife. Robert said, 'If anybody asks you, you're my son, OK?'

'Your *son*?'

'What's the matter, your ears frozen up, too?'

'No, but we don't share anything like the same physiognomy.'

'What's that in human?'

'I mean I don't *look* like your son.'

'I know. And the reason for that is, you aren't my son. All I want you to do, if anybody wants to know, is to *say* that you are.'

Feely frowned. He didn't like the sound of this at all. This sounded suspiciously like part of the conspiracy. First of all they tempt you to deny your brother; now they want you to deny your father, too.

'For Christ's sake,' said Robert. 'I knocked up some Cuban girl, OK?'

'I don't understand.'

Robert took a deep breath. 'It's very simple. I don't want any of the people in this diner to remember us, after we've left. I want us to pass through like ghosts. If we say that we're father and son, we're less likely to make any kind of lasting impression.'

'But why should we?'

'Because this is Canaan, Connecticut, where the straight people live. Because I'm a thirty-five-year-old white guy and you're a teenage Cuban in a stupid hat.'

'OK.' Feely needed the bathroom too urgently to argue any more.

Inside, Chesney's Diner was warm and steamy, with rows of cream-colored Formica tables and red leatherette seats. The radio was playing 'This Old Heart of Mine.'

'Hungry?' asked Robert, breathing in the greasy aroma of breakfast. But without a word, Feely hurried to the door with the little railroad engineer on it.

Robert sat down and sniffed and pulled off his gloves. There were only about a dozen people in there: three huge construction workers in furry caps, their cheeks bulging with food; a spotty young realtor with property particulars spread out all over his dirty breakfast plate; a worried-looking middle-aged woman with a small fidgety boy who kept blowing bubbles into his raspberry milkshake; a black UPS driver; and—at the next table—a bespectacled girl in a khaki stocking-cap and a thick khaki sweater, who was eating yogurt and reading a dog-eared yellow paperback of T.S. Eliot.

An aluminum-trimmed counter ran the length of the railroad cars, with perspex cabinets filled with pound cake and donuts. Behind it, a chimp-like woman in hugely magnifying eyeglasses was busily making toast and clearing up dishes, while a mournful man in a folded paper cap was frying eggs and staring at nothing at all, as if he were waiting to be struck by a divine revelation or a fatal coronary, without too much hope of either.

'This old heart of mine,' sang Robert, along with the radio.

When Feely came back from the bathroom, his hands still wet, a large glass of orange juice was waiting for him. 'I already ordered,' said Robert. 'I hope you like pancakes, and bacon?'

'I can remunerate you.'

'I said I *ordered*, kid. I didn't say I paid.'

The woman in the hugely magnifying eyeglasses came around and poured them both a mug of coffee.

'You traveling far today?' she inquired. 'They say there's more snow on the way.'

'Well, we're not planning on going too far,' said Robert.

The woman stayed where she was, staring at Feely. Feely glanced up at her a couple of times, but didn't say anything. It was like looking down the wrong end of a pair of binoculars.

Robert said, 'Me and my son . . . we just came up to pay our respects at my mother's grave.'

'Oh. Your folks came from Canaan? What's their family name?'

'Baker. But we're from Pittsfield, Massachusetts, originally. We're just passing through.'

'Now, isn't that something! My family on my father's side come from Pittsfield and some of *them* were Bakers.'

Robert said, 'Really?'

'Maybe you know Maggie and Lavender Baker, 1243 Fenn Street. They're my aunts.'

'Sorry, can't say that I do.'

'Well, they tend to keep themselves to themselves, these days. Lavender must be eighty-six if she's a day. But if you're a Baker . . . who knows, we could be blood-related, you and me, and your boy here! Although I'm taking a wild guess that *his* mother didn't come from Pittsfield!'

'You're right there,' said Robert, with forced joviality. Then he added, 'Puerto Rico.'

The woman remained by their table for a little while longer, nodding and smiling, but then the construction workers all heaved themselves out of their seats and stamped their feet and put on their coats and wanted to pay, and she had to return to the counter.

'Jesus wept,' said Robert.

Feely hissed, 'Why did you have to tell her all of that?'

'What? Who cares? None of it was true.'

'But I thought the whole idea was not to make an impression. Ghosts, you said. Now it's lodged in her consciousness that she encountered a father and son who had visited a grave in Pittsfield and their family name was Baker, same as hers.'

'So? I just made the name up.'

'She'll recollect our appearance,' Feely persisted. 'She'll recollect that you're Caucasian and I'm Hispanic.'

'For Christ's sake, Feely, what choice did I have? I'm going to sit there like a dummy and say nothing at all? She'd have recollected us even more, if I'd done that.'

Feely felt trapped, almost panicky. He was convinced that no matter *what* family name Robert had invented, Baker or Jones or Ararallosa, the woman would have pretended that they were blood-related. That was how the conspirators lulled you into a sense of false security. They encouraged you to lie, and they *knew* perfectly well that you were lying, but they pretended to believe you, so that you would paint yourself into an existential corner.

The woman brought their pancakes, a tilted stack of half-a-dozen each, with dripping syrup and melted butter, and rashers of crispy bacon on the side. 'Enjoy,' said the woman. For some reason, Feely looked round at the cook. He was elaborately picking his nose with his little finger.

A Transparent Story

'Listen, Feely,' said Robert, with his mouth full. 'If you're not happy, I'll leave you here, and drive on without you. No problem. It's all the same difference to me.'

Feely toyed with his fork. 'It's just that I don't understand why you want me to masquerade as your son. I'm *not* your son.'

'There's no mystery. I just don't want people to remember seeing me on my own. You don't *have* to be my son. You can be anything you like. My trainer, my accountant, so long as we're together, as a pair. But the way you're dressed . . . "son" just seemed the most plausible, that's all, and even that's stretching it. You look more like my personal goat farmer.'

'Why don't you want people to remember seeing you on your own?'

'Because . . . there's something very important that I want to do. You remember what I said about cataclysmic? I can't explain it to you. Not yet. But I will, when the time's right.'

Feely lifted the top pancake with his fork and then let it flop back onto the stack.

'You're not hungry?' Robert asked him. 'Listen, I'm sorry, I wouldn't have ordered pancakes if I thought you didn't like pancakes. I thought everybody liked pancakes.'

'It's not the pancakes,' said Feely.

'Then what? Come on, you can tell me, I'm a total stranger.'

'It isn't easy to verbalize it.'

'Hey,' smiled Robert. 'I thought you were a walking Webster's.'

'I don't . . .' This was the most difficult admission that Feely had ever made. He looked across at the girl reading T.S. Eliot and for a split-second she caught his eye and smiled, as if she knew exactly what he was going to say.

'I don't know what to give credence to, any more.'

Robert wiped his mouth with his paper napkin. 'You mean like you've lost your religion? Jesus Christ, Feely, plenty of people lose their religion.'

'It's nothing to do with religion. It's me.' He took a shallow breath. 'I can't define my existence.'

'Ah,' said Robert.

'I don't know who I am or where to go, or what to do when I get there. I thought if I headed north . . . but what happens when I can't go any further north?'

'You start going south again. That's the nature of the planet. There's no way off it, Feely.'

'Escape velocity,' said Feely.

Robert painstakingly scooped up the last of his syrup and sucked it off his spoon. 'There is only one way to escape, Feely, and that is to sign up for Mars. But even if you manage to escape, you *still* won't know who you are. Who you are is (a) your family, (b) your friends, and (c) your property.'

'I don't have any family,' said Feely. 'Well, not any more.' He hesitated, and then he added, 'I don't have any friends, either.' He laid his hand on his battered blue folder. 'And this is my only material possession, apart from my hat.'

'Funny, isn't it?' said Robert. 'You and me, we couldn't be more different. You're Cuban, from the city, and I'm just a white dude, from the suburbs. But we've both taken our seats in the same rapidly sinking lifeboat. What a pair of assholes.' He sniffed again, and then he said, 'What's that, in Cuban? Assholes?'

'I don't know. *Zurramatos*, maybe.'

'*Zurramatos*, I'll remember that.' Robert reached into his pocket and took out his business card. 'That was me. Robert E. Touche, Divisional Sales Director, Transparent Rulers, Inc., of Danbury, Cee Tee. Well, I showed you before, didn't I? But that was me. That was who I used to be.

'When I was twenty-three I was going to be an architect. I was going to design houses like nobody had ever seen before. Eat your heart out, Frank Lloyd Wright. But Linda got pregnant before I could finish my studies and Linda wanted to keep the baby so we got married. It was a struggle to make a decent living and so I accepted an offer from Linda's dad to work for a limited period for Transparent Rulers, Inc.

'You know what we made at Transparent Rulers, Inc.?'

Feely shook his head.

'We made transparent rulers. Also transparent set-squares, T-squares, compasses and geometric shapes. We dominated the US market in transparent freedom curves. They used to be called French curves, but you know, after the war with Iraq . . .

'To cut a short story short, "a limited period" at Transparent Rulers, Inc., turned into a year, and then a year turned into seven years. Linda and I bought a house just outside of New Milford and we had two more children and you couldn't have imagined a more contented family. That was me, Robert E. Touche, that was who I was. Divisional Sales Director of Transparent Rulers, Inc. Husband of Linda. Father of Toby, Jessica and Tom. Owner of 1773 Milford Lane. Weekend fisherman. Secretary of the Litchfield Historic Buildings Preservation Society. *Zurramato*-in-chief.

'That was who I *was*, Feely. That was me.'

'So what transpired?' asked Feely.

'What transpired was, *I* suddenly turned up. The real me. The me who was going to be an architect before I made Linda pregnant. The me who loved to take chances, and have a wild time. When I was marketing transparent rulers in Chicago I met a girl. Her name was Elizabeth and she was everything that Linda wasn't. She was passionate and exciting and all of those damped-down fires in me that I thought had gone out for ever, she blew on them, *woofff*, and they burst into flame.

'I felt ten years younger. I saw all of the opportunities that I'd missed out on, all of the chances I could have had. One night Elizabeth and I stood on top of the Hancock Building and we looked out over the city and the lake and there it was . . . the whole world, there at my feet. Glittering. Dark. Calling to me. Here I am, said the world. You can still take me. The world was like a woman with her legs apart.

'You can guess the rest. I went home and I told Linda that I was going off with Elizabeth. I walked out on my wife, my children, my house and my job. But when I got to Chicago Elizabeth wasn't interested in somebody who didn't have an expense account, and she didn't want commitment, and she certainly didn't want me.

'Elizabeth only wanted one-night stands, with other women's husbands.'

48

'That must have been a catastrophe,' said Feely, trying very hard to look sympathetic.

'Catastrophe? I kid you not. It was a bummer of the first water. I crawled back, sackcloth and ashes. But Linda wasn't in any kind of mood to forgive me, and her dad wasn't in any mood to give me my job back. I lost my house and most of my savings, and when I went crazy I lost visitation rights to the kids, too. In the space of seven-and-a-half months, I went from domestic bliss to Dante's *Inferno*.'

He paused, and prodded at a strip of bacon. 'I don't know. Maybe it's all my fault. I don't even know, if Linda *had* taken me back, if I could have stayed with her for any length of time—children, house, job or not. I say "domestic bliss" but once Elizabeth had shown me what I *could* have done, and what I *could* have been, and what kind of woman I *could* have had . . . There was Linda, in her brushed cotton nightdresses, and her hair in rollers, and her moles. And there was Elizabeth, with her shiny black hair, and her lips like a turned-on codfish, and her full Brazilian wax.'

Feely didn't know if he was supposed to say anything. But he could understand what Robert was trying to tell him about the same boat. In spite of the differences in their physiognomy, he and Robert were both adrift on a bottomless, ice-cold ocean, with more snow forecast. They had no oars and no compass, and the water was rushing in fast.

Robert reached across the table and took hold of Feely's left wrist, surprisingly gently, as if he were feeling his pulse. 'There's something I have to do, Feely. It won't take more than ten or fifteen minutes. I want you to wait here for me, and have another cup of coffee. Order something else to eat, if you're hungry. I know you can renumerate me . . .' He paused, realizing his mispronunciation. '. . . *remunerate* me, but I'll pay. This is my treat, OK?'

Feely said, 'Where are you going?'

'I can't tell you, but I'll be right back, I promise you. I won't let you down.'

Feely noticed that there was a small blotch of fresh blood on Robert's BandAid. 'All right,' he agreed. After all, where else could he go?

Mr White Meets His Maker

Ellen was worried. This was the third dose of flu that Randall had contracted in as many months. Now that the new Torrington shopping mall was nearing completion, he was working eleven hours a day, sometimes more, but she always made sure that he wrapped up warm, and that he ate plenty of fresh fruit, and that he took his multi-vitamin pills. But when he had arrived home from Torrington yesterday evening, he had been trembling and coughing and his eyes were glistening pink like an albino rabbit, so she had sent him straight up to bed.

He was still there now, dosed up with Profen Forte, too groggy even to watch daytime TV. She had called Dr Benway, but Dr Benway had told her there was a lot of it going around. 'Bed rest, that's the answer, my dear, but ozone, too! Throw the windows wide open!'

Ellen was worried, but she was also disappointed, because she had been planning on taking Juniper to see Santa Claus today, along with five of Juniper's friends. She supposed she could have left Randall on his own for two or three hours, but he was sweating and shaking uncontrollably, and his temperature was over 100. What if he took a sudden turn for the worse?

Not only that, there was the Leonard thing. Her old boyfriend Leonard had unexpectedly turned up in Canaan in the last week of August, after three years in Los Angeles. Leonard had been tanned and fit, smelling of Lanvin, with shining white teeth and a Rolex watch. He had invited Ellen to lunch at the Mayflower Inn in Washington, just the two of them, for old times' sake, and Ellen had accepted, telling Randall that she was visiting her mother. By chance, Randall's sister had been visiting the Mayflower Inn, too, and had seen them kissing, and it had taken weeks of shouting and slamming doors before Randall had been prepared to accept that they hadn't booked a room and slept together.

Now, whenever Ellen went out, Randall never asked her where she was going, or how long she was going to be, but he always stood in the doorway, watching her leave, with that fatalistic look on his face as if he didn't expect to see her again. Maybe his insecurity had weakened his immune system, and that was why he kept going down with flu.

Seven years ago, when Ellen had agreed to marry Randall, he hadn't been able to believe his luck. He had told her then and he had never stopped telling her, daily. She *was* pretty, in a snub-nosed way, with bouncy blonde hair and wide blue eyes, like a 1950s model for Ivory Soap; while Randall was swarthy and thickset, prematurely balding, and when he put on weight he had a jowly, hungover look. He didn't understand that it was his very ugliness that had attracted her, and made her feel reassured, and protected. But after the Leonard thing, she felt hemmed in, more than protected, and she found it increasingly difficult to act naturally with him. Even going to the market felt like adultery.

Ellen went to the window and knocked. 'Juniper! I want you in now, for breakfast!'

Juniper was still outside, in her little red boots, sticking pine-cone buttons onto her snowman. She turned and waved, and shouted something, but Ellen couldn't hear what it was.

Ellen opened the pantry in her new Shaker-style kitchen and took out the box of Lucky Charms. She poured some into a blue-and-white bowl and set it on the scrubbed-pine table. She didn't believe that Lucky Charms were particularly healthy (too much added sugar and colorings) but Juniper insisted that she would have bad luck if she ate anything else.

'We *all* try to shield our children from harm,' said a serious-looking woman on *The Daybreak Show*, 'but life is full of all kinds of unexpected dangers, isn't it, and we're doing them no favors by pretending that they're never going to get hurt.'

How true, thought Ellen. She went to the window again and gave Juniper another sharp knock.

Juniper came bursting in through the back door, her cheeks red and her nose running. 'I've nearly finished him!' she

51

announced. 'I'm going to ask Daddy if I can borrow one of his hats!'

'Daddy's asleep,' said Ellen, helping her out of her coat. 'But I'm sure he won't mind if you use one of his old fishing hats. Why don't you borrow one of his scarves as well? We don't want your snowman to get cold, do we?'

'His name's Mr White,' said Juniper.

Ellen tugged off her wet boots and stood them beside the boiler to dry. Juniper climbed onto her chair and started to pick out all of the marshmallows in her Lucky Charms.

'When are we going to see Santa Claus?' she asked.

'Well, not today, sweetheart. Daddy has the flu and we have to take care of him.'

'But Janie and Holly and Emily are going to see Santa Claus!'

'I know, but we'll go next week, when Daddy's better.'

'Can't I go with Janie and Holly and Emily?'

'I'm sorry, they don't have enough room in their car.'

'It's not fair!'

'We'll go next week, and I'll take you to Punch's for pizza.'

'It's still not fair!'

Ellen spooned coffee into the cafetière. 'You can finish your snowman, and then we'll make gingerbread, how about that?'

'Mr White likes gingerbread. Mr White likes pizza, too. He likes every kind of food, and that's why he's so fat.'

Ellen looked out of the window. 'He *is* fat, isn't he? Maybe you should put him on the Atkins Diet.'

She was still looking at the snowman when its head exploded. She couldn't believe her eyes. One second it was standing there with its carrot nose and its grin made of broken twigs. The next second it was headless. No sound, nothing. Just *pffff!* and it was gone.

'That's weird,' she said.

Juniper looked up from her cereal. 'What's weird?'

'Your snowman . . . his head's disappeared.'

'Mr White!' said Juniper, in distress. She clambered down from her chair and tried to look out of the kitchen window. It was too high up for her, so she ran through to the living room and looked out of the patio doors. 'Mr White! What's happened to his head?'

'I don't know. I didn't see it fall off. It just . . . *vanished.*'

Juniper came back into the kitchen and started to pull one of her boots back on. 'I have to make him a new head! If he doesn't have a head he won't be able to think!'

'Juniper, finish your breakfast first!'

'No, I have to make him a new head!'

Ellen pulled Juniper's boot back off again. 'I'll tell you what I'll do. While you finish your breakfast, *I'll* make him a new head. Is that a deal? I'm very good at heads.'

'No, *I'm* his mommy, and *I* have to make his head!'

'Maybe so. But I'm *your* mommy and I'm telling you to finish your breakfast.'

Juniper reluctantly climbed back onto her chair and picked up her spoon. When she pouted she looked so much like Randall. But at least she had blonde hair and blue eyes, and Ellen's little tipped-up nose.

'I'll go take a look at him,' said Ellen, slipping on her fur-lined boots, and reaching for her pink quilted coat.

'You won't make a new head for him, will you?'

'No, I promise. You're his mommy. You can make him a new head.'

She opened the kitchen door and stepped out into the yard. The sky was flawless, and the snow was so dazzling that she had to narrow her eyes. There was a clean, bracing smell in the air, as if the whole morning had been freshly washed, and hung up to dry. She crossed the yard, following Juniper's criss-cross footprints, until she reached Mr White.

'You poor unfortunate snowman,' she said. 'What on earth happened to you?'

She looked around. The only trace of Mr White's head were bits and pieces of his carrot nose, which were scattered across the snow almost twenty-five feet away. This was even weirder. If Mr White's head had melted, or simply fallen off, the carrot would have dropped straight downward, intact.

The higher end of the yard was lined with fifty-foot pine trees, which sheltered their house from the north-west winds. Some prankster could have been hiding in the trees, but they would have been too far away to have hit Mr White with a snowball. They could have used a catapult, she supposed— but in that case the pieces of carrot would have been lying halfway *downhill*, in the opposite direction.

With her hands in her pockets, she looked down toward the road, at the lower end of the yard. On the opposite side of the highway stood an old gray-brick building which had once been a furniture store, and a rough stretch of open ground, where there were plans to build a memorial park. There were two cars parked side by side on the open ground, as well as the trailer part of a tractor-trailer, NEW ENGLAND DAIRIES with two smiling cows on it, but there was no sign of anybody, anywhere.

She pushed back her hair. Must have been a freak accident, she thought. A sudden gust of wind. She turned to go back to the house.

At that moment, when her hand was still lifted, she was hit between the eyes by a .308 bullet. The impact flung her off her feet and threw her backward into the snow, her arms and legs spreadeagled in an X. Her blood and her brains were sprayed halfway up the yard, where the bits of carrot were.

Juniper was watching her from the kitchen. She had dragged her chair across to the sink so that she could see out of the window. She hadn't trusted her mother not to start making a replacement head. Mothers *always* interfered, if you let them. When Ellen suddenly jumped backward and fell flat into the snow, Juniper thought that she must have caught sight of her, and was pretending that she was surprised. She ducked down below the level of the draining-board and waited, but nothing happened. After a while she raised her head again. Her mother was still lying in the same place, utterly motionless.

Juniper waited and waited, and then she climbed up onto the sink and knocked on the window. Still her mother didn't move.

'Mommy! What are you *doing*?'

Juniper pulled on her boots and opened the back door. There was no sound, only the high-pitched singing of the wind through the pine trees. She ran across the snow until she reached her mother, and it was then that she saw the hole in her forehead and the pinkish lumps of brains.

Juniper stood where she was, gripping the cuffs of her cardigan, panting. She could see what had happened but she couldn't believe it. 'Mommy,' she said, but she was afraid to touch her.

'Mommy,' she repeated, but she knew it was no use. She waited a moment longer and then she turned and ran back into the house, up the stairs and into her parents' bedroom. Her father was asleep, buried in his patchwork quilt, his face sweaty and red.

'Daddy!' screamed Juniper, tugging at the bedclothes. 'Mommy's been shot! Mommy's been shot!'

Randall opened his eyes and stared at her. 'What? What the hell are you talking about?'

Juniper opened and closed her mouth. 'I think Mommy's *dead*,' she whispered.

Randall stumbled downstairs with the quilt wrapped around him, knocking a picture off the wall. Juniper ran out into the yard and he followed her, barefoot. When he first saw Ellen lying in the snow he said, 'Oh, come *on*,' as if Ellen and Juniper were playing a trick on him, to prove that he wasn't really sick.

But as he came closer, he saw that Ellen's face was luminous white like candle-wax, and that even though her eyes were wide open, and she was looking at him, the hole in her forehead couldn't possibly be fake, and that the blood and the brains weren't just cake-mix and cochineal. She had left him. She had actually left him. Not for an ex-boyfriend. Not to go back home to her parents. She had departed, abruptly, for somewhere else, where neither he nor Juniper could follow her.

He sank to his knees in the snow. 'Call 911,' he told Juniper. His nose was running and his pajamas were stuck to his body with cold perspiration.

Juniper didn't seem to be able to move. Randall took hold of her skinny little elbow and steered her around so that she was facing him. 'Sweetheart . . . call 911.'

The Angle of Death

Jim Bangs from the forensic laboratory laid out fifteen glossy photographs on Steve's desk, and then stood back, his arms folded. He was thirty-one years old, short, with bright chestnut hair that stuck up like a yard-brush, and rimless glasses. His white sleeveless shirt was missing a button, so that his pale bulging stomach was exposed.

'OK,' said Steve. 'What am I looking at?'

'You're looking at the most likely location of the shooter,' said Jim. He had a voice that came right from the back of his throat, as if somebody were half-strangling him. 'Here—in this area in front of the old abandoned diner, right opposite the filling station.'

'OK.'

'The reason for that is, the damage caused to the victim's skull indicates that the shot was probably fired from no more than one hundred fifty to two hundred feet away. There are all kinds of imponderables, like the charge used, and the weapon involved, but Howard Stanton was not killed from any great distance, like for instance he wasn't shot by a sniper concealed way back in this wooded area here.'

Doreen pushed open the office door, carrying an untidy armful of files and a styrofoam cup of cappuccino. 'Did I miss anything?'

'Probable location of the shooter,' Jim repeated, without any hint of irritation. 'The direction in which the victim fell to the ground tells us that the shot came from somewhere between the Branchville turnoff and this roadsign here. There's no natural cover within three hundred fifty feet of the gas station—only the derelict diner, and this old International pickup parked outside of it. This might lead us to conclude that if our perpetrator shot Howard Stanton from anyplace else, apart from the diner, or the pickup, he would have had to be standing right out in the open.'

Steve said, 'It was getting pretty dark, wasn't it, and it was starting to snow, so he could conceivably have stood on the side of the highway without anybody spotting him.'

'True, but it would have taken some kind of nerve, don't you think? The cashier could have looked across the road and seen him at any time, as could Mrs Stanton, if she had turned in his direction, or even Mr Stanton himself. And Route Seven was fairly busy, considering the weather, and the time of day.'

'Did you check the diner?'

Jim nodded. 'We went over every inch of it. It was still shuttered and padlocked, and nobody had forced any of the windows or any of the doors. Nobody had gone up the front steps or stood on the verandah.'

'How about the pickup?'

'It wasn't locked, but there were no indications that anybody had opened its doors in a long time . . . in fact the passenger door was rusted solid. We checked if anybody had climbed into the back of the vehicle and used the roof of the cab to steady a rifle, but there was no forensic evidence for that, either. No footprints in the back of the truck, no elbow-scuffs on the roof of the cab, no fibers, nothing. Besides, the angle of trajectory was way too low.

'However—' said Jim, and with a flourish, he opened an envelope and produced three photographs of the snowy ground in front of the diner. 'We're increasingly convinced that there must have been a second vehicle.'

'A *second* vehicle?' asked Steve.

'That's right. And all the evidence suggests that it was parked right next to the pickup at the time of the shooting.'

'Go on.'

'We found a rectangular area next to the pickup truck where the snow covering was considerably thinner. This indicates that a vehicle was parked there prior to the start of any substantial snowfall, although it had left before the snowfall became really heavy. Unfortunately, the later snowfall obscured any tire-tracks, as did the footprints of half-a-dozen troopers and media folk and rubbernecking passers-by.'

'Any idea what kind of vehicle we're looking for?'

'Something big is my guess. It could have been a full-size sedan, but I'd put my money on a station wagon or a panel-van.'

'Why do you think that?'

'Because the bullet hit Howard Stanton at an upward angle of approximately eleven degrees from the horizontal, which tells us that the perpetrator fired from very low down. Not more than thirty inches off the ground, maybe even lower, if he was firing from the spot across the road where this vehicle was parked.

'Thirty inches is too high for somebody lying flat on the ground, and too low for somebody kneeling. So my guess is that he was lying in the back of his vehicle, and if that's correct it was probably a station wagon or a van, since he could open the tailgate or one of the rear doors to give himself a clear shot.'

Steve opened his desk drawer and took out a flexible ruler. He pulled it out and measured thirty inches up from the carpet. 'OK . . . I see what you mean.'

Jim said, 'We ran some computer simulations this morning, using various types of cars and station wagons and panel-vans. We tried aiming a sniper-type rifle from all of them. With the van and the station wagon, no problem. But even when the front windows of the sedan were fully lowered, the sill was thirty-seven inches off the ground, and the rear windows of most sedans can only be lowered halfway down, for child safety. This means that even if the shooter was kneeling on the front seat of the sedan and firing at an angle through the rear window, he couldn't have made the shot that killed Howard Stanton.'

'Maybe he opened one of the doors,' Doreen suggested.

'Well, we tried that too, but it still makes for a very awkward shot, especially if the shooter was right-handed. Apart from that, there would have been a much greater risk that some-body from a passing vehicle would have noticed him.'

'Are you sure about your trajectory?' asked Steve.

'Within two or three degrees, either way. The cashier witnessed the moment of impact, and he was sure that Howard Stanton was holding his head straight. Even if he had tilted his head to one side, the shot still had to come from a very low firing position.'

Steve leaned back in his chair. 'So you're pretty sure that we should be looking for a panel-van or a station wagon?'

Jim tucked his shirt back into his belt. 'My personal guess is a panel-van. It would give the perpetrator a much higher degree of concealment. Like, when he's taken his shot, all he has to do is close the back door and nobody's any the wiser. In a station wagon he'd have to climb out the back and anybody could see him doing that. If I'm wrong, I'll take you both to Harbor Park and the lobster bakes will be on me.'

Doreen flicked through her notebook. She was wearing a pond-green rollneck sweater that made her look even more tired and liverish than usual. 'I talked to everybody at Howard Stanton's office. They're all very shocked, of course, although my feeling is that Howard Stanton wasn't outstandingly popular. His boss said that he was "meticulous," and his secretary said that he was "very fussy." One of his customers was there, and he said that if it had been possible to cross "i's" as well as dot them, Howard Stanton would have done it. Nobody actually said "pain in the rear end" but the suggestion was there.'

'So . . . he wasn't especially well loved?'

Doreen shook her head. 'They trusted him, for sure, and they respected him for all the business he brought in, but, no, I couldn't find anybody who felt any great affection for him.'

'Do you think anybody felt insufficient affection for him to blow his brains out?'

'Mmm . . . I don't think so. There was an angry young man called Kevin Westenra who told me that he had argued with Stanton over his expenses, but he certainly didn't seem to be the kind of person who would put out a contract, or try to shoot Stanton himself. Besides, Westenra was watching TV at his girlfriend's parents' house in Cornwall when Stanton was killed.'

'Lieutenant-colonel Lynch just called me from headquarters,' said Steve.

'In person? Wow, you're honored.'

'Not really. The media are crawling all over him, and he's very anxious that we don't let this baby go cold.'

'Well, good for him! I hope you told him that we don't

have a single eyewitness, nor any idea why anybody should have wanted Howard Stanton dead, nor any forensic evidence whatsoever. I hope you also told him we didn't even find a bullet yet, and even if we *do* manage to find a bullet we don't have a weapon to match it to.'

'We have one straw to cling to. Jim thinks we're looking for a van.'

'Oh, yes. I forgot. Just as well that there are only one hundred thirty-one thousand commercial vehicles registered in Connecticut, of which forty-seven thousand, two hundred are vans. Otherwise, you know, it might be difficult for us to find.'

'Doreen, you're such a pessimist.'

'I'd rather be a vindicated pessimist than a disappointed optimist.'

'You need to get out more. Socialize. Go to barn dances. Find yourself a man.'

'I don't want any more men, thank you. Why do you think I'm a pessimist? You know, when I was married to Newton, my parents came over to dinner one evening and Newton didn't break wind once. Not once. That was so much more than I could have hoped for, I burst into tears.'

Steve couldn't help smiling. All the same, he felt deeply unsettled. He hadn't come across a homicide so lacking in circumstantial evidence since the Mark F. Rebong case in January, 2000. Mark F. Rebong was the night manager of the Danbury Hilton Hotel, and early one evening he had been shot while driving to work on I-84, for no apparent reason at all.

The more Steve thought about it, the less likely it seemed that the shooter had been specifically aiming to kill Howard Stanton. For instance, there was no way that anybody could have known in advance that Stanton was going to pull into that particular gas station. If Jim Bangs was right, and Stanton had been shot from a vehicle that was *already* parked on the other side of the highway, then the killing was almost certainly motiveless.

Steve didn't like 'motiveless.' 'Motiveless' meant psychos and drifters, who were almost impossible to track down. They didn't have social security numbers, they didn't have credit records, they had no fixed abode and they didn't vote. He swiveled his chair around and looked out of the second-story window. The sun was still shining, but he could see that it wasn't going to stay that way for more than twenty minutes longer. A diagonal band of pale-gray cloud was creeping toward Litchfield from the north-west, and it had that radioactive orange glow, which meant that it was full of snow.

Doreen said, 'What do you want to do? We could put out an APB for troopers to stop any van that arouses their suspicion, for any reason. You never know your luck.'

'Do you know what, Doreen? That's almost optimistic.'

He reached for the phone but before he could pick it up, it rang.

'Homicide, Wintergreen.'

'Detective Wintergreen? This is Trooper McCormack, B Troop, up at Canaan. We have a fatal shooting, sir. Thought you ought to know about it ASAP.'

'When did this happen?'

'About a half-hour ago. A woman was killed in her own back yard. A single rifle-shot, from a distance. It seems to bear some similarities to your shooting down at Branchville, so I guessed you'd want to take a look.'

'Good thinking, Trooper. I can get up to you in twenty minutes. Wait—listen, this is important. We believe that our shooter probably used a panel-van to make his shot from, or maybe a station wagon, so please make sure that your people don't drive or trample over any tire-tracks.'

'OK, I got you. Any idea what kind of a van?'

'Not yet. But you could ask any witnesses if they saw one, or any other vehicle parked in the immediate vicinity. Give me the address.'

Steve jotted down the details on his notepad. Then he put down the phone and said to Doreen, 'Sounds like our shooter's done it again. Get your coat.'

61

Sissy Hears the News

Sissy had just finished her morning bath. She was standing in front of the full-length mirror on the back of her closet door, in her white silk bathrobe with the big splashy poppies on it, combing out her wet hair. Her hair was completely white now, and she had been debating with herself if she ought to try coloring it. Cerise streaks, maybe, to give it some character. Or viridian.

She still found it really strange that her reflection had become so old. She didn't feel any different than she had on the day that she and Gerry had first moved into this house, August 12, 1969. Here was the same bedroom, and the same bed, and the same mirror. She was even using the same comb.

She was still skinny, and thin-wristed. Gerry used to call her 'my ballerina.' But even though her cheekbones were still sharp, her prettiness had collapsed like a crumpled paper bag, and her lips were pursed. And why was she so *colorless*? Did the color fade out of you, as you grew older, the same way it did with furniture?

As she peered at herself in the mirror, the voice of the news anchorman penetrated from the living-room. She lifted her head a little, and listened. The television had been arguing and laughing to itself all morning, and so she didn't know why this particular item caught her attention. Maybe she had been expecting it.

'Thirty-two-year-old Ellen Mitchelson was shot dead in the yard of the Mitchelson family home at 3400 Canaan Road, apparently by a sniper firing from the highway. Her killing was witnessed by her six-year-old daughter Juniper Mitchelson. Randall Mitchelson, her husband, was upstairs sick in bed at the time of the shooting.'

Sissy stopped combing. As she stood listening, the bedroom

gradually began to darken, as if somebody were drawing a curtain across the sky.

'State police detectives have been called in, and the crime scene has been cordoned off while forensic investigators comb the area for clues. However Detective Steven Wintergreen of the Western District Major Crime Squad told WUVN News that it is still too early to speculate on exactly what happened, or what possible motive anybody might have had for killing Mrs Mitchelson.'

Sissy went through to the living room, still holding her comb. A neighbor in a purple wooly hat was talking to a TV reporter. 'It's such a terrible shock . . . you don't think that anything like this could happen in a quiet town like Canaan. The worst of it is, an innocent young girl has had her mother taken away from her.'

Sissy looked across at the coffee table and there lay the Predictor card. La Poupée Sans Tête. It had happened, just as the DeVane pack had said it would. A child had been unexpectedly orphaned.

'Police appealed for anybody who might have seen a van or station wagon or other vehicle parked close to the Mitchelson house at the time of the shooting, or anything else suspicious or out of the ordinary, even if it seems to have no direct relevance to Mrs Mitchelson's death.

'The killing of Mrs Mitchelson follows the shooting yesterday of forty-seven-year-old realtor Howard Stanton, who was gunned down by an unknown sharpshooter at the Sunoco gas station on Route Seven near Branchville . . . again, with no obvious motive.'

Sissy slowly sat down. Maybe Trevor was right, and the cards were nothing but hocus-pocus. Maybe she was deluding herself, and looking for some kind of magical answer to the meaning of life when there *was* no answer.

She picked up the cards and reshuffled them. She was tempted to read them again, but she decided not to. Supposing they were going to tell her that something *worse* was going to happen?

She looked across at the photograph of Gerry on the table beside her. It had been taken at Hyannis, in the early summer of 1971. Gerry was wearing a yachting cap and he was giving the thumbs-up. At the end of that year, Sissy had gone to bed, twice, with a handsome painter called Victor Raven. Gerry had never found out about it, and she had never confessed it. But now and again, when she was reading Gerry's cards, she had turned up Le Corbeau Infidèle, the unfaithful raven, and almost every time that happened, Gerry's car had refused to start, or he had lost his wallet, or he had brushed up against poison ivy.

She had never been sure if she ought to blame the raven card for Gerry's mishaps, or if they were nothing more than coincidence. Maybe she blamed the card as a way of blaming herself, because she felt so guilty. Maybe, after all, none of the cards had any significance whatsoever, except in her imagination, and her imagination was fading, like her hair, and her skin, and the color of her eyes. On the other hand, La Poupée Sans Tête had come up, the card that signified a child's sudden bereavement, and what had happened? Bang. A mother had dropped in the snow.

Almost absent-mindedly, she unwrapped another Cherry Mash. She wished Trevor hadn't bought them, because they reminded her that she was self-indulgent and weak, in the same way that the raven card had reminded her that she was self-indulgent and weak, and faithless, too.

Feely Finds Serenity

Feely waited over an hour-and-a-half at Chesney's Diner and the sun shone bright through the windows but there was still no sign of Robert. He ordered another cup of coffee (his fourth) and a large slice of lemon-curd sponge cake. Now and then he glanced up at the vivid yellow photograph of the 'extra-fluffy 4-egg omelet with melted Jack cheese,' but the chef hadn't yet made any effort to wash his hands, and Feely couldn't stomach the thought of unknowingly eating a booger.

The girl in the khaki stocking hat suddenly slapped her book shut. 'He's not coming,' she announced.

Feely turned and blinked at her. 'Pardon me?'

'My friend. He was supposed to meet me here an hour ago.'

'Oh,' said Feely. He had thought that she was referring to Robert.

'He promised to meet me here at nine exactly and what is it now?'

Feely looked out of the window. 'The roads are still pretty gelid. Maybe he's been hampered by a snowdrift.'

'He could have *called* me, couldn't he? It's not like he doesn't have the latest state-of-the-art Sony cellphone or anything.'

'Maybe you should try calling *him*?'

'Are you serious? I wouldn't demean myself. If he thinks so little of me that he can't be bothered to meet me when he says he's going to meet me, then I'm certainly not going to go crawling after him on my hands and knees like I care or something.'

Feely nodded, and sniffed. 'I know what you mean. You can't expect other people to hold you in higher estimation than the estimation in which you yourself hold yourself in.'

'Excuse me?'

Feely found himself going hot. Although she was wearing such dull, baggy clothes, the girl was quite good-looking, if you liked overweight girls. She had a broad face, with wide-apart eyes, and very full lips. Her eyebrows were unplucked, and Feely could see that she bit her nails, but to Feely that was part of her attraction. She looked natural, unlike his sister Gloria who spent hours in front of the mirror with a pair of tweezers and ended up looking like some yuca dancer's Thursday-night girlfriend.

Feely said, 'What I meant was, you're probably making the most sagacious choice. You know, by not phoning him.'

'Oh,' said the girl, although she didn't seem to understand the connection between 'phoning' and 'estimation.' She was silent for a moment, and then she added, 'Your friend's taking his own sweet time, too.'

'My friend? Oh, he's not my friend. He just picked me up.'

The girl blushed. 'I'm sorry. I didn't mean to pry or anything.'

'You're not. You didn't.'

The girl sat looking at him for almost half a minute, as if she wanted to say something, but couldn't.

'What?' said Feely, at last.

'I'm sorry. You kind of threw me off balance, that's all. I never met a guy who does what you do.'

Another long silence. Then Feely said, 'I wish you'd illuminate me. What exactly *do* you think I do?'

'Well, you know . . .' The girl rolled her eyes toward Robert's empty seat.

Feely turned toward the empty seat too, and then turned back again. 'What—you think—? Him and me? Hey, you've construed that totally erroneously! I was hitch-hiking, that's all, and Robert was the only one who had the empathy to stop for me.'

The girl stared at him. 'I'm *so* sorry! When you said he picked you up . . . oh, I could *die!*'

'Hey, don't be mortified,' said Feely. 'It's an easy misapprehension to come to. I mean, him and me, we're not exactly congruous, are we? He said that I should impersonate his son, in case people might think what you just thought, but, you know, I thought, what's all *that* about?'

The girl was so embarrassed that she cupped her hands over her face. 'I'm so sorry. I really am. You don't even *look* gay. Oh God, I didn't mean it like that, either! You're not, are you? Or *are* you?'

'No, I'm not.' Feely couldn't believe the way this conversation was going. It was like trying to eat very long spaghetti and everybody's staring at you and you never seem to get to the end of it. 'I mean, I'm *definitely* not. I don't have any familiarity with the guy at all, except that he used to sell these transparent rulers and he walked out on his wife.'

She took her hands away from her face. 'And now he wants you to pretend that you're his son?'

'Yeah.'

'Don't you think that's *strange*?'

'I don't know. He said he didn't want people to notice us, that's all. He said we should be like ghosts.'

'Well, I think that's strange. I noticed the two of you as soon as you walked in the door, and I thought: *strange*.'

She paused, and then she held out her hand. 'My name's Serenity, by the way. Serenity Bellow.'

'Serenity? That's a very mellifluous name.'

'Mellifluous? Where do you learn all these *words*?'

Feely released her hand. 'Out of the dictionary,' he admitted.

'You have to be *kidding* me.'

'Well, I didn't learn *all* of them out of the dictionary. Some of them I found . . . you know . . .' His eyes shifted sideways. ' . . . in the thesaurus.'

The girl slowly sat back, her eyes bright, her mouth wide open with surprise and delight. Feely couldn't understand what was so funny. Where else would you learn words from, except for the dictionary, or the thesaurus? They were all there, from aardvark to zymurgy, and all you had to do was memorize them. Or was he being hopelessly obtuse? Maybe everybody else acquired their vocabulary some other way that nobody had told him about. Maybe, when you were little, your father was supposed to whisper into your ear all the words you needed to know, that's if you had a father, and not Bruno.

'I'm reading T.S. Eliot,' said Serenity, holding up her book.

'Hey. Cool.'

'You don't know who he is, do you?'

'I've heard the name.'

'You know all of these incredible words and you never read T.S. Eliot?'

Feely shook his head.

'How about Ezra Pound? Did you ever read anything by Ezra Pound?'

'Not exactly,' said Feely.

'What *have* you read?'

'Well, *Moby Dick*. My English teacher Father Arcimboldo gave it to me when I was in school.'

'What did you think of it?'

'Actually, to tell you the truth, with *Moby Dick* I never proceeded a whole lot further than the middle of page one. Like I'd already seen it on TV with Captain Jean Luc Picard in it so I knew pretty much what was going to happen in the end, so I wasn't exactly enthused to read the central portion.'

'T.S. Eliot is wonderful,' said Serenity. 'Just listen to this.

"*To communicate with Mars, converse with spirits,*
To report the behavior of the sea monster,
Describe the horoscope, haruspicate or scry,
Observe disease in signatures, evoke
Biography from wrinkles of the palm
And tragedy from fingers; release omens
By sortilege, or tea leaves, riddle the inevitable
With playing cards . . ."

Feely listened until she had finished. Then he said, 'That's very unusual. I never heard anything like that before.'

'You like it?'

'I think so. It's very unusual, the way the words are joined together. It's kind of like a different language. *Harus*—what was that? That's a word I don't know.'

'*Haruspicate*. I had to look it up myself. It means when you tell the future by poking around in some animal's intestines. That's what they used to do in Ancient Rome. Like, if Caesar wanted to know if it was a good idea to invade Persia, the priest would cut open some sheep and stir its intestines with a stick.'

'And that's how they told the future? They haruspicated. That's a great word. Haruspicate. "Want to go out tonight, dude? I don't know. Hold on for a moment while I har-*us*-picate."'

Serenity closed her book. 'What's your *name*?' she asked him.

'Fidelio Valoy Amado Valentin Valdes.'

'Wow.'

'Don't worry about it. Most people who know me call me Feely.'

'*Feely*. That's cool. Where do you come from, Feely?'

'New York City. El Barrio. I guess you'd call it Spanish Harlem.'

'Really? So, like, what are you doing here in Canaan?'

'I'm in transition, that's all. And waiting for my ride to come back, wherever he's vacated himself to.'

'You didn't eat your breakfast,' said Serenity, nodding toward his untouched stack of pancakes.

'No. My partiality was kind of extinguished.'

'Your what was what?'

'I was about to eat them when I saw the cook,' said Feely, and mimed his nose-picking.

'Oh, *gross*. I just had the eggs and Canadian bacon. *Urrghhh!*'

'It's probably OK. Like, the human digestive system is very resilient. I expect you could digest a considerable quantity of other people's mucus without any deleterious effect.'

Serenity stared at him. 'Tell me something, Feely, are you for real?'

'What do you mean?'

'You're not putting me on, are you? You use all these words, and it's like you *nearly* know what they mean but not quite.'

Feely frowned at her. 'I don't think I'm exactly following you.'

'I don't know. I'm confused. I can't work out if you're serious.' She hesitated, and then she laid her hand on his shoulder. 'I'm sorry. I'm not trying to bring you down or anything.'

'Let me tell you something,' said Feely. 'My Uncle Valentin was a singer. He was my genuine uncle, my father's brother, nothing to do with Bruno. My genuine father walked out when I was three maybe, or maybe four. I'm not really acquainted with why or when and it was never any use asking my mother because quite frankly she doesn't know shit from Wednesday. That doesn't mean I don't love my mother and hold her in reverentiality. I do. I hold her in great reverentiality. But I remember my Uncle Valentin and he was sitting halfway down the stairs smoking a little cigar and playing his guitar and I came and sat next to him, and he sang me this song. The song was all about this little mouse, and how he devoured books instead of cheese, so that he was full of words, and because he was full of words instead of cheese he became king of the mice.'

'That's sweet.'

'Well, you can call it sweet if you like, but it became entrapped in my conscience. And especially when I was at school and I was bullied every day, and Father Arcimboldo told me that an accurate word is as equally impactive as a punch in the nose if not even more so. Well . . . on 111th Street, there wasn't very much opportunity to employ accurate words in context. I learned them all, but mostly I had to keep them to myself, because the people there are totally impermeable, they're either stoned or stupid. So if I use any incorrect nuances that's possibly the cause of it. But now I'm out of there. I can use all the vocabulary I know.'

Serenity said, 'You are really the most extraordinary person I ever met. Do you know that?'

'I'm just making good my escape, that's all.'

'So where are you headed? I mean, eventually?'

'I'm going north.'

'Sure. But where? Massachusetts? New Hampshire? Don't tell me you're going to Canada?'

'No particular destination. I think you have to pursue your mirage, that's all, and I have this mirage of someplace north, someplace very hygienic, you know, where it's too cold for people not to tell the truth.'

Serenity looked up at the clock. 'Do you think your friend's coming back? I don't think he's coming back. I think he's just offed and left you.'

'Well, in that case I'll have to find another ride. To be

70

honest with you he kind of intimidated me. He was pretty much inebriated and we nearly crashed, and then we got lost.'

'Why don't you come home with me?' Serenity suggested. 'My parents are away in San Diego for the holidays so I have the whole house to myself. You could have a bath and something to eat and you could borrow some of my brother's old sweaters. Well, you could *have* them, if you want to. He's working in Stamford now, for this law firm, and he's put on so much weight. They're never going to fit him again.'

'I'm not so sure,' said Feely. 'I did promise Robert that I'd wait.'

'Hey, what for? You don't owe him anything, do you? And he sounds like a total whack-job to me.'

As if to make up his mind for him, Feely's stomach made a loud growling noise, followed by a gurgle. He and Serenity looked at each other for a moment and then they both burst out laughing.

Trevor Gets Angry

Sissy hadn't expected Trevor to call around again so soon. She had dressed and pinned up her hair and she was sitting in the living room smoking and watching the TV news when she heard the crunching of car tires on the frozen snow in her driveway. She heaved Mr Boots off her feet, where he had been sleeping, and went over to the window.

'Oh rats,' she said. She stubbed out her cigarette in the Martha's Vineyard ashtray and waved her arms around frantically to get rid of the smoke.

Trevor came in through the kitchen door, stamping his feet on the mat. He was dressed in a quilted jacket the color of French mustard, and a brown wool balaclava.

'Hey, I was just passing,' he said. 'I had to see a client in Torrington so I thought I'd call by to see if you'd made up your mind.'

He pulled off his balaclava and his hair stuck up, just like it did when he was a little boy. Sissy had actually licked her finger to paste it down for him before she realized what she was doing.

'Would you like tea?' she asked him. 'Oh—and *before* you start sniffing, I had a cigarette this morning. Just one.'

Trevor rolled up his eyes, as if she were beyond redemption. 'The real thing is, Momma, I need to know if you're coming to Florida or not. My friend at Globe Travel has offered me a real good price on the tickets but I have to book them by the end of today.'

'Oh, I see. You're sure you won't have any tea?'

'Momma, you can't put this off any longer. Jean and I, we could have said to ourselves, so what, if the silly old woman wants to spend Christmas all by herself, freezing her buns off in Connecticut, that's her lookout. But we're worried about you, Momma, and we want to take proper care of you.'

'Yes,' said Sissy. She could see Gerry smiling at her from the fireplace. *Oh Gerry, I'm so sorry that I betrayed you. And I was such a coward, I couldn't tell you what I'd done, even when you were lying on your deathbed.*

Trevor said, 'Come with me today. Pack your bags and I'll come back to collect you when I've finished at the office. You can stay with us in Danbury until the nineteenth, and then we'll all fly off together.'

'Do you really think you can put up with me that long? Me and my smoking and my fortune-telling?'

'Momma, Jean and me have discussed this right down to the smallest detail. Jean is just as keen to have you come to Florida as I am. Listen, we're exactly the same with Jean's parents, Ned and Marilyn, we visit them regularly, we make sure they have everything they need. We believe that we have a duty.'

Sissy could see herself in the mirror at the end of the hall; and in the glass-framed pictures of Italy beside the living-room door; and reflected in the windows. So pale, so old. So many different Sissys.

'My heart's here, Trevor. This is where I always spend Christmas.'

'Your heart has angina, Momma.'

'It's the cards, too. I know you'll get angry. I know you won't understand. But this morning a woman was shot dead up at Canaan and I believe that the cards predicted it.'

Trevor stared at her. His hair was still sticking up at the back. 'For God's sake, Momma, this doesn't make *any* sense at all.'

'The Headless Doll, that was the card that came up, and when the Headless Doll comes up it always means that a child is going to be orphaned. And that's what happened.'

'Momma, this is insanity! The cards are just cards, they only mean what you want them to mean! Look—we really don't mind. If you don't want to come to Florida, then don't! But why not come straight out and say so, instead of making this ridiculous pretense that the cards are telling you not to?'

'But they *are*! They're trying to tell me that something dreadful is going to happen! Can't you see? It's already started, and it's going to get ten times worse!'

'All right!' Trevor shouted. 'All right! Supposing the cards *are* right! Supposing they really *can* predict what's going to happen, and it's going to be terrible! What do you think *you* can do about it? Hmh? Tell the police? Call up the National Guard? "I'm a sixty-seven-year-old widow and my cards tell me that something terrible is going to happen!" What do you think they're going to say to that?'

Sissy went across to the coffee table, picked up her pack of Marlboro, took one out and defiantly lit it. She blew out smoke, and then she said, 'You and Jean, you believe you have a duty. Well, I have a duty, too. I love you, Trevor, and you know I love Jean and little Jake. But the people around here, they're going to need me in the next few weeks, and that's why I have to stay. I feel it in my bones: there's no other way of explaining it.'

Trevor looked around the room; at the clutter of pictures on the walls; at the antique chairs with their scatter-cushions; and the gaggle of occasional tables; and the old carpet-bag that Sissy kept her sewing in; and the week-old newspapers stacked beside the fireplace.

'It's all right,' said Sissy. 'You can throw this all away, when I die. I won't be upset. But it's my life, and I want to go on living it.'

Trevor puffed out his cheeks, and then he said, 'OK, if that's the way you want it. But I don't understand you at all. It's like—I don't know. I just can't follow the way you think.'

'I *am* your real mother, if that's what you're getting at. I was there when you were born.'

'Very funny, Momma. Look . . . if you change your mind before six o'clock today, give me a call, will you?'

He pulled on his balaclava and for a moment Sissy wanted so much to say to him, make sure you've got your lunch money and your clean handkerchief and don't be home too late; but those days had long gone, and all the photograph albums in the world could never bring them back.

The Headless Doll

The wind began to rise, so that the snow in the Mitchelsons' back yard was whipped up into little dancing fairies.

Jim came trudging up to the swing-set and leaned against the upright. His cheeks were bright red and there was a clear drip swinging on the end of his nose.

'Well?' said Steve. 'What have you got?'

Jim took out a scrumpled-up bit of tissue and blew his nose. 'I'd say that the shot was fired from a vehicle parked next to that New England Dairies trailer. Again, I'd say that it was probably a van or a station wagon, because the shot came from very low down.'

'Any tire tracks?'

Jim shook his head, emphatically. 'The surface is all rubble and broken brick, and there wasn't sufficient snow covering for the vehicle to leave any kind of recoverable impression.'

'So we're only guessing that there *was* a vehicle?'

Trooper MacCormack gave a dry little cough. 'Sure. But I'd say that given all the variables it's a reasonable guess.'

Trooper MacCormack was a handsome, mature man with silver hair and a light winter sun-tan, and noticeably large ears. He was experienced, and he was efficient, and Steve had never seen a crime scene so meticulously cordoned off and protected. The only trouble was, Trooper MacCormack spoke in such a measured, expressionless drawl that Steve found it very hard to concentrate on what he was saying.

'We've talked to seven different witnesses and none of them saw any individual on foot anywhere in this vicinity within the time-frame of Mrs Mitchelson's shooting, nor did they notice any individual on that waste ground with or without a weapon of any description.'

Steve almost felt like saying 'Amen.' Instead, he looked around and asked, 'Nobody saw a *vehicle*, either?'

'Correct,' agreed Trooper MacCormack. 'But that doesn't preclude the possibility that a vehicle was there. If you were approaching Canaan from the south, any vehicle parked in that location would have been shielded from your direct line of sight by that trailer; and if you were leaving Canaan it would have been mostly concealed behind that furniture store. You would have had to have turned your head to see it, even if it was there, and why would you.'

Steve took out a stick of Doublemint, made stiff by the cold, and folded it into his mouth. 'If a panel van had been parked there, with one or both of its rear doors open, I think *I* would have noticed it.'

'Yes, but with respect you're a detective and you notice that kind of thing because you've been trained to. You would have said to yourself why does that panel van have its rear door open when there are no stores or warehouses nearby for goods to be loaded or unloaded. Your average individual goes around all day and wouldn't notice if a pink gorilla walked past them. That's a scientific proven observation.'

'I'd still like to find one person who actually saw a van parked there. Just one.'

'Well, we're still appealing for witnesses, sir, and you never know.'

Doreen came out of the house and balanced along the narrow path that had been marked out with yellow tape by the crime scene unit. 'Steve,' she said. 'Do you want to talk to Mr Mitchelson, and the little girl?'

'Absolutely.' He turned to Trooper MacCormack and said, 'Excellent work, Trooper. You'll keep me posted, right?'

'You bet.'

Steve followed Doreen into the house. The kitchen was crowded with troopers and reporters and photographers, and the boarded floor was a mess of wet footprints. Steve elbowed his way through to the living room. A female trooper opened the door for him, and then closed it behind him.

The living room was chilly and very silent. It was decorated plainly, with magnolia walls and a polished oak floor, and brown leather furniture. A sulky fire was smoldering in the grate, giving off more smoke than heat. Randall Mitchelson was standing by the window wearing a thick blue woolen robe, his hands in his pockets. Juniper was sitting on the floor close to the fire, clutching a Bratz doll.

'Mr Mitchelson? I'm Detective Steven Wintergreen, Western District Major Crime Squad.'

Randall turned around. 'Hi. I won't shake your hand. I have this appalling flu.'

Doreen hunkered down next to Juniper and said, 'That's a really cool dolly. What's her name?'

'Izzy,' said Juniper.

Randall said, 'Her aunt's on her way here now. Ellen's sister. She's going to take care of her for now.'

'We'll need to talk to your little girl,' Steve told him. 'But we'll have a specialist in child witness interviews . . . you know, somebody who won't upset her.'

'Upset her? She saw her mother shot dead, right in front of her eyes.'

'But *you* didn't see anything? Or hear anything?'

Randall blew his nose. 'The first I knew about it was Juniper shouting at me.'

'Mr Mitchelson . . . can you think of anybody who might have wanted to harm your wife, for any reason whatsoever?'

'She was a wife, she was a mother. That was all.'

'She hadn't fallen out with anybody lately? She hadn't been involved in any local politics, or any personal disputes?'

'She was very critical of all the money that was being spent on restoring Union Station. She thought that it ought to be spent on other things, like play areas for kids, and traffic calming. But that was all. I can't see anybody wanting to kill her for that.'

'OK,' said Steve, making a note. 'And what about your personal relationship?'

'What do you mean?'

'Were you and Ellen getting along OK?'

'Of course. What are you trying to suggest?'

'I'm not suggesting anything, sir. I simply have to ask you these routine questions.'

Randall stared at him in disbelief. 'You think that *I* had her killed? She was my wife. She was the mother of my child.

How can you think that *I* had her killed? How do you think that I'm ever going to find a woman like Ellen, ever again? Jesus.'

Steve waited for a moment while Randall blew his nose again. Then he said, 'Financially, things are OK?'

'Financially? What does that have to do with somebody shooting my wife?'

'I mean, your business is OK? You don't have too many outstanding debts?'

'I don't see the relevance.'

'Can you please just answer the question, sir?'

'All right, I have debts, but nothing too serious. Fifteen, twenty thousand dollars. I'm a freelance surveyor, I've been working on the Paugnut Mall at Torrington. I don't get paid until the second stage is completed, but that's not an insurmountable problem.'

'Was your wife insured?'

Randall lowered his head and pressed his fingers against his forehead as if he were starting a migraine. Steve waited and said nothing, because he knew how enraged *he* would be, if somebody had asked him the same question.

Doreen said, 'Did your mommy give you this doll?'

Juniper nodded, solemnly. 'I'm going to buy her a black dress because of Mommy being shot.'

Eventually, Randall said, 'The answer to your question, Detective, is yes, she was insured, but not for very much. And her value to me was far greater than all the money in the world. Now, I think I'd like you to leave.'

'Just one more question, Mr Mitchelson, if you don't mind. Do you know anybody who owns a panel van, or have you noticed a panel van anywhere around here in the past few weeks, parked, or driving especially slow?'

'Most of my contractors run panel vans.'

'OK . . . can you do me a favor, then, and draw up a list of all of your contractors, especially those you know for sure have panel vans?'

'You don't seriously believe that one of my contractors—?'

Steve put away his notebook. 'Mr Mitchelson, I don't seriously believe anything at the moment. There appears to be no motive for your wife's death, and so far we have no suspects.

I have to assume that anybody and everybody might have done it.'

Randall gave him a bunged-up nod. 'Yes. I understand. I'm sorry. It hasn't really sunk in yet. I keep expecting to hear her singing in the kitchen. She couldn't sing, you know. Couldn't hold a tune.'

Steve said, 'Sure. I'll talk to you later. And I'll let you know if there are any developments. If you can just work on that list.'

Juniper said, 'I put drops of water on Izzy's face, for tears.'

Welcome to the House of Fun

Serenity paid for Feely's coffee and his uneaten pancakes, even though he insisted over and over that he had enough money. 'Forget it,' said Serenity. 'You're going to need every cent for going north, aren't you? Supposing you need to make a down-payment on an igloo?'

'You don't really believe that my intentions are serious, do you?' asked Feely, as they walked across the slushy parking lot.

'Of course I do. I think you're wonderful. It's so refreshing to meet somebody who can just say, "That's it, I've had it up to my neck with this,"' and simply put their shoes on and walk out the door. It's so *hopeful*.'

She reached a bright orange Volkswagen Beetle, and unlocked it. 'Come on, hop in.'

Feely climbed into the passenger seat, carefully laying his cardboard folder on the floor.

'What's in there?' asked Serenity.

'I can show you. I've only ever shown it to one person, Father Arcimboldo, but I don't think he comprehended my rationale.'

'You thought a lot of this Father Arcimboldo, huh?'

'Father Arcimboldo changed my life. Father Arcimboldo made me realize that I wasn't a victim.'

Serenity backed out of her parking space and turned out of the station parking lot onto Railroad Street. She drove for only three-quarters of a mile before she took a right across a grade crossing into Orchard Street. Halfway along Orchard Street she stopped at a white-painted house surrounded by sugar maples. There was a Shogun SUV parked outside, covered with a blue waterproof sheet. Serenity parked close up behind it and climbed out.

'Welcome to the house of fun,' she said. 'Or it is when my mom and dad are away.'

'This is a really salubrious neighborhood,' said Feely, looking around. He had seen streets like these in movies, but he had never actually visited one in real life. Serenity's house reminded him of the house in which Jamie Lee Curtis was babysitting in *Halloween*.

Serenity went up the steps to the front verandah and opened the bottle-green door. Feely followed her, bemused. There was a brass knocker on the door with a face like a snarling wolf and he reached out and touched it on the nose.

'That's for protection,' Serenity explained. 'The front door faces east, which is where the Mohawks used to believe that all the evil spirits came from, so you put this wolf on the door to warn them off.'

'Very sagacious,' said Feely. He believed in the power of charms and talismans. His mother had lost her lucky pendant, the one that her mother had given her when she was dying of cancer, and a week after she lost it she met that *papayona* Bruno at a dance. If meeting Bruno wasn't bad fortune, Feely didn't know what was.

Serenity led the way into the house. It smelled of furniture polish and marijuana. It was only a modest four-bedroomed dwelling, with a living room and dining room combined, and a smallish kitchen, but it was the most spacious house that Feely had ever been in. It was so comfortably furnished, too, with a big gold-braided couch, and matching armchairs, and a huge TV in a polished oak cabinet. Above the fireplace hung a painting of a Spanish dancer in a crimson dress.

'This is very opulent,' said Feely, turning around and around. 'This is very classy indeed.'

'You think so? I think it looks like 1968. If I had my way, it would be all white leather and chrome.'

'Yes, but it's the comfort. The opulence.'

'If you say so. You want a cup of coffee? No, I guess you don't, after all that coffee you drank at the diner. How about a beer? Take your coat off, relax.'

Feely took off his thin brown windbreaker and Serenity hung it on a peg in the hallway. Underneath he was wearing a faded maroon sweatshirt with a picture of Compay Segundo on it, and baggy black track pants.

Serenity sniffed. 'I hate to say this but you smell like a dead raccoon.'

'I'm sorry. We had to sleep in the car. I didn't even brush my teeth.'

'Listen, why don't you take a bath and I'll wash your clothes for you?'

This was like a dream. Feely hesitated, but then he thought, this is where my destiny has brought me, all this way, and I shouldn't refuse what my destiny is offering me. He felt as if he were being passed from hand to hand, like a runaway slave being smuggled to the north by the underground railroad.

Serenity disappeared upstairs for a few minutes, while Feely sat on the very edge of the couch watching Channel 24 news. On the coffee table next to him there was a red glass dish full of Hershey's miniatures but he didn't have the nerve to take one, especially since there was a framed photograph of Serenity's parents right next to them, grinning at him. Serenity's mother looked just like Serenity, only bleached-blonde, with a hairband. Serenity's father looked like Beau Bridges, except he had less hair.

In the dining room stood a large lighted tank swarming with all kinds of tropical fish, tiny shiny blue ones, yellow-and-black striped ones, and big fat green ones with bulging eyes. Feely wondered how something could be so ugly and live. Then he thought of Mrs Castro who ran the corner store on 113th and Lex, with her squint and her mustache and her *famban barretoso*.

The TV reporter was saying, '. . . single shot from a .308 caliber bullet fired from a distance of one hundred thirty yards . . .'

The hot-water system in the house was making a deep rumbling noise, like an approaching avalanche. Serenity appeared and said, 'Your bath awaits, my lord!'

She had taken off her khaki hat and her thick khaki sweater and she was wearing a blue-and-white striped T-shirt and navy-blue ski pants. Even though nobody could have called her skinny she had a surprisingly good figure, big-breasted and wide-hipped, but her stomach didn't bulge too much and her ass was ample without being enormous and her ankles were very trim. Her hair was cut in a long black bob, and she had back-brushed it so that it was shaped like a bell. She looked even prettier than she had in the diner, in a big-sisterly way.

Feely followed her upstairs. On the landing there was a stained-glass window with a picture of fields, and a river, and skies piled high with cumulus clouds. A flock of ravens had gathered at the far corner of one of the fields, as if they were picking over a dead body.

'That's a really mesmerizing window,' said Feely, his face lit up yellow and blue, but all Serenity did was smile.

'Go on,' she told him. 'The bathroom's through there.'

The bathroom was tiled in white and green, with a polished wooden floor. In the center stood an old-fashioned tub with brass faucets and shower attachments and claw feet. It was brimming with bubbles, so strongly scented that they made Feely sneeze.

'Wild Hyacinth,' said Serenity. 'My grandmother gave it to me last Christmas. I know it's kind of overwhelming, but it should get rid of the smell of dead raccoon.'

'Thanks,' said Feely. He stood in the steamy sunlight and looked at the bath with a mixture of awe and unreality.

'There's a nice big towel here. If you want to shave, you can use my razor.'

'Thanks.'

Serenity waited. 'I'll need your clothes.'

'Oh.'

Feely struggled out of his sweatshirt. Then he sat down on the little cork-topped seat beside the bath and took off his damp-stained shoes and his rancid gray socks. Serenity took his socks between delicately pinched fingers and said, 'Ew. If Saddam had had *these*—'

Feely hesitated.

'Shorts?' said Serenity.

'I'm embarrassed.'

'Oh, you think I've never seen dirty shorts before?'

'I'm not wearing any shorts.'

'OK then, I'll just take your pants.'

Feely stood up, turned his back to her, and stepped out of his pants, leaning on the side of the bathtub to stop himself from overbalancing. He handed his pants to her, awkwardly, with one hand, but as he did so she grabbed hold of his wrist and swung him around, and then grabbed hold of his other wrist so that he couldn't escape.

'Why so *shy*?' she teased him. She looked him up and down, at his skinny flat chest with his nipples like flattened sultanas and his bony hips. She nodded down at the tarnished silver spider that hung on a chain around his neck.

'What's this? This is kind of creepy.'

'My grandfather gave it to me. He said that spiders spin the web of destiny, up into the sky. If you climb up the web of destiny, you get to heaven.'

'The web of destiny,' she repeated. Then she looked at him intently and said, 'Feely?'

'I'll, uh—I'd better get washed,' he said, trying to twist his hands free.

'First—' she began, and Feely thought, *What's she going to say? Don't tell me that she wants me to chingar her. I can't believe my luck. I'm scared. Don't say that she wants me to chingar her. I'm terrified.*

She let go of his wrists. 'First, I think you should take off your hat.'

'My what? Oh, sure. Sorry.' He took off his Peruvian peasant's hat and handed it to her.

'OK if I wash this, too?' she asked him. 'It won't shrink or anything?'

'I don't think so.'

'All right, then. Enjoy your bath. Don't drown, will you? I don't know what I'd tell my parents, if you drowned.'

Feely washed himself all over, twice, scrubbing his fingers with the nailbrush, and then he washed his hair. Afterward he lay back in the tub and allowed himself to float. He had never felt as clean as this, ever. He felt as if he washed off his past life completely—El Barrio, and his family, and all the dirty streets of New York City. Here beginneth my new existence. Simple, saintly, and truthful, and every sentiment expressed in words of the utmost limpidity. He almost felt as if he should step out of the bath and dress in a seamless woolen robe of softest white, like Christ.

Sola vaya, El Barrio. Goodbye and good riddance.

He was still floating when Serenity came into the bathroom. He sat up, and hurriedly scooped foam between his legs to cover himself. Serenity said nothing but held out a cold can of Miller Lite.

'What?'

'Take it. I can make you something to eat in a minute, if you like.'

She herself was smoking a very anorexic joint. She sat down beside the bath and sucked at it two or three times, flicking it occasionally to keep it alight.

'Do you have a girlfriend, Feely?' she asked him.

'A girlfriend? No.' He had used so much soap that the bubbles were rapidly crackling into oblivion and he had to keep his knees tight together to preserve his modesty.

'Have you *ever* had a girlfriend?'

'Oh, for sure! So many I couldn't count. Girls, they were all over me like flies. But before I left New York City, I broke it off with all of my girlfriends. They were upset, yes, some of them were crying, but I wanted to think about my destiny with total perspicuity, do you know what I mean?'

'You wanted to see things clearly,' said Serenity, nodding and sniffing up smoke.

'That's right. Like—deciding to go north, that was a highly spiritual decision. You can't be spiritual and have a girlfriend, not coevally. You never heard of any saint with a girlfriend, did you? You don't think, there was Saint Sebastian tied to the top of a tree and they were shooting all of the arrows into him, he had some girlfriend screaming and crying leave him alone, that's my boyfriend, leave him alone!'

'But now?'

'Now?'

'Now that you've made up your mind to travel north. Are you going to start going out with girls again or are you going to stay celibate?'

Feely didn't know how to answer that. The truth was that he had only ever had one girlfriend, his cousin Antonia, who was nice-looking but slow. All of those flashy girls on 111th

Street in their bouncy halter-tops and their sequin micro-skirts, they used to mock him because he didn't have a car and they couldn't understand a word he was talking about. It was no use trying to explain to these girls that there was more to life than yuca dancing and screwing and having babies at the age of seventeen. Couldn't they see their own mothers, beaten and degraded and worn out before their time, and only sixteen years older than they were? Didn't they *get* it?

Two weeks ago, after a great deal of maneuvering on the couch, Feely had tried to put his hand in Antonia's sweater, the red fluffy one. Antonia had immediately taken his hand away and told him that she had been screwed by almost every boy in her class at school, as well as three of her uncles, and most of her father's friends, and that she didn't want to screw Feely because screwing was boring, nobody said anything interesting while they were screwing and you couldn't even read a magazine, while Feely always made her feel clever and special and pretty.

Afterward he had stood on the corner of 111th Street with his hands in his pockets, oblivious to people who bumped into him. Greasy old men with no teeth could get to screw his girl-friend, but he couldn't. There must be a word for that. *Cabrón* was probably the nearest you could get, in Spanish. What was the English word for *cabrón*?

Serenity said, 'What do you want to eat? Do you like melon?'

Captain Lingo

Serenity sat watching him as he ate his second bowl of Cap'n Crunch, biting one of her fingernails.

She said, airily, 'I have this kind of an on-and-off thing with my boyfriend. I miss him, you know, when he's away, but whenever he comes back, he really gets on my nerves. His name's Carl Roedebaker, and he's something to do with golf resorts. I mean, he's so *handsome*, but I don't know—' She pulled a face, as if she couldn't make up her mind which sweater to wear.

'I don't know anything at all about golf,' Feely admitted. 'To me, you know, golf is like a gulf.'

'Golf is the opiate of the people.'

'So you don't think you'll marry him, this guy?'

Serenity shook her head. 'I don't want to marry anybody, not yet. I want to be a great writer first. I want to write a tragic novel that makes people actually weep while they're reading it and even consider suicide. Carl thinks that a tragedy is twenty-five last-minute cancellations from the Enuresis Association of Twin Forks, Minnesota.'

'But he's handsome.'

'Sure. But so are you, in a different way.'

Feely was dressed in a dark-blue Lacoste polo shirt with a snowy white collar, and a pair of stone-colored chinos that were three waist sizes too large for him. His wet hair was combed straight back from his forehead, although it was beginning to get curly again, as it dried.

'You really like that stuff?' said Serenity, as Feely finished his cereal and put down his spoon.

'I never tasted it before. Cap'n Crunch. It's good.'

Serenity put his bowl in the dishwasher. 'So . . . what do you think is the saddest thing that can happen to a person?'

'The saddest thing of all? Oh, no question. Being alone, that's the saddest thing of all. When you don't have nobody to say "Look at that!" to, or "What do you think of that?"'

'You don't feel like that now, do you?'

'Not now.' Pause. 'I *did*.'

'But why? You're a very attractive young guy. I mean you're way interesting.'

'I don't know. I always felt all my life like everybody in the world knew something that I didn't, and they weren't going to tell me what it was. I could never work out if anybody felt really affectionate toward me or if they were just dissimulating, you know? Even my mother. I remember I hugged her once but I saw her face in the mirror while we were hugging and she looked like she was thinking, how much longer do I have to stand here pretending that I love him?'

'Maybe you were hugging her too hard but she didn't like to say so.'

'No,' said Feely, emphatically. 'That was the face of somebody who wanted to be doing anything else in the world rather than hugging me. And do you know what she did afterward? She cleaned the toilet. She would rather have been cleaning the toilet than hugging her first-born son. The prosecution rests.'

Serenity traced a circle on the back of his hand, over and over. 'Have you had enough to eat?'

'Oh, sure. I'm stuffed. I'm going to have to acquire myself some of that Cap'n Crunch. I mean you could devour it straight out of the box, right? You wouldn't necessarily have to be furnished with a bowl and milk and everything?'

Serenity's finger kept on circling, and circling. 'Sure . . . you can eat anything straight out of the box, if that's what turns you on.'

'Do you have any more milk? I could really relish another glass. Back home, the milk always used to taste cheesy, or garlicky.'

'Ew.' Serenity stood up and went to the fridge. 'You were going to show me what was in your folder.'

'I don't know. It's not very cataclysmic.'

'I don't mind.'

Feely picked up the cardboard folder and laid it on the

kitchen table. He opened it up and carefully took out twenty large sheets of paper, each of them crowded with cartoon drawings. On the first page, a muscular man was bursting through a huge leather-bound book. He was dressed entirely in white, with words printed all over him; and he had a fan-like mask that was made out of folded paper. 'With nothing but the power of words . . . I can exterminate all evil!' he was shouting. The huge book was resting on stacks of other books, which between them formed the letters CAPTAIN LINGO.

Serenity looked through the first four or five pages in amazement. 'You drew all of these yourself?'

'Penciled, inked, and colored. *And* did the lettering.'

'They're incredible. You're a majorly good artist.'

'I'm not very good at hands, though. Look at his fingers, they look like five frankfurters.'

'They *don't*. These are wonderful.'

'I had the idea for Captain Lingo after Father Arcimboldo told me about words being much more lethal than guns and bombs. The story is that Captain Lingo is trying to defend New York City against the Grunters.'

'The Grunters?'

'These ugly purple guys here with the spots and the sloping foreheads. They can only speak in grunts, that's why they're called the Grunters. They're trying to rip up every single book and every single newspaper so that people forget what words are and have to grunt when they want anything. Like, there's a special grunt for "food" and another grunt for "money" and another grunt for "sex." But there are no grunts for words like "freedom" or "liberty" and there isn't even a grunt for "no." If people want something, they grunt, and if that doesn't work, they grab it anyhow. Food, money or sex.'

Serenity held up a drawing of a girl with a mass of curly black hair and eyes like a leopard and enormous breasts. 'Who's this, then? Your fantasy woman?'

'That's Captain Lingo's assistant, Verba. She gets caught by the Grunters and they torture her, and rape her. But she escapes and she finds out that the Grunters are controlled by the Hoarders, who are storing up all the words for themselves, so that only *they* can understand what's transpiring. *Own the words, own the world.* That's their motto.'

Serenity said, 'This is very deep stuff. Have you ever thought about showing it to anybody, like maybe Marvel Comics?'

'I don't know. I don't think it's so good.'

'I think it's so *brilliant*. I'll bet if they published this, you'd make a fortune.'

Feely carefully tucked his cartoons back into their folder. Serenity said, 'Where do you think you got it from? All this word thing?'

'Maybe my father, I don't know. He was a musician, like my Uncle Valentin. He played in restaurants and clubs, like that. But I don't know much about him. I don't even know if he's alive or dead. I think most probably he's dead, but my mother won't say. Either that, or she doesn't know.'

Serenity took hold of his hand and separated his fingers, one by one. 'I talk to my parents sometimes about T.S. Eliot and Ezra Pound and there's this certain look in their eye which tells you that they're not really listening and they don't under-stand and not only that, they don't *want* to understand.'

'Haruspicate,' said Feely, with satisfaction.

Serenity half stood up and leaned across the table and kissed Feely on his open lips. 'The web of destiny,' she replied. 'The box of Cap'n Crunch.'

She kissed him again, and then she licked his cheeks, and his nose, and his eyes, so that his eyelashes stuck together, and he was blinded with saliva. He was breathless. He didn't know what to say.

It was then that the doorbell rang and the doorknocker banged and a voice shouted out, 'Feely! Are you in there? Feely, this is Robert! Why the blue hell did you run out on me like that?'

Home is the Hero

Steve went home at two o'clock that afternoon because he was hungry and tired and he badly needed to change his shirt. He lived only two-and-a-half miles away from the Western District headquarters, on Litchfield Ponds Road, but in the time it took him to drive there, it started to snow again, in earnest.

The road was utterly silent and lined with naked trees. The only sign of life was old Mr Brubaker, in a fake-fur hat, salting his driveway. Steve lived at the very end of the road, in the nondescript square three-bedroomed house that his grandparents had built in the 1950s, and then added to, with verandahs and a sunroom and an ugly kitchen extension that Steve couldn't afford to replace.

He parked his Chevy Tahoe next to Helen's Bravada. As he climbed out, he heard the front door slam, and his son Alan came down the steps, shrugging on his parka. Alan was skinny and fair, quite unlike Steve, with a sharply turned-up nose and his hair messed up in that 'just woke up' look.

'What are *you* doing home?' Steve asked him. 'Aren't you supposed to be in school?'

'I'm sick, OK? I'm taking the day off.'

'You're *sick*? What's the matter with you?'

'Strep throat.'

'Well, if that's true, which I very much doubt, the best place for you is inside, keeping warm.'

'I have to run this errand for Mom.'

'Oh, yeah? What errand?'

'Listen, what is this? Are you *interrogating* me?'

'I just asked you what errand, that's all.'

'What's it to you? I'm not one of your goddam suspects.'

'Don't use language like that with me. You're damn well taking advantage again. Just because I didn't happen to be

91

home this morning, you thought you could do whatever you damn well liked.'

'Oh, whatever,' said Alan, and tried to push past him.

Steve snatched Alan's collar and twisted it around. 'You're going nowhere.'

'I see. Am I under arrest or something? You didn't read me my rights.'

'Get back in the house,' said Steve. He could feel his anger banging inside his brain.

'I'm running an errand for Mom, OK?'

'I said, get back in the house.'

'And I said, I'm running an errand for Mom, or have you gone deaf?'

Steve shoved Alan, hard, so that he fell back into the snow. Alan lay there for a moment, his eyes closed, and then he opened them and started laughing. 'You're so sad, aren't you? You're so predictable! You're supposed to be a police officer, steady under pressure, and what happens? You can't even talk to your own son without going psycho!'

There was a moment when Steve thought that he could handle it, that he wasn't going to lose his temper. But then Alan climbed to his feet and brushed the snow off his storm jacket and gave him the finger.

'You are nothing but a loser, man. I mean, look at you.'

Steve slapped him, hard, across the side of the head. Alan didn't fall down this time, but he clapped his hand against his ear and said, 'Shit. You psycho.'

'Get back in the house,' said Steve.

'Oh, so that you can beat up on me where the neighbors can't see you? No thanks! You psycho.'

Steve turned around and, sure enough, Mr Brubaker was standing in his driveway with his sack of salt, staring at them. He gave Mr Brubaker a half-hearted salute but Mr Brubaker didn't wave back. 'Alan, this is your last warning,' he said. 'Get back in the house.'

'Or what?'

Steve wiped his nose with his glove. He couldn't believe the hatred that he saw in Alan's face. Hatred for what? He had adored this little boy, when he was young. Every fall they had walked through the leaves together, kicking their feet up.

Every summer weekend they had gone fishing together on the lake. Night after night Steve had made up stories for him, about gingerbread men who ate their own toes for breakfast, and stroked his hair while he fell asleep.

And now? Now they could barely sit at the same breakfast table together. When Steve walked into the room, Alan walked out.

'It's simple,' said Steve. 'Either you get back in the house or don't bother to come back at all.'

Alan stood there for a moment, still nursing his ear, then he turned round and started to walk away.

'Where are you going?' Steve demanded.

Alan didn't answer, but kept on walking.

'You listen to me, mister! I want to know where the hell you're going!'

Without looking around, Alan gave him the finger again.

Steve stood and watched him while the snow began to fall thicker and thicker, and Mr Brubaker stood and watched both of them. Although it wasn't even 2:30, the sky was the color of corroded zinc, and there was that end-of-the-world feeling. Eventually Alan disappeared into the gloom.

Steve was tempted to drive after him, but he didn't think he could handle any more anger. 'Kids today!' Mr Brubaker called out.

Steve gave him another wave. He had never felt so inadequate in his life.

'My dad used to hit me with a hickory stick!' said Mr Brubaker. Then he added, 'Hard enough to raise lumps!'

Steve unlocked the front door and went inside. The house was chilly and smelled of woodsmoke and wet washing. He looked into the living room. The fire was lit, but it obviously hadn't been burning for very long, and Barry their marmalade cat was lying on the hearthrug looking deeply aggrieved.

Steve went through the kitchen and found Helen in the laundry room. The floor was a half-inch deep in water, and there was laundry dripping everywhere.

'For Pete's sake. It looks like Lake Naugatuck in here.'

'I tried to wash the Indian throw. It's jammed up the washing machine and I can't get it out.'

93

'You tried to *wash* it? You're supposed to take it to the cleaners.'

Helen looked close to tears. She was a small woman, for a big man like Steve. Her blonde hair was tied back with a scarf, which made her features look even finer. The first time that Steve had seen her, dancing through a lawn sprinkler on a summer afternoon, he had thought that she looked like a pretty little elf. And she had clear turquoise eyes, which she had inherited from her Swedish mother, the color of the sea, at Hyannis, in July.

'Look,' said Steve. 'You start bailing and I'll see if I can't get this darn thing disentangled.'

'I feel so *stupid*. I thought it would save us money if I washed it myself.'

Steve took off his coat and rolled up his sleeves. 'I can't stay long. I just wanted to take a shower and grab something to eat.' He reached inside the washing machine and gave the throw a hefty tug. Somehow it had managed to wrap itself around the paddles in a wet and inextricable knot. 'If I can't get this free now, you'll have to call Pushnik.'

'How's it going with those shootings?' Helen asked him. 'I saw you on the news just now. That was terrible, that woman being killed.'

Steve gave the throw another heave. 'It's much too early to say if they're connected. Jim Bangs thinks they could be. The shooter used the same caliber bullet, and the MOs were very similar. Apart from that, though, we don't have much evidence at all. What Lennie used to call NSN, NHN, NKN. Nobody saw nothing, nobody heard nothing, nobody knows nothing.'

Helen said, 'Come on, Steve, leave this. Go take a shower and I'll make you a cheese-and-ham sandwich. You want tomato?'

'Just let me give it one more—' Steve told her. He reached right inside the tub and pushed the paddles anticlockwise, an inch at a time. Then he wrenched the throw violently from side to side as if he were Tarzan, fighting an anaconda.

'You'll tear it!' Helen protested. 'You'll break the washing machine!'

But Steve suddenly found the strength to twist the throw

94

clear of the paddles, and it came free. He dragged it out of the tub and dropped it into the sink.

'My hero,' said Helen.

Steve said, 'Let it dry out, then I'll take it to the cleaners. Marjorie owes me a favor, anyhow. She'll probably clean it for free.'

He went back into the kitchen and dried his hands. 'By the way, what was Alan doing home?'

'Alan? He said it was a home study day.'

'Oh, really? He told me he had a strep throat. I asked him what he was doing outside, if he was so sick, and he said that you'd asked him to run an errand. Not to mention using all kinds of bad language and giving me the finger.'

'You two didn't fight?'

'It wasn't really a fight. Kind of a scuffle.'

'Oh, Steve.'

'For God's sake, tell me when we *don't* fight. I don't understand that kid at all. He has a good home, a good education. If he needs anything, all he has to do is ask for it. Yet he struts around like a total punk.'

'He's rebelling, that's all. He's trying to show his independence.'

Steve unbuttoned his shirt cuffs. 'He can show his independence as much as he likes, so long as he doesn't show it around here. So long as he's living with us, I expect him to show some respect.'

'Steve . . . you don't realize sometimes that you throw a very big shadow. It isn't easy for Alan to come out from under it.'

Bare-chested, Steve put his arms around her waist and kissed her. 'We should have had a girl. Then she would have looked like you, like the little fairy that fell off the top of the Christmas tree.'

Helen kissed him back. 'You think we should have had a *girl*? You don't have the first idea what trouble is, until you've had a girl. She would have had her tongue pierced, and a tattoo, and skirts so short she was flashing her fanny. You wouldn't have had time to solve any crimes. You would have been following her everywhere, making sure that she didn't smoke pot or have unprotected sex. Or any sex at all, for that matter.'

'What do you think I am? Some kind of control freak?'

'Go take a shower. You smell like stale detective.'

He was halfway up the stairs when his cellphone rang. He wrestled it out of his pants pocket and said, 'Wintergreen.'

'Detective? This is Trooper MacCormack. We have ourselves an eyewitness. A young guy who saw a van parked opposite the Mitchelson property, at the approximate time of the shooting.'

'That's good news. Where is he?'

'Right here, at Lakeside Road. What do you want me to do? Bring him down to Litchfield?'

'No, that's OK. I'll come on up to Canaan. Is he happy to wait?'

'No problem. He's going through coffee and frosted donuts like there's no tomorrow.'

Steve had the fastest shower on record. He toweled himself dry, pulled on the clean woolen underwear that Helen had laid out for him on the bed, buttoned up his shirt, laced up his boots, and he was ready to go. Helen pushed a sandwich into his mouth as he opened the front door, and handed him two more sandwiches in a brown paper bag.

'Be careful,' she said. He kissed her, slid on the icy front steps, and landed on his butt in the snow.

'I said "be careful!"' she laughed.

He brushed himself off and tried to laugh, too, but he had bruised the base of his spine and anyhow he didn't feel like laughing.

Ask No Questions, Tell No Lies

A few minutes before three o'clock, Sissy heard a knock at the kitchen door, but before she could open it, Sam Parker came in, his cap and his shoulders covered in snow. He stamped his feet on the mat and clapped his gloves together like a performing seal.

'Hi there, Sissy! I'm on my way to Torrington and I just dropped by to make sure you didn't need nothing or nothing!'

Sam was going to be seventy on Christmas Day. He was a widower, who lived about a half-mile away, overlooking Lake Waramaug. He was stocky, and short, with a big head and a little mustache, like Clark Gable. Sissy had been close friends with his wife Beth, and watching Beth waste away from motor neurone disease had been one of the most painful experiences of her life.

'I'll tell you what, Sam, I could use some mayo, but don't trouble yourself if you're not going into a food store.'

'No, I can bring you some mayo. Hell of a day out there. I wouldn't go nowhere at all if I didn't have to.'

'Like a cup of coffee before you go?'

'Thanks for the offer, but I don't want to be making too many comfort stops, not in this weather.' He looked through to the living room, where Mr Boots was lying in front of the fire. 'Hi there, Boots! Look at you! Don't know why they call it a dog's life, when he's indoors warming his nuts and I'm out driving in twenty below.'

Mr Boots barked, and thumped his tail against the rug.

'I reckon that dog's more human than most humans,' said Sam. He tiptoed into the living room in his snow-boots and roughly tugged at Mr Boots' ears. 'Look at those eyes! There's real genuine intelligence, behind those eyes! I'll bet he could give you a mean game of backgammon, if God had given him fingers, 'stead of paws!'

It was then that Sam saw the DeVane cards laid out on the coffee table. He turned around to Sissy and said, 'Still telling your fortunes, then?'

Sissy gave him an almost imperceptible nod. It had been the DeVane cards which had first warned Sissy that Beth was seriously ill. Beth had been losing her balance and dropping things, and at first she had thought it was nothing but her natural clumsiness. But Sissy had turned up La Pierre D'Achoppement, the Stumbling-Block, which showed a woman tripping up and falling into a chasm, at the bottom of which pigs were tearing at the flesh of living people.

At Beth's request, Sissy had told her fortune with the cards from the day that her illness had been diagnosed, and she had been able to predict Beth's gradual deterioration with dreadful accuracy. Her muscles wasting away; her inability to walk; to dress herself; or to take herself to the toilet. Her inability to chew her food, and swallow; and worst of all, her inability to speak.

Beth had wanted to be ready for each stage in her illness before it happened, and Sissy had told her, although she had lied about the day she was going to die.

Sam took off his glasses, polished them with his scarf, and then peered at the cards with interest. 'So what's in store for us? All good news, I hope.'

'To be honest with you, no. The cards have warned me that two storms are coming, although I don't exactly know what that means, not yet. Then *this* card came up . . . the Headless Doll, which meant that some child was going to be orphaned. The next thing I heard of, some poor young woman in Canaan had been shot dead by a sniper, and her poor little girl lost her mother.'

'I heard about that on the news. You really think this card predicted it?'

'Yes, I do. And I think these other cards are connected with it, too, although I still don't understand how.'

'Hmm,' said Sam, standing up straight. 'Hard to know what to do about it, I'll bet.'

'I thought of calling the police, but Trevor said that they wouldn't take any notice.'

'No, I don't suppose they would. Besides . . . you remember what it was like with my Beth. You told her what was going to happen to her, but there wasn't nothing she could do to stop it, was there? And nothing *I* could do, neither, although I would have given my life, if it would have made any difference.'

Sissy reached out and laid a hand on his sleeve. 'Sam,' she said, and he knew exactly what she meant.

'Maybe you should ask the cards about it, theirselves,' he suggested. 'Like, what should I do to stop this thing from happening, whatever it is?'

'I don't know. They're very good at telling the future, but they're not particularly helpful. In fact they're downright abusive, at times.'

'Why don't you try it, all the same?'

'OK. Why don't you take off your boots?'

She sat down on the couch while Sam went back into the kitchen to take off his boots and his coat. She didn't need to do a full reading. All she had to do was lay two more cards on top of the two Predictor cards, and then a third card across them, horizontally. The first two cards would tell her if there was any point in her trying to change the future, and the third card would tell what she actually had to do, if there was.

Sam came back in as she was turning up the first card. 'Les Trois Araignées,' she said, holding it up.

'Hm. Looks like three spiders to me.'

'That's exactly what it is. Three spiders. But if you look close, you can see that they're all spinning the same web. This means that whatever is going to happen next, it depends on three things, or more likely three people, all working together.'

'Is that good or bad?'

'Could be either. Two spiders are white and one spider is black, which means that one spider has evil intentions while the other two are comparatively harmless. But if the black spider can persuade the two white spiders to work for evil, then the three of them could do very great wickedness between them. If you look closer, you'll see that there are tombstones in the background, hidden in the grass.'

Without a word, Sam took a pack of Marlboro out of his

shirt pocket, shook out two, and lit them. He passed one to Sissy and they both sat in silence for a moment, blowing out smoke. 'I see you're beating that craving just as good as me,' he remarked.

Sissy turned over the second card. This was unexpected. Les Menottes, the Handcuffs, which showed a shallow stream, under a gibbous moon. A naked woman being led across stepping-stones by two men wearing pointed hoods. The woman's wrists were fastened together with a decorative chain of assorted flowers: roses and chrysanthemums and daisies. There was a strange distracted smile on her face, as if she were thinking about something very pleasurable.

'So what does this mean?' asked Sam. 'Hanky-panky in the park?'

'I've never turned up this card before, not in all the years I've been telling fortunes. These three people are *very* intimately linked. Maybe not related, maybe not lovers, but very close to each other in some way. The handcuffs are only made of flowers, which tells us that the woman has been willingly enslaved. This card may be throwing some light on our spiders . . . explaining what their relationship is. But look at the moon. The moon means madness. Whatever these three people are doing together, it's a kind of collective lunacy.'

Sam coughed, and cleared his throat. 'I think you've about lost me here, Sissy. Spiders, handcuffs. I don't know. When you were reading Beth's cards, it all seemed a whole lot clearer.'

'That's because we were close to Beth, and we knew what was happening to her. But these people, whoever they are, we don't know anything about them at all. Not yet, anyhow. But we will. You wait and see. By the time we've finished, we'll know them better than they know themselves.'

'Well, if you say so. What's the last card? I'd better be making tracks soon, before this snow gets too deep. Four inches, that's what they forecast. Up in Maine they got eight.'

Sissy took a deep drag on her cigarette and set it down in the big blue ashtray. She turned over the third card, and it showed two people standing in a heavy snowstorm, each with one hand raised beside one ear. Les Écouteurs Dans La Neige. The Listeners in the Snow.

'Two people,' said Sissy, and she could feel her cheeks flush. 'Two people, standing in the snow, listening.'

'What does that mean?'

'I think that's you and me.'

'How do you figure that? They could be anybody.'

'But it's the last card, it's the one that's supposed to tell me what to do now.'

Sam made a face. 'OK. One of those people may be you, but there's nothing that says that the other one's me.'

'Yes, there is. This card tells me what I'm supposed to do *now*. And it's snowing, isn't it? And you're the only other person here.'

'So what are we supposed to do?' said Sam. 'Stand out in the snow and listen?' He held his hand up to his ear like one of the characters on the card.

'We could try it.'

'Sissy, you know how much I respect what you can do with these cards. But I don't think you have the first idea what any of this means.'

Sissy held her head in her hands and stared at the snow card as if she expected it suddenly to speak, and tell her what it meant. She was sure that the figures on the card were Sam and herself. But Sam was right. She didn't have any idea what it signified, or what she was supposed to do about it, even if she did.

All the same, she had an overwhelming feeling that the cards were trying to tell her something important. They gave her the same sensation that she got when the phone rang in the small hours of the morning. Whoever was calling, and whatever they had to say, you just knew that it wasn't good news.

'Put your coat back on,' said Sissy.

'What?'

'Put your coat back on, we're going outside.'

Sam crushed out his cigarette. 'OK, if you say so. But I think you're sending your beagle down the wrong rabbit-hole.'

He shrugged on his coat and put on his boots, while Sissy buttoned up her blue fur-collared parka. 'Do you want a Cherry Mash?' she asked him, holding out the bag. 'Trevor bought them for me.'

'No, thanks. I just ate lunch.'

'Oh, go on, it gives me an excuse to have one.'

They both unwrapped a Cherry Mash, and then they stepped outside into the snow. It was so silent that they could hear a snowplow clearing the highway, over two miles away. 'So what do you think we're supposed to be listening for?' asked Sam.

'I wish I knew,' said Sissy.

They waited and waited, and Sam did a little shuffle to keep his feet warm. 'I can't stay too much longer, Sissy. I have to go to Torrington before the bank closes.'

'Well, OK,' Sissy conceded. 'Maybe I got it wrong. Maybe I should do the cards again, to see if I've made a mistake. The cards can be sly, you know. They won't lie to you, but they can lead you up the garden path.'

'Beth was like that.'

'Beth? I can't believe it.'

'Oh, she never told an untruth, not once. But she had a rare talent for making you think what she wanted you to think.'

'Yes,' said Sissy. She took his arm and they went back inside, into the kitchen. 'I guess you'd better be on your way.'

But at that moment, the clock in the hallway chimed three. And at the same time, with what seemed like unnatural loudness, the anchorwoman on the TV news said, 'State police detectives say they have a new witness to the shooting yesterday of Mrs Ellen Mitchelson, who was gunned down in her own back yard in Canaan by a single rifle shot. So far they are refusing to identify the witness, or to say exactly what fresh information he might have given them, but they say they are hopeful of making an arrest "within hours rather than days."'

'However, police are still asking people in Canaan to keep their eyes and ears open for anything that strikes them as suspicious.'

'Eyes and ears open,' said Sissy. 'Sam . . . we've been listening in the wrong place.'

'What are you talking about, Sissy? Listen, I really have to make tracks.'

'We should have been listening around Canaan, where that woman was shot.'

'Well, how do you know that?'

'I just do. I can feel it. And they said so, on the TV.'

'So what are you going to do about it? It's snowing like a bastard out there. You're going to wander around Canaan with one hand held up to your ear, expecting that you're going to hear what?'

'I don't know. I just know that I have to go there.'

Sam took hold of both of her hands. 'No, Sissy. This is just a senior moment, that's all. You're letting yourself get carried away.'

'Sam . . . I can't describe it to you. I feel like I'm *quivering*, like a compass needle.'

'Listen to me, Sissy, you know what that quivering is? It's your need to show the world that you're still useful. I get it from time to time, just the same as you do. It's because we've found ourselves old and alone, without even a partner to appreciate us, and we feel like we're surplus to requirements.'

'You're wrong, Sam. You're so wrong. I have to go to Canaan.'

Sam released her hands. 'You can go, Sissy. I'll even take you there, if you like. But it's a copper-bottomed waste of time.'

Sissy went back to the coffee table, and turned over the next card in the DeVane deck. She peered at it through her spectacles, and then she handed it to Sam and said, 'There! If that isn't proof, I don't know what is!'

Sam looked at the card skeptically. La Famille du Déluge. It showed a mountain landscape, under a thundery sky, and in the distance Noah's Ark, tilted at an angle. In the foreground stood Noah and his wife, as well as his sons, Shem and Ham and Japheth, and their wives, and *their* children, too. Ham was resting his hand on one of his son's shoulders, but the boy had his own hand raised to his ear.

'I don't get it,' said Sam, handing it back.

'Shame on you, Sam, not knowing your Bible! Ham's son was called Canaan. And look what he's doing. He's *listening*. It's Canaan, listening, get it?'

'Oh, come on, Sissy, you're putting eight and six together and making nineteen.'

'All right, if you don't believe me, I'll call Dan Partridge and ask *him* to run me up to Canaan.'

'Dan Partridge? That lunatic? There's no way you're driving up to Canaan in no blizzard with Dan Partridge.'

Sissy kissed him on the cheek. 'Then it looks like *you'll* have to take me, doesn't it?'

Incy Wincy Spiders

Feely opened the front door. Robert was standing in the porch, hunched up with cold, his coat-collar pulled up to cover his mouth. There was no sign of his car outside, so Feely looked up and down the street, but he couldn't see it anywhere.

'What is it?' he asked.

'What do you mean, "what is it"?' Robert protested. 'I went back to the diner to pick you up, and you weren't there!'

'Well, no, I was here.'

'Oh, you were here. Great. You couldn't have left a message or anything?'

'I didn't think you were coming back.'

'Did I tell you I was going to come back?'

'Yes, you did. But you said twenty minutes.'

'Christ almighty.' Robert shook his head in disbelief. 'Aren't you going to ask me in?'

'I don't know.' Feely turned around to Serenity, who was standing a little way behind him.

'Hi there,' said Robert. 'I'm Robert Touche.'

'How are you doing?' said Serenity.

Robert explained, 'Fine, I'm good. How are you? Feely and me, we were kind of traveling together.'

'So he told me.'

'I thought he was going to wait for me back at the diner but when I came back he wasn't there so I asked the woman behind the counter if she'd seen him leave and she said yes she'd seen him leave with you and you lived here on Orchard Street.' He took a breath and said, 'Serenity, right?'

'That's right.'

Robert cupped his hands in front of his mouth and blew on them. 'Pretty damn nippy out here, Serenity. Do you mind if I come inside?'

105

Serenity turned her mouth down and shook her head. 'I don't really think so.'

'Ha! Well, OK! It's just that I wanted to ask Feely here if he was traveling any further. You're still headed north, right, Feely, and I'm still headed north, so you're welcome to come along. I'm not twisting your arm or anything. You're good company, that's all. But if you're staying here . . . or you want to hitch a ride with somebody else, that's totally up to you. Totally.'

Serenity reached up behind Feely's back and began to twist his curls with her fingers. 'What do you think, Feely? Do you want to chill out here for a while? Or do you want to go along with—what did you say your name was?'

'Robert Touche. But call me Robert. Or Touchy, if you like. That's hilarious, don't you think? I pick up this one guy in the middle of a blizzard and he calls himself Feely. And people are always pronouncing my name wrong and calling me Touchy. So Touchy and Feely. That's hilarious, don't you think? Well, I can tell you're laughing on the inside.'

Serenity said, 'What do you want to do, Feely? Like he says, it's totally up to you.'

'He was the only one who had the benignity to stop for me,' Feely admitted.

'You see?' said Robert.

Feely wanted to go on heading north, but he wasn't sure that he wanted to go on heading north with Robert. He didn't believe that Robert would ever let him down. After all, hadn't he come looking for him now, to see if he still needed a ride? But there was something desperate about him that made Feely uneasy. Something dangerously unpredictable, and accident-prone.

Robert jiggled around and said, 'Maybe you could let me in for just five minutes so that I can thaw out my feet and we can talk it over.'

'OK, then,' said Feely. The wind was slicing through the front door and the wind-chimes in the kitchen doorway were jangling as wildly as alarm bells. 'Serenity . . . is that OK with you?'

'Sure,' said Serenity, without enthusiasm.

Robert stepped inside and Feely closed the door. 'I didn't see your car,' said Feely.

'I parked it round the corner, out of sight. You remember

last night, when we had that minor contretemps with that truck? I don't really want the truck company making any claims against my insurance. You know what it's like.'

Without taking off his coat or his boots he headed directly for the fireplace and stood in front of it, with his hands outstretched. 'I'll tell you something, Feely, when I walked into the diner and saw that you were gone, I really thought that I was never going to see you again.'

Feely said, 'I got talking to Serenity.'

'That's a beautiful name, Serenity. Beautiful name for a beautiful girl.'

'Oh, please,' said Serenity.

'I'm sorry, Serenity. But I'm a salesman by nature. That means that if something impresses me, I say so. If you took me to see the Mona Lisa, I wouldn't just stand in front of it with my mouth hanging open. That's not me. I don't believe that we should repress our natural responses. I think it's like some kind of illness. You have a beautiful name, don't you, you can't argue with that, I mean your parents thought of it, not you, but as it turns out you grew up to suit it, and if you think I'm being cheesy by saying so, then please accept my apology, but all I did was make a truthful honest comment.'

Serenity said nothing but sat back on the couch. She patted the cushion and Feely sat down next to her.

'Incredible,' said Robert, looking around the room. 'Landed on your feet, then, Feely? New clothes! Look at you! Looks like you've taken a shower, too.'

'Feely's a very special person,' said Serenity.

'Oh, yes,' said Robert. 'That's for sure.'

'So, you're headed north, too?'

'I'm not really headed anywhere, to tell you the truth. But north is as good a direction as any, don't you think?'

'If you say so.'

'Well, with respect, you don't really understand what the hell I'm talking about. It's only twelve days to Christmas and here I am, driving around Connecticut in a snowstorm, not really headed anywhere.'

'I'm sorry, Robert,' said Serenity. 'What you're doing and where you're headed, that's not my business. Added to that, I don't majorly care.'

'Sure,' said Robert. 'I understand. Why should I expect you to care? If we all went around caring what everybody else was doing, shit, we wouldn't have the time to care for ourselves, would we?'

'I'm not interested,' Serenity retorted. 'I only let you in because Feely wanted to let you in, but if you've warmed up now, you're more than welcome to leave.'

Robert came away from the fire and hunkered down beside the couch, so close that Feely could smell the Jack Daniel's on his breath, and the cigarette smoke on his coat, and his pungent socks.

'People complain about racial prejudice, you know that? Blacks complain about it, Hispanics complain about it, Koreans complain about it. But do you know who suffers the most racial prejudice of all? The white middle-class white-collar male, that's who suffers more than anybody else. You invited Feely into your home, right? Look at him. He's Cuban. He's young and he's poor and he's good-looking. He's like a lost dog, so you feel sorry for him.

'For all you know, Feely's a crack addict, or he's suffering from HIV. The chances are, both. But you don't think about that. All you think is how cute he looks and how funny he talks. But me? One look at me and your hackles go up. White middle-class male. Ignore the fact that I'm statistically likely to be honest, and responsible, and caring, and church-going. Ignore the fact that I'm also a human being.

'You don't care that I'm driving around in a snowstorm twelve days before Christmas, with noplace to go? Why should you? I'm a white middle-class white-collar male, and I can look after myself, right, plus every other workshy bastard who's living on welfare. I don't need anybody's sympathy. I don't need a warm fire and anybody's love, even when it's twenty-five degrees below and all my friends have turned their backs on me and I can't even afford a bed-and-breakfast.'

He stood up. 'I screwed up, OK? I know I screwed up. But does that mean that I have to lose my two little girls, and my house, and my car, and all my possessions? I didn't do anything, except I had carnal relations with another woman! That's all I did! I cheated on my wife! That's all! I would have got more respect if I had cut her head off!'

Serenity said, 'OK. I didn't know. I'm sorry.'

'Well, like you said, it isn't your affair.'

Robert went back to the fireplace and chafed his hands together. 'I guess my blood's started circulating again . . . if young Feely doesn't want to come with me, I'd better hit the bricks. I've got miles to go before I sleep . . . many very necessary things to do.'

'How about a drink?' asked Serenity.

'No, thanks. I reach this particular level of drunkenness when I drive like an angel. Any more and I start to get a little dangerous.'

'OK,' said Serenity.

There was a long silence. Robert stayed by the fireplace, still rubbing his hands. Serenity looked at Feely and Feely looked from Robert to Serenity and back again, as if he were waiting for one of them to say something.

'Adios, then,' said Serenity.

But Feely said, 'Look—it's snowing again.'

Serenity and Robert both turned to look out of the window. Feely was right. The snow was coming down thick and heavy.

'You can't drive in this,' said Feely. 'It's far too aleatory.'

Robert went over to the window. 'You're right. It is pretty damned aleatory.' He paused for a moment, and then he said, 'Guess I'd better find myself a bed-and-breakfast. I don't want to spend another night in the car.'

'Oh, all right,' said Serenity. 'You can stay here until the snow eases up. But on two conditions.'

'Anything.'

'Condition one is, you go out and chop some more logs for the fire. Condition two is, when you've done that, you take a shower and change your clothes.'

'Serenity, you're a queen. I just hope that my daughters grow up to be like you.'

'I'm an idiot. My parents would go Chucky if they knew.'

Robert picked up the framed photograph of Serenity's dad and mom. 'I don't know. They look like good people to me.'

'Well, looks can be deceptive. They're so dated, those two. My dad's favorite song is "Voulez-Vous Coucher Avec Moi."'

'Hey,' said Robert. 'Mine too.'

The Laughing Tree

'This is the guy,' said Trooper MacCormack, showing Steve and Doreen into the interview room. 'Denis Bodell, plumber's assistant. He was a passenger in his boss's van when they drove past the Mitchelson place at the time of the shooting.'

Denis Bodell was sitting at the interview table with a cup of coffee and an empty box of Krispy Kreme donuts. He looked not much older than twenty or twenty-one. He had curly ginger hair and ginger eyebrows. He was wearing a green-and-red sweater and jeans with a sharp crease pressed into them.

Steve approached him and Denis looked up with a small, hopeful smile.

'Denis? My name's Detective Wintergreen and this is Detective Rycerska. We'd like to thank you for coming in.'

'Hey, you're welcome. I saw it on the TV that you was appealing for witnesses, and I said to Mr Johnson, that's me, I'm a witness, and Mr Johnson drove me right here, no stopping.'

Steve dragged out a chair and sat down. 'Mr Johnson, that's your boss?'

'That's right. We was on our way to the Rheinhold place to thaw out some frozen pipes.'

'And you were passing the old warehouse around the time that Mrs Mitchelson was shot?'

'Eight twenty or thereabouts, that's right.'

'So tell us what you saw.'

'I seen a van parked right opposite, next to a trailer. I never would have thought nothing of it, 'less I saw it on the TV and how you was appealing for witnesses.'

'OK . . . you want to tell us what this van looked like?'

Denis Bodell nodded, and nodded, and kept on nodding.

110

'Go on, then,' said Doreen, impatiently. 'Tell us what it looked like.'

'It was white, with a tree on the side of it.'

'Did you recognize the model?'

Denis shook his head. 'I'm not too sure. Could have been a Savana.'

'License plate?'

'Didn't look. I mean there wasn't any reason to.'

'So what about this tree on the side of it? What did that look like?'

'It was brown, and it was leaning over, like it was blowing in the wind. It had red leaves on it and some of the leaves were flying away, and it was laughing.'

'Excuse me?'

'There was like a face on it, if you understand what I mean, and the face was laughing.'

'I see.' Steve wrote down, *laughing tree*. 'How about writing? Was there a company name on the van, anything like that?'

'There was writing, but I couldn't tell you for sure what it was.'

'If you close your eyes, and really try to picture that van in your mind, can you give me any idea at all what that writing might have said? Was it a long word, or a short word? What letter did it start with?'

Denis screwed his eyes tight shut. Steve and Doreen waited for over thirty seconds before he opened them again. 'I think . . . double-yah.'

'You think it started with a W?'

'That's right. Double-yah. In fact, I'd put ten dollars on it.' Steve jotted down a few notes. Then he looked across at Denis and said, 'Which way was the van parked? Was the front end facing the highway or was it facing away from the highway?'

'It was facing away.'

'And were its rear cargo doors open or closed?'

'Open.'

'One of them or both?'

'I think one of them.'

'And did you glimpse anything inside?'

'No, sir. We was driving past, that's all, and I only caught a quick flash.'

111

'OK,' said Steve. 'If I were to ask you to draw the tree that you saw on the side of the van, do you think you could do that?'

'I don't think so. When it was art, the teacher used to make me wash her car.'

'Well, maybe we can have a police artist draw it for you?'

'Sure, that's cool. I can do that.'

Steve stood up. 'All right, then, Denis, if you can wait here just a little longer. I want to thank you again for being so public-spirited.'

Denis stood up, too, and primped up his curls. 'Do we do the TV now?'

'I'm sorry?'

'The TV. Like, me telling everybody what I seen and everything.'

'I'm sorry, Denis. This isn't going to be on TV.'

Denis looked baffled, and Steve suddenly realized why he had pressed his jeans.

'You thought this was going to be on TV?'

'No. Well, yes.'

Doreen said, 'That isn't the only reason you came in, is it? To be on TV? I mean, you really *did* see this van?'

'Oh, sure I did. White, just like I said, with a laughing tree on the side of it. And a word beginning with double-yah.'

Steve and Doreen left him in the interview room and went out in the corridor. Doreen said, 'What do you think?'

'I'm not sure. But it doesn't sound like he's making it up. When people make things up, they're either very vague, or else they're much too specific. He clearly saw the van and he clearly saw the tree, but he didn't see the license plate and he couldn't be sure about the lettering.'

Trooper MacCormack came up. 'I've, ah, talked to Lennie Johnson, Denis Bodell's employer. According to him, Denis is reliable and honest, even if you can't trust him to put on his pants the right way up. His words.'

'OK, then,' said Steve. 'Let's put out an APB for a white Savana-type van, carrying a brown logo of a laughing tree, and a word that might begin with W. Maybe we'll catch this bastard before he uses some other poor sucker for target practice.'

Echoes of Tragedy

Sam drove so slowly that by the time they reached Cornwall Bridge, Sissy's lower back was aching and she was beginning to wish that she hadn't come. Snow was still falling, but only thinly now, and the snowplows had just been through, so the main roads were mostly clear. In spite of that, Sam drove at a steady 27 mph, and slowed down even more whenever he approached an intersection. 'Never know . . . somebody might come whizzing out on skis, or a snowboard . . . happened to my younger brother Marlon. Crushed his pelvis, and he walked like a rocking-horse for the rest of his life.'

Sissy said nothing but sat deeply huddled in the big black sable coat that she had inherited from her mother. It had a huge collar and it brushed the ground when she walked, although it hadn't when she was younger, and taller. Her mother had worn it for the opening night of *The Most Happy Fella* in 1956, and it smelled like it.

Sissy had once wondered if Sam might make a good companion for her sunset years. He was handsome, after all, and he had a ribald sense of humor. But as they crawled toward Canaan on Route 7 that afternoon, she knew that she could never stand to go anywhere with him, if this was how he normally traveled around.

'Sam . . . do you think you could give it a little more gas?' she asked him.

'I don't want to tempt fate, Sissy.'

'I don't want you to *tempt* it, just try to catch up with it.'

Eventually, however, they drove into Canaan. They passed the yellow-painted Mitchelson house. Sissy recognized it from the TV news, although it looked smaller in real life. Two state police cruisers were parked outside, as well as a TV van, and the yard was still fenced off with tape.

'Would you stop here, just for a moment?' Sissy asked Sam.

Sam drew up outside the old furniture warehouse. Sissy opened her door and climbed out, and stood in the snow for a minute. It was so quiet that she could hear the police radios squawking. The cards had told her to listen, but she wasn't at all sure what she was supposed to be listening for. But she felt confident that she was supposed to be here, and that she had come to the right place.

A young trooper came across the road. 'You can't park here, folks. Crime scene. You'll have to move on.'

'This is where that young woman was shot, isn't it?'

'Just move on, please.'

Sissy turned slowly around. *Completeness*, she thought, although she didn't know why. *Completeness, like a happy family.*

The trooper said, 'Ma'am . . . I don't want to have to book you.'

'Of course not, I'm sorry.'

But as she climbed back into Sam's boxy old Jeep, she shivered, and it wasn't just the north-west wind, blowing off the snow. She turned her head and looked back toward the rough piece of ground next to the New England Dairies trailer, and she could almost sense that there was somebody there. Somebody who felt very lonely, and disaffected. Somebody who felt that the world had turned its back.

'Something wrong?' asked Sam, as they pulled away from the side of the road and drove toward the town center.

'I don't know . . . I had the strangest feeling. It was like when a bad card comes up.'

'Where do you want to go now?'

'Let's just keep on heading north. I've got that quivering again.'

Sam pulled a face. 'I hate to say this, Sissy, but this is just about the wildest wild goose chase I've ever been on. You and I should be sitting in front of the fire with blankets over our knees, sipping some of that coffee of yours, the one that's half coffee and mostly vodka.'

'Oh come on, Sam. Stop talking like a geriatric.'

'Why not? I *am* a geriatric.'

Sissy said, 'Did you ever look at me and think, "I wouldn't

mind getting into the sack with Sissy, and having carnal relations"?'

'Sissy . . . that's not the kind of question a woman like you should be asking a fellow like me!'

'Why not?'

'Well . . . even if I ever did think about you improperly, and I'm not saying that I ever do, I hope I'd be gentleman enough to keep my improper ideas to myself.'

'What's improper? We're both single, aren't we?'

'Sure. But that isn't the point.'

'That's precisely the point. So why don't you answer the question?'

They were approaching Union Station. The snow was whirling off the top of the station tower like a long white scarf. As they came closer, Sissy thought she heard somebody whisper '*Tea-leaves.*'

'Stop,' she said, as they passed close to Chesney's Diner.

'What is it?'

'I can hear voices.'

Sam listened, and then he frowned at her. 'I don't hear nothing.'

'They're very indistinct.'

'I got my hearing-aid turned up.'

Sissy closed her eyes tight and inclined her head toward the diner. 'Whoever it was . . . they're not here now. They've gone. But they were talking here before.'

'What do you mean?'

'It's like an echo. Like when somebody's hammering, very far away, on a snowy afternoon, and they stop hammering, but you can still hear it.'

'Can you hear what they're saying?'

'Not too clearly. "Tea-leaves," I think.' She listened again. 'And "horoscopes," I definitely heard "horoscopes." And somebody talking about crying.'

Sam turned up his hearing-aid until it whistled with feedback. 'I still don't hear nothing.'

Sissy said, 'It must be a conversation that somebody had here earlier. It's like their words are still here, waiting for me to hear them.'

'You're sure you're not imagining it? Who else talks about tea-leaves and horoscopes, except for you?'

115

'Sam . . . I can *hear* it. That's why the cards sent me here. They want me to listen, so that I can understand what's going on.'

She climbed down from the Jeep and stood in the parking lot, her head lowered and both hands cupped over her ears. A man walking in a bobbly ski-hat stopped and stared at her. Maybe Sam was right, and all that she could hear was the wind blowing, and the rattle of plastic sheeting around the half-restored station. But she was sure that she picked up the words 'playing-cards' and 'tragedy.'

Tragedy, there it was again; and it wasn't the wind. Then, *north*.

She lifted her head. The wind made her eyes water, but she didn't move for almost a minute. *North*, she could feel it. She had never in her life felt so certain about one of her intuitions. It couldn't have been clearer if it had been written in the snow.

She got back into the Jeep and slammed the door. 'North,' she said. 'We have to follow the main highway.'

Sam looked at her solemnly. 'I *did*, as a matter of fact.'

'I'm sorry?'

'I *did* look at you one time and think that I wouldn't mind taking you to bed, for carnal relations.'

'Oh.'

'As a matter of fact I thought it two or three times. But especially that one time. It was the first week of July, and there was a wind blowing, and you were standing in your yard in a yellow cotton dress with blue flowers on it, and you hadn't fixed your hair up, so that it was all flying up in the air.'

'You should have said something.'

'No, Sissy. Some things are better left as daydreams. I've seen myself in the mirror, doing my press-ups, and believe me, that's not a sight to stir any woman's libido.'

Sissy reached across and squeezed Sam's hand. 'Let's go north. I get the feeling that whatever it is, we're coming pretty close to it.'

Blood on the Snow

Feely followed Robert around to the side of the house. Robert said, 'You fell on your feet here, kid, that's for sure.'

'I didn't think you were coming back.'

'You should of trusted me. I never let anybody down, ever. I never let my children down, I never let my friends down. I know I let my wife down, but that was just a misfortune of marriage.'

'A vagary,' said Feely.

'Yeah,' said Robert. 'That too.'

He bent down and pulled up the garage door. Inside, one of the spaces was taken up by a beige Toyota Corolla, while the other space was stacked with sawn-off logs. At the back of the garage was a long workbench, and rows of shiny tools, screwdrivers and wrenches and tenon saws, all pedantically hung up according to size.

'Neat freak,' said Robert. But Feely had never seen inside a suburban garage before, except on TV, and he stood and looked at it in wonder.

Robert found a long-handled ax, cleaned and oiled and fastened to the wall. 'OK, Feely, you going to give me a hand here? You can carry the logs outside, and I'll split 'em.'

Feely was touching the tools on the workbench. He couldn't imagine what most of them were for, but he was fascinated by the way they shone, and the way they smelled. Robert came up behind him and laid a hand on his shoulder.

'Know what this is? A vise. Every man has his own secret vise.' Feely blinked at him, but he said, 'Joke. Get it?'

They went outside, into the snow. There was a chopping block by the side of the garage, under the trees. Feely carried out logs while Robert swung the ax around. 'You know what?

This feels so good. You don't realize how much you're going to miss all of those simple chores, until your home gets taken away from you. Splitting logs, burning the leaves, clearing out the gutters. And your kids, playing in the yard while you're doing it. And your wife, you can see her through that brightly lit window, baking a cake.'

'You really miss it, don't you?' said Feely.

Robert shrugged, and then he said, 'No. Who gives a shit?'

He propped a log on the chopping block, stood back, and swung at it. The log split neatly in half, and the whack of the ax echoed and re-echoed around the street. Feely picked up one of the fallen halves and balanced it back on top of the chopping block, so that Robert could split it again.

'Hold it up straight,' said Robert.

'Hold it? You might cut my hands off.'

'Didn't I tell you to trust me?'

Feely nervously held the log up, but just as Robert brought the ax down, he whipped his hands away, and the log toppled sideways.

'You think I'm going to hurt you?' said Robert, in exasperation.

Feely kept his hands tucked firmly into his armpits. 'Not with any premeditation. But you might do it inadvertently. And you've been drinking.'

'For Christ's sake. I'm an expert. I've been splitting firewood since I was big enough to pick up an ax.'

Robert picked up the piece of firewood and held it steady with his left hand. He closed one eye, to get his aim, and then he swung the ax down with his right. He split the firewood, but he also chopped off the top of his left index finger, just below the first joint, and the tip of his middle finger, just below the nail. Blood spattered sharply across the snow, and onto Feely's new pants.

'Shit!' screamed Robert. 'Shit! Shit! Shit!'

He held up his hand and blood was spurting out in two pulsing jets. 'I cut my fingers off! I cut my freaking fingers off!'

Feely took one look at him, open-mouthed. Robert was shouting and waving his hand around and it was so much like a cartoon that Feely started to laugh. He could almost believe that Robert had chopped his fingers off on purpose, to entertain him.

'What the blue hell are you laughing at?' Robert screamed at him. 'You think this is *funny*?'

He clamped his right hand over his left hand, trying to stop the bleeding, but blood streamed into his sleeve and dropped across the driveway.

'Give me that!' Robert reached out and dragged off Feely's white woolen scarf. He wrapped it tightly around his fingers and then he held his arm up high, as if he were giving a salute.

'Hey, Robert, that's my new scarf,' Feely protested, as he saw the blood soaking through it. 'Serenity just gave me that.'

'Oh, I'm sorry, you'd rather see me bleeding to death in front of your eyes?'

'It was so funny,' said Feely. 'You went *wop!* And then you went *huh?* And then you went *argghh!*'

'You distracted me, you clown. If you hadn't distracted me—*Look for my fingers!*'

'What?'

'Look for my fingers, you moron! I can stick them back on!'

'Oh,' said Feely. He looked all around the chopping block, but he couldn't see any sign of them, only blood and bits of firewood. Robert pushed him aside and started searching for himself, his left arm still lifted, his right hand ferreting into the snow.

'There—there's one of them,' he said, at last, holding up the tip of his middle finger. 'Fill your hand with snow. That's right, fill your hand with snow. That'll keep it from decomposing.'

Feely held out a handful of snow. Robert carefully laid his bloody fingertip in the middle of it, and said, 'Don't lose it, OK? Whatever you do, don't lose it.'

Feely looked down at the fingertip in disgust. The nail had been bitten and for some reason that made it all the more revolting. Almost immediately, Robert found the other fingertip and laid that in Feely's hand, too. 'How are you going to fix these back on?' asked Feely.

'I'm going to stick them with BandAids, what else?'

'Do you think they'll take?'

'There's a good chance, isn't there? The cuts are still fresh, they'll heal up just like normal cuts.'

Feely shrugged. In his opinion, Robert ought to go to the emergency room, and have his fingertips sewn back on by doctors.

'What's the matter?' said Robert.

Feely said, 'I think you ought to go to the emergency room, and have your fingertips sewn back on by doctors.'

'Well, yes, smartypants, you're absolutely right. But the fact is, I can't.'

'I could call 911.'

Robert said, 'Feely, I am supposed to be a ghost. I am supposed to be traveling around unseen and unnoticed.'

Feely looked at him standing in the driveway with his left arm raised and a bloody scarf wrapped around his fist. He would only go unnoticed if nobody happened to be looking. Fortunately, Orchard Street appeared to be deserted, except for a red Jeep parked twenty yards down the street, with exhaust fluffing from its tailpipe.

'We'd better go inside,' said Feely.

At that moment, the front door opened and Serenity appeared. 'How are my two lumberjacks getting on? We've almost finished our last basket of logs!'

'Not too good,' said Feely. 'Robert's had a misadventure.'

'He distracted me!' Robert retorted. 'You can't take this retard anywhere.'

Feely went over to the front door and held out his handful of pink-stained snow. 'See? He chopped his fingers off.'

'*Ew*,' said Serenity. 'Ew ew ew squared.'

Robert, in pain and frustration, kicked over the chopping block.

The Watchers

'That's them,' said Sissy, lighting up her third cigarette. 'You're sure about that?'

'Absolutely positive. Don't you remember the cards? Two men cutting wood. Then La Faucille Terrible. The man poking his eye out, and the other man laughing. What you just saw, that was exactly what the cards predicted, coming to life.'

'Not exactly. That guy didn't poke his eye out with a pruning-hook, did he? He walloped his hand with a damn great ax.'

'Sam, those cards were first published in 1763, but they clearly foresaw that a man would hurt himself while he was working and another man would laugh at him, over two hundred forty years later. I don't think we need to be too picky about exactly how he did it, do you?'

Sam lit a cigarette, too. 'Do the cards foresee that we're ever going to give up smoking?'

'Well, *I'm* going to, I don't know about you.'

'I'm not so concerned about me. It's you I'm worried about.'

'I'll give up when I'm good and ready. Who are you, my dad?'

'Sorry,' said Sam. 'It's just that—'

'I know, Sam. You care about me. You wouldn't have driven me all the way up here, if you didn't care about me. But this is really, really important. It's hard to explain it to anybody who doesn't feel it for themselves, but what's happening here . . . it's people's lives, Sam. People are going to die, if we don't do this. I mean it.'

'So what are we going to do now?' Sam asked her.

'There's not much we *can* do, not today. But at least we know who we're dealing with, and that's going to make it much easier to predict what's going to happen next.'

'Do you think that those people had something to do with that woman getting herself shot?'

121

'I'm certain of it.'

'Shouldn't you tell the police?'

'I may do, if the cards tell me that they're going to do it again. Just at the moment, though, I don't have any proof, do I? Only a quivering feeling, and a quivering feeling won't stand up in a court of law, will it?'

'Do you know something?' said Sam. 'You're a very rare woman, Sissy Sawyer. I think I'm going to take you into New Milford this evening, and treat you to dinner.'

As they sat there, Feely reappeared from the house, went across to the garage, and brought down the up-and-over doors. Then he kicked snow across the driveway, so that it concealed the blood spatters from Robert's severed fingers. Finally he picked up three of the logs that Robert had intended to split, and carried them inside.

'Les Trois Araignées,' said Sissy. 'One black, and two white, but all of them spinning the same web.'

'I think you should talk to the police,' said Sam.

'And say what? "Excuse me, officer, my two-hundred-year-old deck of cards tells me that three people are going to be causing all kinds of mayhem in the Canaan area." Come on, Sam. They wouldn't stop laughing for a week.'

'Don't be so sure. From what I read, the cops are much more ready these days to listen to oddballs.'

'Oh, *thanks.*'

'No, no, I didn't mean to be rude. What I meant was, they don't dismiss things out of hand these days, just because they're unconventional. They use psychological profilers, don't they, and psychics, and even mediums. Remember that young boy who went missing in Wyantenock Park, last summer? They used an Algonquin shaman to find him.'

'OK, but I need to read the cards at least one more time. I don't want to send the police off on some fool's errand, do I? And I don't want to look like a fool myself.' She looked at her watch. It was almost a quarter of four now, and it was beginning to grow dark. 'So where are you taking me to dinner?' she said, with sudden enthusiasm. 'How about Adrienne's? I haven't had any of their home-raised pheasant pot pie since Gerry went on his way.'

Ghost Van

'**W**e've identified the van,' said Doreen.

Steve was frowning at his PC screen. He was reading up on random snipers, including Lee Boyd Malvo and John Allen Muhammad, who had terrorized Washington, D.C., and the unknown rifleman who was picking off innocent passers-by in Ohio.

Doreen handed him a computer printout. 'It's a 1998 Ford Econoline, first registered to Waterbury Tree Surgeons . . . hence the letter 'W' that our witness says he saw. Motto: 'A healthy tree is a happy tree.'

'Waterbury Tree Surgeons went out of business in February, 2002, and the van was sold to Peter Koslowski, of Meriden, who ran a two-man removal outfit. It was involved in a traffic accident on November 11, 2003, and Koslowski sold it to Middletown Auto Spares, for scrap. Middletown Auto Spares have records showing that it was stripped and broken down for usable parts, but presumably somebody stole it before that could happen.'

'OK,' said Steve. 'I need to know the name of every single individual who was working at the auto wrecking company when the van was first brought in there, and their employment record.'

'Done,' said Doreen. 'Trooper MacCormack and his people are checking through them now.'

Steve pointed to his PC screen. 'See this? I've been reading through the case histories of random sniper incidents. All the way back to the freeway shootings in Los Angeles in 1976.'

Doreen leaned over his desk and peered at it with interest. 'Learn anything useful?'

'Oh, sure. I learned that every case is completely different

123

in every material respect, except for one thing: the mentality of the perpetrators. Random snipers are without doubt the saddest, most clueless individuals on the planet. Look here—this is Malvo, one of the Beltway Snipers. He said that he wanted ten million dollars to stop shooting people. The idiot really believed that he was going to get it.'

'So what do you think *our* sniper is after?'

'Money, revenge on society, notoriety. Maybe nothing at all. The only thing these case histories tell me is that he isn't likely to be very bright, and one day soon he'll give himself away—either because he's careless, or incompetent, or he's so intent on shooting somebody that he allows himself to be spotted—or else because he *wants* us to find him, so that he can have his moment of glory.'

'He won't get too far in a van with a laughing tree painted on it.'

Steve shut his PC off. 'You know what I think? I think people have lost their self-respect. They don't feel like they're worth anything any more, and maybe they're not. They're uneducated, inarticulate, and they don't have any ambitions any more. The only way they know how to make an impression is by hurting other people, or killing them.'

'You're having more trouble with Alan?'

Steve looked at her sharply. 'You know me better than anybody, don't you?'

'I went through it myself, Steve, with my Damien. The drinking, the drugs, the language. He'll grow out of it.'

'I don't know. I'm just glad that I'm not his age, not these days. It seems like nothing's sacred, any more.'

Trooper MacCormack rapped loose-knuckled on the door. 'Detective Wintergreen? I think I may have something here. There was a mechanic called William Hain working at Middletown Auto Spares from September 4, 2002, until January 16, 2003. According to his personnel file, he was repeatedly warned for lateness and careless workmanship, and for generally having an attitude.

'Mr Koslowski's damaged van was collected from his premises in Meriden on January 13, 2003, and towed to Middletown. On January 15, William Hain entered into the company's record books that it had been dismantled. The next morning he called in sick and that was the last that Middletown Auto Spares ever saw of him.'

'The dates fit,' said Doreen.

'Yes,' said Steve. 'And William Hain sounds like the kind of guy who considers that the world owes him a favor. Do we have any other information on him?'

'Only his personnel file. He gave his address as 7769 Lamentation Mountain Road, Middletown. His date of birth was May 12, 1974, and his social security number was 046-09-6521. When he first applied for a job at Middletown Auto Spares, he gave references from Green Peak Engineering and Kyle's Auto Repair, both in Hamden.'

'Right, then,' said Steve. 'Send somebody to Middletown Auto Spares, and let's check those references, too. There may be somebody at one of those auto shops who knows William Hain, or remembers him. More than anything else, I want a description.'

He stood up and lifted his coat off the back of his chair. 'Doreen—you and me can go to Lamentation Mountain.'

He was halfway down the stairs when his cellphone rang. 'Wintergreen.'

'Steve, hi, it's Roger Prenderval, in Torrington.'

'How's it going, Roger? What can I do for you? I'm kind of tied up right now, with the Mitchelson case.'

'I thought you ought to know that we picked up your boy.'

'Alan? What do you mean, you picked him up?'

'I'm sorry to tell you that we had to arrest him. Thought you'd rather know, before Helen.'

Steve stopped. Doreen stopped, too, but he waved his hand at her and said, 'I'll meet you in the parking lot.'

'Trouble?' asked Doreen.

'Just give me a minute, OK?'

Trooper Prenderval said, gravely, 'He's been arrested on suspicion of sexual assault.'

'Sexual assault? My Alan? Are you serious?'

'I'm sorry, Steve. We had a call from a house in the Burntwood district. It seems like the owners returned home unexpectedly and caught Alan trying to climb out the kitchen window. Their daughter was upstairs naked in a state of shock and she claims that Alan was trying to force her to have sexual intercourse against her will.'

'Do you believe that?'

'I'm sorry, Steve, it doesn't make any difference what I believe. The girl has made the complaint and her parents are howling for blood.'

Steve pressed his fingertips against his forehead. He was beginning to feel a headache coming on—one of those headaches that made his left eye blurry.

'Are you still holding Alan now?'

'We'll be bringing him down to Litchfield in maybe twenty minutes. I thought you'd probably want to see him before we charge him.'

'Who's the girl? I wasn't even aware that he *knew* any girls. Not that intimately, anyhow.'

'Her name's Kelly Kessner. Her parents are Richard and Davina Kessner.'

'Kessner Realty?'

'That's them.'

'God almighty.'

Steve had only met Richard Kessner two or three times, at charity functions. But he remembered him as being a loud, bullying man with a permanent tan and dyed, bouffant hair. The sort of man who always tried to crush your fingers when he shook your hand. He couldn't remember Davina Kessner, though, and as far as he knew he had never met their daughter Kelly.

'Is Alan there? Can I talk to him?'

'Hold on, Steve. Let me ask him.'

'Don't *ask* him, Roger, *tell* him. I want to talk to him, OK?'

There was a lengthy pause. Through the window, Steve could see Doreen standing impatiently next to his car. He raised one finger to indicate that he wouldn't be long.

'Steve? It's Roger. Alan says he doesn't want to talk to you.'

'I'm sorry, Roger. He *has* to.'

'You want me to hold a gun to his head? He absolutely refused.'

'I don't believe this. What did he say?'

'You want the exact words?'

Steve hesitated for a moment, and then said, 'No, thanks, Roger. Just tell him I'll be back in about an hour. And tell him not to worry. It sounds like the whole thing was some kind of stupid misunderstanding.'

'OK, Steve. Talk to you later.'

Children of the Absent Gods

For Feely, the afternoon passed like a dream, or a home movie of somebody else's life.

Serenity microwaved a frozen chili that her mother had left for her, and the three of them sat cross-legged on the hearthrug in front of the fire and ate it with serving spoons, straight out of the big blue Tupperware bowl. Robert hadn't been able to chop any more firewood so Feely had wedged one huge log into the fireplace, which was burning with a furious roar.

'Are you kids happy?' Robert asked them.

Serenity only licked her spoon and gave him a suggestive smile, but Feely said, 'Absolutely—I'm happy.'

'Then now's the time to start worrying,' said Robert. 'And you know why? Because the happier you are, the worse it hurts when it all turns to shit. Which it inevitably will.'

He spoke very slowly, and very emphatically. He had not only drunk three-quarters of a bottle of Mr Bellow's Maker's Mark, but he had taken eight Tylenol tablets to dull the pain in his fingers. With Feely's reluctant help, he had stuck his fingertips back on as accurately as he could, using BandAids and Scotch tape, but he still kept complaining that they were throbbing, and that they felt 'loose.'

Feely felt full now, and weary, and he was finding it hard to stay alert. But he couldn't take his eyes away from Serenity, sitting opposite him. Her hair was shining in the firelight, and her eyes sparkled, and the shadows fondled her breasts. He wished he could sit here for ever, just staring at her.

'I don't know . . .' he said. 'Fate's been very benevolent, so far as I'm concerned.'

'You think?'

'Sure. Ever since I bought my ticket at the Port Authority, I really feel like somebody's been taking care of me. Like in

Hercules, The Incredible Journeys, you know, with the gods looking down from the clouds and making sure that I achieve my desideration.'

Robert gave a dismissive *pfff!* 'You really believe in gods? Let me tell you, kid, there are no gods left. Not one. Even before the birth of Christ the gods saw what men and women were turning into, and they bailed.'

'Oh, I think you're wrong,' said Serenity. 'I don't think the gods have gone. I think they're in hiding, that's all, until we come to our senses. But they still keep an eye on us.'

'Yeah—look at everything that's happened to me,' Feely agreed. 'Meeting you, meeting Serenity. You can't tell me the gods didn't have something to do with it. Look at us here now, man, in front of the fire, don't try to tell me that all three of us congregated here just by happenstance?'

'You're full of crap,' said Robert. 'The trouble with human beings is, we're all still looking for signs. We need meaning in our lives! We need oracles, and predictions, to tell us what to do next! So we keep on looking for clues, or marks, and when we find them . . . poor pathetic souls that we are, we think that we've discovered the answer.'

He looked at Feely with unfocused eyes, and then at Serenity. 'But I've discovered the real answer, children, and the real answer isn't in signs, or riddles. The real answer is . . . transparent rulers.'

'*What?*' said Serenity.

'Transparent rulers,' Robert insisted. 'Just like the gods, they're invisible, but they still have the measure of us.'

'There's no answer to that,' said Serenity.

'Exactly,' said Robert, 'because it's a universal truth.' Then he said to Feely, 'Get me another drink, will you, kid? I think my legs are permanently locked. No wonder the Japs lost the war. Once they sat down to eat they couldn't get up again.'

Feely uncrossed his legs, took Robert's glass, and went across to the drinks cabinet on the other side of the living room. As he passed the widescreen TV, he saw a small yellow house, with a TV reporter standing in the back yard. The caption along the bottom of the picture said NEWS 24: SNIPER KILLS CANAAN WOMAN.

'Hey, Robert!' he said. 'Lookit—on the TV! Isn't that the

same house we passed by this morning, where that little girl was making a snowman?'

Robert swiveled around and squinted at the screen with one eye. 'Yes, Feely, you're right. That's the very house. What about it?'

'Looks like a woman got herself killed there, by a sniper.'

Robert looked up at him, with one eye still closed. 'What are you trying to say to me, Feely? That I gave them the evil eye? Are you trying to suggest that it was *my* fault, that woman getting shot?'

'Of course not. Why should I? I just think it seems kind of epiphenomenal, that you should say what a happy house that actual specific house was, and the very same day it's visited by doom.'

Robert shook his head. 'Wouldn't have happened, if she'd owned a transparent ruler. She would have seen it coming. The snowman, too, poor bastard.' He tried to turn back toward the fire, but he fell sideways onto the rug, with his legs still locked together. 'God, I must be drunk.'

'Why don't we get you to bed?' Serenity suggested.

'My legs are stuck. Help me sort my legs out.'

Between them, Feely and Serenity disentangled his legs. 'Come on,' said Serenity. 'You could use some sleep.'

'I need another drink,' said Robert. 'If I have another drink, I'll sober up.'

Serenity ignored him. 'Come on, Feely, help me to get him upstairs.'

It took them almost five minutes to drag Robert up to the guest bedroom. He kept trying to turn around and go back downstairs again, and even when they got him to the top he decided to cling onto the banisters like a stubborn child.

'I'm sober! I've sobered up! Listen to this: "Since inquiry is the beginning of philosophy, and wonder and uncertainty are the beginning of inquiry, it seems only natural that the greater part of what concerns the gods should be concealed in riddles."'

'You couldn't say that unless you were drunk,' said Serenity, prying his fingers free from the banister-rail.

'What? You girls—you think you know everything! You

think you control our lives! Nothing could be further from the spoof! You can't do squat unless we allow you to! You can't even menstruate unless we say so! Men are the sole arbiters of everything that walks, flies, sinks, shits, or swims!'

Eventually, Feely and Serenity managed to force Robert through the bedroom door, and push him onto the bed. Once he had collapsed back onto the pink-and-white quilt, he stopped struggling, and lay back with his eyes closed. 'I think I need a little sheep,' he slurred. 'Feely, get me another drink, will you? Make it a large one. Not one of those goddamned . . . small ones.'

Serenity knelt down beside the bed and laid her hand on his forehead. 'Get some rest, OK, Touchy? You've had a pretty bad day, one way and another.'

Robert opened his eyes again, and stared at her. 'You're not Elizabeth, are you? No, I thought not. Pity. You know what Elizabeth said to me? She said, "Whatever you want, Robbie, you just tell me what it is, and I'll do it." Now, how many women do you know who would say something like that? And mean it?' He nodded, and kept on nodding. 'And *mean* it? You see where I'm coming from? And *mean* it?'

His eyes closed, and he fell into a drugged and drunken sleep. He didn't snore. In fact he didn't even seem to be breathing, but Serenity laid her hand on his chest and said, 'He's OK . . . I can feel his heart beating.'

Feely surprised himself by feeling jealous. He wouldn't have minded if Robert were dead.

The Return of Captain Lingo

They left the bedroom and Serenity closed the door. 'I think I'm going to my room now. I want to wash my hair and all. If you want to stay up and watch TV, fine.'

'Hey, it's not even nine o'clock yet. Don't you maybe want another drink, and we can maybe converse some more?'

'Actually, Feely, I'd like a little time on my own.'

'Oh . . . OK.'

Serenity smiled at him and chucked him under the chin with her finger. 'Don't be disappointed. You look like you could use some sleep, too.'

Feely shrugged and looked around. 'I just like this so much. Whatever Robert says, I feel happy here. I feel hygienic, and also warm, and not at all inclined to be mendacious.'

'You're something, you know that?'

'Everybody is something.'

'I know. But you're *really* something.'

'I don't know. Robert says you have to do a cataclysmic deed if the world is going to pay you any attention.'

'A cataclysmic deed? Like what?'

'I don't really know. But Robert says that when you do it, everybody has to go *ho-o-oly shit!*'

Serenity laughed. Then she took hold of his hands and kissed him on the lips, just lightly. 'You know, sometimes I stare at my parents' eyes real close up and I try to see if there's anything inside them. My dad says "What the hell are you staring at?" and I say "I'm trying to see into your soul." He thinks I'm cracked, but there's a poem by Lawrence Ferlinghetti and this woman says, "I feel there is an angel inside me . . . who I am constantly shocking." I love that poem. But when I stare at my parents I think that what you see is all they are. No angel inside. No devil either. They're like hollow people, *knock-knock*, they're empty. I wonder if they were always like that, or if their real selves decided to escape one day, like you escaped, and went north.'

Feely nodded. He couldn't find the words to answer her. He nearly said, 'I love you,' but he didn't know how she would respond. If she laughed at him, he thought that he would probably shrivel up and die of humiliation, like a slug with salt on it.

Serenity turned and opened the door to her room. 'Maybe I'll come down later, when I've washed my hair. Help yourself to anything you want. You know, beer, Cheezos.'

'Sure. Thanks.'

Feely went downstairs to the living room. The log that he had wedged into the hearth had left a smoky mark right up the middle of the white-painted fire-surround, and up the wall, too. He picked up the poker and levered the log sideways, so that it wouldn't stick out so much.

On the TV news, a detective with dark rings under his eyes was saying, '—one or two promising leads, and we're expecting some developments within the next twenty-four hours. We're keeping an open mind as to motive, but it seems increasingly likely that Mrs Mitchelson's shooting was a random act of violence by a very disturbed individual.'

Feely sat down at the dining table and opened his blue cardboard folder. Captain Lingo wouldn't have had any trouble telling Serenity how he felt. But Feely was beginning to think that maybe words weren't everything. You could know every single word in the English language. You could know 'piaffer.' But if you didn't know how to say 'I love you' without the risk of humiliating yourself, what was the point? For the first time, Feely wondered if Father Arcimboldo might have not been telling him the whole truth.

He pulled out a clean but slightly crumpled sheet of art paper, and took the top off his thick black felt-tipped pen. He sketched Orchard Street, and the Bellow house, and the snow. Captain Lingo was walking up toward the front door. He was turning around to Verba and saying, 'I feel magnetized toward this house, Verba . . . there's somebody here I have to talk to.'

Verba said, 'Very well, Captain Lingo . . . I'll meet you later.'

In the next frame, the front door was opened and Serenity was standing there—an idealized Serenity: slimmer, more bosomy, with much more hair, and feline eyes. 'I don't know why,' she was saying, 'but I've been expecting you.'

Captain Lingo and Serenity go into the living room. Captain Lingo says, 'You and me have origins of such disparity that it beggars belief that we have even found ourselves in the same room together, let alone the same continental mass.'

Serenity says, '*Mmm . . .*'

Captain Lingo takes Serenity in his arms. 'If each word of love was a flower, I would be presenting you now with the most abundant bouquet that the world of horticulture has ever had to offer.'

Serenity says, '*Ohhhh . . .*'

In the last frame, Captain Lingo kisses Serenity and says, 'You are the dictionary definition of "perfection."'

Feely spent over an hour filling in the background details. When he had finished, he sat back and looked at his work with satisfaction, because he thought he had drawn it very well—especially his idealized Serenity. But he also looked at it with self-doubt, because he wasn't at all sure that Serenity would like it. She might even be insulted, because he had drawn her waist so tiny and her breasts so big.

Even so, he was determined that he would show it to her. If he couldn't find a way to tell her that he had fallen in love with her, then Captain Lingo could do it for him. All he needed was courage, and maybe a drink. He went across to the cocktail trolley, unscrewed the cap from the Maker's Mark, sniffed it, and then took a swig straight from the bottle. Then he stood there for almost half a minute, his eyes crowded with tears, his lungs on fire, coughing and coughing and coughing.

Holy Mary Mother of God, why would anybody want to drink that stuff on purpose?

When he had wiped his eyes and blown his nose on a piece of kitchen towel, he went upstairs. It was very quiet on the landing. He leaned his head against the door of Serenity's bedroom, but he couldn't hear anything. No television, no hair dryer, nothing.

Now he didn't know what to do. If Serenity was asleep, he supposed that he could creep into her bedroom and lay his drawings on her bed. That would be pretty romantic, wouldn't it? He could gently shake her awake and the first thing she would see when she opened her eyes would be Captain Lingo, telling her that she was the dictionary definition of perfect.

But what if she wasn't asleep? What if he walked into her bedroom and she thought he was trying to come on to her? He stood outside her door for over a minute, and then he hesitantly knocked. He waited, and waited, but there was no answer. Maybe he hadn't knocked loud enough. He tried knocking a second time. He waited, but there was still no answer.

It was then that he lost his nerve. He should have gone in and laid his drawings on her bed, but he didn't have the *cojones* even to take hold of her doorknob. I'll show her the drawings tomorrow at breakfast, he consoled himself, even though he knew that his chance was already passing him by. Tomorrow at breakfast would be too late, and Robert would be there, with a ten-megaton hangover and his hand still hurting.

Feely didn't know how long he stood outside her door, trying to make up his mind what to do, but it seemed like about an hour. He was so tired that his neck began to creak. In the end, he tiptoed his way along the landing to the guest bedroom, so that he could check on Robert.

He opened the door, and at first he couldn't work out what he was looking at. The bedside lamp was on, and the pink quilt had slid off the bed and was heaped on the floor. On the bed itself, naked except for a pair of khaki knee-high socks and a green glass necklace, was Serenity. Behind her, also naked, was Robert. He was holding his bandaged hand out sideways as if he were a motorist, signaling to turn left. His white buttocks were clenched together with effort. The air in the bedroom was almost unbreathable with the pungency of marijuana.

Feely stood in the open doorway feeling as if he had walked into the wrong universe. Robert turned around and saw him, and for a split second he looked mildly surprised. But then he gave him an exaggerated grin, all teeth, and said, 'Hi there, Feely!' He didn't even look embarrassed.

'I'm—' said Feely, and reached for the door handle. He just wanted to blot it all out.

134

But—'Feely!' Robert called him. 'Wait up! Where the hell are you going, Feely?' and now Serenity opened her eyes and saw him, too. Her cheeks were apple red and her forehead was shiny with perspiration, and she smiled at him, like everything was perfectly normal.

'Come on, Feely,' said Robert. 'Don't be shy and retiring. Come on in. We're all friends here, aren't we?'

'I, uh—'

'Come on, Feely! Not like you to be lost for words! We're having a good time here, aren't we, Serenity? We're having a bee-aye-double-ell *ball*! Why don't you join us?'

Serenity giggled. 'Come on, Feely!' she repeated. 'Come on, Feely!' Then—to the tune of 'Hang On, Sloopy'—she sang, 'Come on, Feely—Feely, come on!'

Feely opened his mouth and closed it again. He had never experienced such an avalanche of emotions, all at once. Embarrassment, jealousy, lust, anger, rage and elation. He felt as if God had opened the top of his head and poured them all in, without even giving him the chance to say *stop!*

'Don't you Cubans know how to have fun?' Robert taunted him. 'I thought Cuba was the land of sex and rum and sex and big fat cigars and sex! Here—come and have a piece of this! How can you refuse?'

Feely lifted up his drawing. 'I did this for you,' he said, so weakly that he could hardly hear his own voice. Robert and Serenity obviously couldn't hear him either, or didn't care. Robert circled his right arm around Serenity's flabby waist. He heaved once, he heaved twice, and then he rolled right over onto his back, his left arm still extended, so that Serenity was lying on top of him, facing upward. She kicked her legs and screamed and laughed and shrilled out, 'You're crazy! What are you doing? We're going to fall off the bed!'

Robert laughed at Feely, over Serenity's shoulder; and Serenity laughed at him too.

'Here it is, Feely, the promised land. Come and stake your claim.'

'Come on, Feely—Feely, come on!' sang Serenity.

Feely didn't hesitate. He dropped his Captain Lingo drawing onto the floor. He reached behind him and dragged off his polo shirt, inside-out, and dropped that too.

'Yayy!' Robert encouraged him, as he unbuttoned his chinos. But then, 'Don't forget your socks, Feely! There ain't nothing more guaranteed to put a girl off than a naked guy wearing nothing but his socks!'

Feely tugged off his socks, and then he stumbled out of his pants. He had to grab the end of the bed to stop himself from falling over. But then he was standing there naked and skinny, and so excited that he could hardly breathe.

'Here it is, Feely!' said Robert. All the same he wasn't sure what Robert and Serenity expected him to do. Feely climbed onto the end of the bed, but he felt inexperienced and thin and unsure of himself and he was convinced that they could actually see his heart beating, under his ribcage.

'Give the kid a helping hand, will you, darling?' wheezed Robert. 'I'm dying of asphyxia under here.'

Serenity lifted herself up a little, even though Robert grunted and said, 'Squashed to death by an overweight bimbo, that's what they'll put on my headstone!' She reached out and took Feely's hand, and drew him closer. 'Come on, Feely,' she whispered. 'Feely, come on.'

Feely edged himself closer and closer, and then Serenity guided him inside her. She felt so warm and liquid that Feely thought that there was no sensation in the world which could possibly feel more ecstatic. And she was still looking at him, and still smiling, and she seemed to be so calm and matter-of-fact.

Then they were all together. Robert heaved his hips up, and Serenity arched her back, and at the same time she grasped Feely around the waist and pulled him into her. This was like nothing he had ever felt before, nothing he had imagined before . . .

And suddenly it was over. Robert slumped and let out a deep groan of defeat. 'God, I'm too drunk . . . God, I'm far too drunk.' All three of them collapsed and lay there with their arms and their legs entangled. Feely could see a hand and at first he thought it was his, but when it wriggled its fingers he realized it was Serenity's. Robert was breathing noisily against his neck.

As he lay there, it slowly crept into Feely's mind that he loved these people. Not just Serenity, because she was a girl, and her breasts had looked enticing in the firelight; but Robert,

136

too; for all that he was so cynical, and he drank so much, and he had nearly killed them both. And it wasn't because they had all had sex together, either. It was the closeness. It was the feeling of being in a family, where they could say whatever they wanted and do whatever they wanted. Feely suddenly understood that he had reached the place where he was going. Here, on this bed, with Robert and Serenity, this was the north.

Eventually Feely sat up. He reached out and stroked Serenity's hair, and then her shoulder. She looked at him and said, 'I'm hungry again. Are you hungry?'

'It's that dope you smoke,' said Robert. 'Personally, I couldn't eat another thing.'

With that, he let off a loud, complicated fart. Serenity let out a shout of laughter and fell on top of him, and Feely started laughing, too. For nearly five minutes, the three of them lay on the bed, laughing until they had to bang each other on the back.

But Robert suddenly stopped laughing and said, 'Shit!' and then 'Shit!' and started ferreting wildly through the sheets.

'What's wrong, man?' Feely asked him.

'My fingers!' said Robert, in desperation. 'My goddamned fingers have fallen off!'

The House of Loathsome Things

It took them nearly two hours to find 7769 Lamentation Mountain Road, and by then Steve's left eye was throbbing so much that he could barely open it. He knew it was stress, and he knew he should probably take something for it, but he had never liked pills. His mother had always taken pills. So far as she was concerned, pills were the answer to everything, from chronic disappointment with her choice of husband to a fallen Parmesan soufflé.

When they saw headlights on the Berlin Turnpike less than a mile up ahead of them, Doreen realized that they must have passed the house already. She turned the Tahoe around and drove slowly back the way they had come.

'You shouldn't have come,' she said, peering through the windshield as if she were a lookout on a whaler. 'Alan's really going to need your support right now.'

'I know that, Doreen. But this is a homicide, or even a double homicide. It doesn't matter who's involved, homicide has to be a higher priority than sexual assault.'

'Have you heard yourself? He's your son!'

'I know. But if he did it, then he deserves whatever he gets.'

'You don't really think that he assaulted that girl, do you? It sounds to me like she made it up, so that her parents wouldn't give her a hard time for playing mummies and daddies while they were out.'

'Doreen—I don't know. I haven't heard the evidence.'

Doreen drove in silence for a while. But then she said, 'I don't entirely blame you. I mean, kids these days. It's about time they carried their own cans. They always seem to expect that we're going to do it for them, and then they get chippy with us when we say no.'

Steve was wiping his nose. 'That doesn't make me feel any better. But, thanks.'

They turned a rising left-hand bend, and as they did so they saw a track running off to the right, between overgrown bramble bushes. The bushes were thick with snow, which had effectively camouflaged the track when they were approaching it from the opposite direction. Doreen stopped the SUV and said, 'Logically, 7769 should be here.'

'Well, let's give it a try.'

They bumped and jostled their way down the track, with branches scraping against the Tahoe's doors, and snow dropping from the overhanging trees. After about a half-mile, they found themselves in a clearing. It was strangely luminous, because of the snow, and Lamentation Mountain was rising to the north-west, barely visible, like a bad memory.

At the far side of the clearing there was a small single-story house, painted pale green. It had a low, shingled roof and a verandah all the way around it. Not far away from the house there was a shed made of rusty corrugated iron, and resembling a disused pig-pen.

'Doesn't look like there's anybody home,' said Doreen.

They drove slowly up to the house and stopped. Steve climbed out of the SUV and took out his flashlight and his gun. Doreen climbed out, too.

'Maybe we should come back with a search warrant,' she suggested.

'I don't know whether we'd get one.'

Their footsteps crunched on the snow as they crossed the yard at the front of the house. A washing-line was suspended from the verandah to a skinny, leafless tree. There was a green plaid shirt on it, and three pairs of boxer shorts, all frozen solid. 'Hope he thaws those out before he tries to put them on,' said Doreen.

They went up the steps to the front door and knocked. Each knock echoed from the trees on the opposite side of the clearing.

While they waited, Steve looked around. It was hard to tell if anybody still lived here. There was a sagging canvas chair, and a rusted table with a hammered-glass top, and a child's scooter with no back wheel, but they could have been abandoned long ago.

Steve opened the screen door and tried the door handle. To his surprise, the door wasn't locked. 'Maybe he wasn't expecting visitors.'

'Maybe he doesn't have anything worth stealing.'

'Still,' said Steve, 'we'd better check the place out, just to make sure that nobody's broken in.'

He opened the front door and went inside, and Doreen followed him. They found themselves in a chilly living room. It was sparsely furnished, but there were plenty of signs that somebody was still living here. The fire in the hearth had gone out, and it was heaped with soft gray ashes, but the ashes were still faintly warm. There was a damp, sagging couch, upholstered in worn brown velveteen, and the cushions were still out of shape where somebody had been lying on them. There was a stool next to the couch with an ashtray on it, crammed with cigarette butts, as well as the plastic tray from a microwaveable fruit pie, and an empty Miller bottle.

Steve flicked his flashlight left and right. The walls were papered with large green flowers, faded by years of damp and sunlight. Next to the fireplace there was a calendar from Middletown Auto Spares, still turned to August, with a color picture of a 1957 Chrysler 300F on it—'red-hot and rambunctious.' On the opposite wall there was a large photograph of a hairy-legged spider, torn out of a magazine, and a yellowed black-and-white photograph of a couple standing outside a hardware store. By their hairstyles, and the way they were dressed, Steve guessed that the photograph had been taken sometime in the late 1960s.

Stacked in one corner of the room were at least a dozen copies of *Guns & Ammo*, as well as several of *Hot Rod*, and three numbers of *Hustler*.

'You can tell a pin-headed male chauvinist by the books he reads,' Doreen quoted.

'Who said that?'

'I did, just now. These are the same magazines my Newton likes to look at.'

Steve went through to the kitchenette. It was fitted out in yellow and scarlet Formica, and every shelf and work surface was crowded with half-empty tubs of margarine and dirty plates and unwashed coffee cups and torn-open packs of instant pasta and curled-up Kraft cheese slices. The old Westinghouse cooker was thick with dark brown grease and there was a saucepan on it which was filled with rancid gray foam.

'Well,' said Doreen. 'We're not looking for Mr Clean.'

Steve opened and closed the kitchen drawers. He was looking for boxes of ammo, but all he found was filthy knives and forks, an egg-whisk that still had egg on it, used batteries, rubber-bands, and the same detritus that everybody keeps in their kitchen drawers, like business cards from screen-door salesmen, and take-out pizza menus.

He opened the door to one of the bedrooms. As he did so, Doreen said, 'Don't come into the bathroom, not unless you have a really strong stomach. He had a dump this morning but forgot to flush.'

The bedroom wasn't much better. There was no undersheet on the bed, only a heavily stained and misshapen mattress which looked as if it had been rescued from a roadside ditch. A coffee-brown candlewick bedspread was lying on the floor, along with a heap of dirty socks and work shirts. A small dressing table stood beside the bed, its veneer lifted by damp. There was an economy can of Right Guard spray deodorant on it, and a bottle of Aramis aftershave.

'At least he *knows* that he smells bad,' said Doreen.

Steve opened the door to the second bedroom. It was in total darkness, but his flashlight caught the smeary glint of glass. He took a cautious step forward. The room was surprisingly warm, unlike the rest of the house. As he took another step forward, however, he was overwhelmed by the worst stench that he had ever smelled in his life. It was thick, and leathery, and rotten: like natural gas, and putrescing fur coats, and raw chicken that had gone past its sell-by date. He covered his face with his hand, but even so he couldn't stop himself from retching.

'Oh God,' he said, taking a step backward.

'What is it?' said Doreen. Then, immediately, 'Sweet Jesus. What's that *smell*?'

'Here, the windows are covered, let's have some light.'

Steve groped around the door-jamb until he found the light switch. There was a single fluorescent tube hung diagonally across the ceiling. It flickered for a few seconds, and then it

141

sprang into full brilliance. Doreen made a desperate *haaahhh* noise, like a terrified child.

The room was filled with tables of assorted sizes, and each table was stacked with glass fish-tanks. The fish-tanks, however, didn't contain fish, but spiders, and snakes, and giant snails, and centipedes, and enormous slugs, and some glutinous creatures that Steve couldn't even put a name to. All of the windows were covered with corrugated cardboard, and there was a small electric storage heater standing in the center of the room to keep the temperature up in the seventies.

As Steve looked around, his hand still clamped over his face, one of the largest spiders jumped against the glass of its tank, and he couldn't stop himself from jerking back. Everything else seemed to be moving, too. A brown centipede with rippling legs; and scores of cockroaches; and a pale beige slug which kept rolling its eyes in and out.

Steve ducked his head down and quickly checked under the tables, just to satisfy himself that there were no rifles or ammunition concealed there. Then he switched off the light and closed the door.

Doreen was standing in the middle of the living room, fanning herself furiously with her hand. 'I'm going to have nightmares about this for the rest of the year. I mean, where does this guy get *off*?'

'Maybe he identifies with spiders and centipedes. Insects kill things at random, don't they, without any qualms about it?'

'We really have to find this guy, don't we? If his pet collection is anything to go by, he's seriously nuts.'

Steve took a last look around. There was nothing else they could do here, not tonight. They couldn't even admit that they had been here, and searched the place.

'Come on,' said Doreen. 'We should get you back now.'

Steve nodded. He stepped outside the house and found to his relief that his headache had almost gone.

They climbed back into the Tahoe, and Doreen started the engine. She had only just released the parking brake, however, when they saw headlights jostling toward them, over the snow.

'Holy moly,' said Doreen. 'It's him!'

The Heartless Coachman

Mr Boots was waiting for her by the back door when she returned, his tail drumming against the washing machine.

'I know, fellow,' she said, tugging his ears. 'You must be starving. I'm sorry I was out for so long.'

Sam stayed outside. 'You don't need me to come in, do you, Sissy? I'd best be getting home.'

'Don't you want a drink? It's the least I can offer you, for driving me all the way to Canaan and back. How about a brandy?'

'I don't think so, Sissy. I'm just about ready for a mug of warm milk, and the latest Clive Cussler.'

Sissy went back to the doorstep. Snow was spiraling out of the sky, onto his shoulders. 'What happened to us, Sam? When did we lose our licentious youth?'

'The only licentious youth I know is working behind the counter at Quinn's Drugstore.'

Sissy leaned forward and kissed him. 'Thanks, Sam. I'm going to read the cards again tonight, and see what's going to happen next. You don't mind if I call you, do you, if I need you?'

Sam kissed her back, and squeezed her hand, but somehow this attempt to show her how much he felt for her seemed desperately sad, and all Sissy could do was give him a regretful little smile, and turn her face away.

Mr Boots prodded her with his cold wet nose, behind the knees, just above the top of her boots. 'OK, fellow, I'm coming. Thanks for everything, Sam. You're an angel.'

Sam said nothing. He was obviously aware that something wasn't quite right between them, but he didn't know what. Or else he *did* know what, and didn't want to face up to it. When it came down to it, warm milk and Clive Cussler were so much more comfortable than vodka and Sissy Sawyer.

143

Sissy opened up a pack of Bil-Jac senior dog food, chicken and oatmeal flavor. Mr Boots didn't like it as much as Alpo's hearty beef, bacon and cheese, but the vet had warned Sissy that he needed less fat and more fiber at his age, and in any case it usually gave Sissy a quieter night.

She lit a cigarette and built up the fire, which had sunk down to nothing but a few glowing embers. Then she sat in Gerry's old armchair, still wearing her coat, smoking and thinking. She couldn't get those three people out of her mind. Les Trois Araignées. She could still see the older man, chopping his hand; and the younger man, laughing. If she had taken a photograph, and reversed it left-to-right, and changed the ax into a pruning-hook, it would have been almost an identical reproduction of La Faucille Terrible, right down to their facial features.

But what had exhilarated her, and bewildered her, and tired her so much, was the way in which she had been drawn toward them. Not only to Canaan, but to Orchard Street, to the very house where they were staying. She couldn't explain it. She had always been highly sensitive to other people's feelings. As she had told Mina Jessop, she could feel true love through a cinderblock wall. But the magnetism which had pulled her today was stronger than any emotional force which she had experienced before.

She glanced sideways at the deck of cards on the coffee table, as if she didn't want them to catch her looking. She wasn't sure that she was ready to consult them again, not tonight. She had always known that they were powerful, but she had never realized that they could not only predict the future, but intervene.

The cards had told her that somebody was going to die, and Ellen Mitchelson *had* died, in just the way that the cards had foretold it. The cards had told her who had done it, and where to find them. All she needed now was proof.

She placed her hands on the arms of Gerry's chair, where *his* hands used to rest, and said, 'What would *you* do, darling?'

The clock ticked, and the fire hissed, and she could hear Mr Boots' claws scrabbling on the kitchen floor as he finished his food; but that was all. She believed that Gerry was here, and that he was listening to her. But he was telling her that

144

this was a decision which she had to make on her own. She could leave the cards in their box, and try to forget about Les Trois Araignées, or she could see what tomorrow had to bring.

She lit another cigarette from the butt of the first. Then she reached across the table and picked up the deck of cards. She didn't have any choice. Gerry knew that, as well as she did. If she didn't read the cards, she might as well give up, like Sam.

She opened the box, tipped out the deck, and shuffled them. *'Pictures of the world to be,'* she whispered. *'I beg you now . . . please speak to me.'*

She didn't lay out a full arrangement. All she needed to know was what was going to happen next—something factual that she could take to the police, to convince them that she wasn't a dotty old woman. She turned up three Ambience cards, and stared at them in resignation rather than disbelief, although they were scarcely believable. The two storm cards again, and the man in the chest. This was no coincidence. The odds against these three cards coming up together were astronomical.

As she picked out the fourth and last card, the Predictor, Mr Boots came in, licking his lips. He stood next to her, and shook himself, and shivered.

'What do you think, Mr Boots? Do I turn this card over, and see what it says, or do I call it a day? I could still go to Florida, you know, and forget all of this.'

Mr Boots cocked one ear. Then he barked, once. He hardly ever barked, even at the mailman.

'What does that mean? Should I turn this card over or not? One bark for yes, two barks for no.'

Mr Boots continued to stare at her but didn't bark at all.

'OK, I get it. I have to make up my own mind, just like Gerry told me.'

She took a deep drag at her cigarette, and blew out smoke. Then she closed her eyes tight, and turned the card over. When she opened them again, she was looking at Le Cocher Sans Coeur. It showed a horse-drawn coach, driving along a country road. Inside the coach sat three people, two men and a woman, and they were all laughing and making merry. But their coachman, who was sitting up above them, had been struck in the chest by a spear. It had passed right through his body, and his heart was impaled on the point.

The coach was rolling on its way, with the team of horses still oblivious to the coachman's death. A sign by the side of the road said *Catastrophe, 3 milles*.

So what did this mean? A man would be killed while he was driving a vehicle, but the vehicle would carry on going— much to the hilarity of two other men, and a woman.

She stared at the card for a long time and then she put it down on the table. Mr Boots made a whining sound and shook his head. 'You're right, Mr Boots, this is very bad news. The thing is, what the hell am I going to do about it?'

Steve Gets Angry

As the van approached them, it slowed down, and steered to the left of them, and stopped. It was too dark for them to see the driver, not yet, but they could clearly see that the side-panel had a laughing tree painted on it, with its leaves blowing away, and the faint words 'Waterbury Tree Surgeons', painted over in white.

Steve said, 'Pull up here.' He pulled his gun out of his shoulder-holster and opened the Tahoe's door. Doreen opened her door, too, and jumped down onto the snow.

'Cover me,' said Steve. He ducked down and ran across to the rear of the van. Then he made his way toward the front, holding his gun in both hands and pointing it directly at the driver's window.

'State police!' he shouted. 'Come on out with your hands up!'

There was a long moment of silence. Steve looked across at Doreen, who was crouched down behind the Tahoe's door. He was just about to shout again when the van door was opened up.

'Come out of there real slow!' Steve called out. 'I want your hands out in front of you where I can see them!'

The door opened wider, and a big man in a bulky blue windbreaker appeared, with both of his hands held up. He was wearing a brown furry cap with flaps that covered his ears, and a stripy scarf that covered most of his face.

'Comin' out!' he said, in a surprisingly high voice.

'Hit the dirt!' Steve told him.

'What?'

'You heard me! I said hit the dirt!'

'But it's snow,' said the man, plaintively.

'Hit it!'

147

The man got down on one knee, and then the other, and then reluctantly laid himself flat on the ground, with his arms and legs spread. The snow was over four inches thick, and he was half buried. He spat snow out of his mouth, and complained, 'I'm freezin' my nuts off here, officer. What am I s'posed to have done?'

Doreen came out from behind the Tahoe's door and kept the man covered while Steve quickly patted him for weapons, and then went through his pockets. All he found in his windbreaker was a Swiss Army penknife, a half-empty pack of Juicy Fruit chewing gum, a broken ballpen, two M&Ms wrappers and a ring-shaped metal clip that looked as if it had something to do with automobiles.

In the back pocket of the man's jeans he discovered a worn-out red-leather wallet. It contained a Connecticut driver's license in the name of William Kenneth Hain, 566 Pequabuck Road, Plainville, CT; an Exxon card with oily fingerprints on it; forty-seven dollars; a photograph of a round-faced girl with a mole on her cheek; and a green novelty condom that had been there so long that it had left a circular impression on the leather.

'You're William Kenneth Hain?'

'Yes, sir.'

'Put your left hand behind your back, William.'

Hain did as he was told and Steve handcuffed him. 'Now your right.'

'Can I get up now?'

'Sure, you can get up now.'

Steve helped him onto his feet. He pulled William Hain's stripy scarf down from his chin and shone his flashlight in his face. He had bright blue near-together eyes, and bushy blond eyebrows, and a hooked nose. He was clean-shaven but his cheeks had several cuts on them, and his skin was rough, as if he needed to buy some new razor-blades.

'What's this about, officer?' he asked, in his high-pitched voice.

'William Kenneth Hain, I'm arresting you on suspicion of the homicide of Mrs Ellen Mitchelson. You have the right to remain silent—'

'*Homicide?* What is this? You're suggestin' I *killed* somebody?'

'—but anything you do say can and will—'

'I didn't kill nobody. How am I s'posed to have killed them? You just been through my pockets . . . you think I killed somebody with that little bitty penknife? The big blade snapped off years ago.'

'Will you just shut up and let me finish telling you your rights.'

'But I'm innocent. I didn't do nothin'.'

'Tell me later, OK? Do you own a rifle?'

'No, sir. I used to have an airgun once but it got busted.'

'Do you own any kind of firearm? Handgun, maybe?'

'No, sir.'

'Is this your van?'

'Sure it is. Why?'

'You want to tell me where your documents are? Insurance, pink slip, all that stuff?'

'I lost them. I didn't get any replacements yet.'

'The truth is you stole this van from Middletown Auto Spares, didn't you? It was supposed to be dismantled but you took it home?'

'OK, I admit it. But they was only going to take it apart. That doesn't mean I killed nobody, does it?'

Steve said, 'Get in the vehicle. We're taking you in. Doreen, would you call headquarters and ask them to send out a crime scene unit to go over Mr Hain's van, and his property; and would you call Trooper MacCormack up at Canaan and tell him that we've picked up our suspect.'

'I have pets,' William Hain protested. 'I can't just leave my pets.'

'You mean that roomful of creepy-crawlies?'

'There's a red-striped hobo spider in there, and that's a real rare arachnid; and there's a dusky slug; and a swallowtail seahare, too.'

'Well, William, if you're telling the truth, and you didn't kill anybody, you'll be able to get back to them before you know it.'

'I didn't kill nobody, I swear to it.'

Steve escorted him over to the Tahoe and put him in the back seat. 'Now, you're not going to give me any trouble, are you?'

'You won't let my pets go hungry, will you? I know that some people don't care for them too much, but they got feelings, just like dogs and cats.'

'We'll take care of them, don't worry.'

'You'll even take them walkies, won't you, Steve?' said Doreen, as she climbed back behind the wheel. 'Come on, slug, come on boy! Fetch!'

'I think you missed out the bit about the lawyer,' said William Hain, helpfully, as they settled into their seats.

Back at headquarters in Litchfield, Steve left Doreen to book William Hain while he went upstairs to see what had happened to Alan.

He walked with squeaking shoes along the second-floor corridor, looking in one door after another, until he found Alan sitting in one of the interview rooms with Roger Prenderval. He opened the door and said, 'Hi. Sorry I took so long.'

'Steve,' said Roger, getting up from his chair. Steve had known Roger since they were rookies together. Roger was short and stocky with gray brushcut hair and he always wore a natty little bow-tie, but you always got the feeling that if he hit you, he would hit you very hard.

Steve said, 'Hi, Roger. Thanks for sticking around.'

'No problem. Least I could do. How did it go? Did you get your man?'

'We got him all right. I'm not so sure he's the guy we're really looking for, but we got him.'

Alan looked pale and spotty and his hair was all messed up. There were several buttons missing from his shirt and the shoulder of his red Adidas top was torn. He kept his eyes fixed on the wastebasket in the corner of the room, and his only acknowledgement that his father had just walked in was a loud, catarrhal sniff.

'Alan?' said Steve. Alan continued to ignore him. 'Are you OK, buddy? Do you want to tell me what happened?'

Alan said nothing, but sniffed again, and shuffled his feet. Steve turned to Roger and said, 'What's the situation here? Are the Kessners still pressing charges?'

Roger nodded. 'Mr Kessner says it was attempted rape.'

'And what do *you* say?' Steve asked Alan.

Alan shrugged.

'Come on, Alan, this girl must have invited you into her home. Were you dating her before?'

'Depends what you mean by dating.'

'I mean, were you going out together? Were you having sex?'

'Today was the first time.'

'OK, but she invited you into her home. Then what?'

Alan shrugged again. Steve said, 'I'm trying to help you here, Alan. But I can't help you if you don't tell me what happened.'

'I tried to get into her pants, all right? Satisfied?'

'OK . . . but was she willing or unwilling? Did she say no?'

'I don't know, I can't remember. What do you care?'

Steve pulled out a chair and sat down next to him. 'Have you been smoking dope?'

'Oh dear,' said Alan, turning his head and staring at him like Johnny Rotten. 'What if I have? Are you going to charge me with that, too?'

'Alan, for Christ's sake, this is serious. You could get five to fifteen years for this.'

'Dad . . . I was smoking puff and Kelly was smoking puff and we went upstairs to her bedroom and I told her that it was time that she and me got physically connected. You know, pole into hole. I was trying to do exactly that when her parents came home early. I tried to get out of there but Mr Kessner caught me in the kitchen with no pants on. I mean it was me that had no pants on, not him.' He sniffed again, and then he said, 'Satisfied?'

'No, I'm damn well not satisfied. What I have to know is, was Kelly a willing partner or did she at any time say no?'

'I don't remember, OK? She might have said no and then again she might not.'

'Alan—how the hell can I help you if you won't help yourself?'

Alan swiveled his head round again. 'Hasn't it occured to you that I don't *want* your help? In any case, you're not interested in *me*, you're only interested in *you*. You don't want to see it in the papers, that's all. "Decorated detective's son sent to slammer for pulling down turquoise see-through panties of unwilling daughter of pillar of the community."'

Steve took a steadying breath. 'Listen to me, Alan.'

'Why should I?'

'I said listen to me! You and me, we haven't been getting along too well for quite some time now. I'm not going to pretend that we have. But father and son butting heads, that's natural. It's all part of growing up. So let's try to be grown-up about this, shall we? You don't want to be convicted of a sexual offense, believe me. It'll stay on your record for the rest of your life.'

'And yours too,' Alan retorted.

'What are you talking about?'

'Don't you get it, you idiot? If they find me guilty, then everybody will know who's really to blame. *You*—because you're a crap father, and a hypocrite. You go around judging people like you're God, but what are you? Just a boring, plodding, uninspiring loser.'

Steve lifted his right hand but Alan pointed to the red bruise on his cheek and grinned at him. 'Don't have any answers, do you, Dad? If people upset you, all you can do is hit them. Very articulate, not.'

Steve glanced up at Roger and Roger pulled a face that meant 'leave it.' Steve stood up and pushed his chair back in. 'Just think about what I've said,' he told Alan. 'I'll be here for most of the night if you want to talk to me again.'

Alan shook his head as if that was the most desperately pathetic thing that anybody had ever said to him. Steve knew that Alan had got the measure of him, and what made him feel inadequate. He wondered if his own father had ever stood and looked at him and felt such anger and such helplessness.

Cataclysm Time

Feely was having a dream that he was back in the family apartment on 111th Street. It was utterly silent, and cold, and through the grimy windows he could see snow falling. He had the feeling that something was terribly wrong, but he wasn't sure what.

He walked out of the kitchen into the living room. There was nobody there. Bruno's three-legged chair was empty. The candles clustered around his mother's shrine had all burned down.

'Who's there?' he called, but his voice didn't even echo.

Suddenly, however, he heard a toilet flush. He looked around and Bruno appeared from the bathroom, carrying a newspaper, his beige suspenders hanging loose from his waistband. When Bruno turned around, his eye sockets were empty, and his face was a glistening mask of blood.

'Feely?' croaked Bruno.

Feely shouted out *'Aaaahhhh! Aaaaaahhhh! Aaaaahhhh!'*

'Jesus Christ,' said Robert. 'That was right in my ear.'

Feely sat up, panting. At first he couldn't think where he was, but then he looked around and saw the pink wallpaper and the little pink-upholstered armchair and the dressing table, and he realized that he was in the guest bedroom in Serenity's house. In bed. With Robert. There was no sign of Serenity.

Robert rolled onto his back, and looked up at the ceiling, and let out a groan. Then he lifted his left hand and stared at it. The fingertips had gone, and the BandAids were thickly crusted with black blood. 'God, this hurts. You don't even know.'

'I said you should have gone to the emergency room.'

Robert turned his hand this way and that. 'I couldn't, could I? They would have wanted to know who I was.'

'Sure. You have your anonymity but now you're doomed to be a cripple.'

'What are you talking about, cripple? I've lost the tips of my fingers, that's all.'

Feely looked down at him, and smiled.

'Something funny?' said Robert.

'No . . . I was thinking how one seminal event can change the way you look at your destiny, overnight.'

'What are you talking about?'

'Last night . . . the three of us together.'

'Well, I guess you could accurately say that was a seminal event.'

'But didn't it make you feel different?'

Robert frowned at him. 'I got to take some more painkillers. This is *throbbing*, you know?'

'I'll get you some, OK?'

Feely found his pants on the floor and went to the bathroom. He took a long pee, admiring himself in the mirror in the bathroom cabinet. He was sure that he looked different, slightly more handsome. He turned his face sideways, and lifted one eyebrow.

He returned to the bedroom with a glass of water and a foil strip of Tylenol tablets. From downstairs, he could smell coffee, and hear Serenity singing along to REM. '*Only to wake up . . . only to wake up . . .*'

'Take your time,' Robert grumbled.

'I'm sorry,' said Feely, sitting on the side of the bed. 'Here.'

Robert shook five tablets into the palm of his hand and clapped them into his mouth. 'God, this hurts. As if God hasn't punished me enough.'

'Serenity's making coffee.'

'Good. My mouth feels like the inside of a vacuum-cleaner bag.'

'Last night . . . that was amazing, wasn't it? It was . . . *revelatory*.'

Robert stared at him.

Feely said, 'I can't believe that we've become so close . . . I mean, when you picked me up on Route Six, you were a total stranger, right, and the snow was so thick that you might not even have seen me. But you *did* see me, and you stopped.

And last night . . . the three of us . . . it was revelatory.'

'If you say so,' said Robert, cautiously.

'Yes,' said Feely, and without warning kissed him on the cheek.

Robert immediately dragged up the corner of the quilt and wiped his face. But he could see by the beatific smile on Feely's face that he wasn't making a pass at him. Feely looked shiny-eyed and truly inspired.

'*Coffee!*' called Serenity, from the foot of the stairs.

'OK, sweetheart!' Robert shouted back. 'Just give us a minute!'

Feely stood up, but Robert said, 'Wait up for a second, Feely. There's something I want to talk to you about . . . something I need you to do.'

Feely hesitated, and then sat down again. 'Sure,' he said.

Robert cleared his throat. 'You remember we were talking yesterday about making your mark. Doing something cataclysmic.'

'Sure I do. *Ho-o-o-oly shit!*'

'That's right. Well, the thing is, I've started doing something cataclysmic already.'

'Yeah?'

'I've already started making my mark . . . showing those bastards that I'm not quite as crushable as they thought I was. Because they thought I was *crushed*, you know, when they took my kids away from me, and my house, and my job, and everything that made me the man I was. They thought, that's Robert Touche ground down for good.'

'That's right,' said Feely. 'But you're going to show them, aren't you? You're going to manifest your resilience.'

'Like I said, Feely, I started already! The day before yesterday.'

Feely blinked at him. There was something in the tone of Robert's voice that was starting to unsettle him, like somebody trying to laugh when they've had their legs torn off.

'That guy who was shot, at the gas station, down near Branchville.'

'Yeah?'

'That woman who was shot, at that yellow house, here in Canaan.'

155

'I don't understand,' said Feely.

'It was me,' said Robert. 'I shot them. Me.'

'You shot them? *You* shot them?' Feely was totally bewildered.

'That's right. I shot them.'

'But—' Feely looked desperately around the room, as if there was an explanation pinned to the wall somewhere. '*Why?*'

'I just told you why. I had to do something cataclysmic— something to show those bastards that I wasn't crushed. And I had to make them understand that their happiness can be smashed apart just as easily as mine was. It's no good them feeling smug, and safe, and superior. Fate can come and whack them just like it came and whacked me. Right out of the ether. *Whack*, for no apparent reason.'

'That's, ah—Robert, that's horrendous.'

'Of course it's horrendous! That's the whole freaking point! Don't you think it was horrendous, what happened to me? They didn't even have the humanity to put me out of my misery!'

'I don't know. You actually *shot* those people? I find that really, really hard to assimilate.'

'You'd better assimilate it, because I'm going to go on shooting people, one person per day, for every day they're making me suffer.'

'Really?'

Robert nodded.

Feely looked down at his fingers, silently counting. 'Seven people a week, Robert. That could add up to be an awful lot of people.'

'It could and it couldn't. It depends how long it takes them to recognize what they did to me, and show some genuine remorse.'

'I don't know, Robert, this is a shock.'

'It *is* a shock. It's supposed to be a shock. That's the holy shit factor.'

Feely looked at Robert. That round, tired face, and that gnomon nose. It was hard to imagine him deliberately shooting an innocent person. But he knew that even the gentlest person could be driven to extreme measures. Robert's happiness had been bulldozed, all around him, for making one misjudgment, and who had allowed that to happen? The same people who had allowed Bruno to beat his mother, and Jesus to die of an overdose, and Feely's brother and sister to spend the rest of their life in squalor.

Robert was right. Society couldn't tear a man's life to little pieces, not as comprehensively as that—and not expect him not to retaliate.

'So . . . you're going to shoot one person every day?'

'More than that. I'm going to shoot one *happy* person every day.'

'Man.'

Robert shifted on the mattress, and gritted his teeth because of the pain in his fingers. 'You don't approve? You don't think I'm right to seek revenge?'

'No, no. I think you have an overflow of justification. What they did to you: your wife, and her lawyers, nobody should do that to nobody. I mean they treated you like ordure. I was treated like ordure, so I can understand how you feel.'

'So you're not going to call the cops on me?'

Feely shook his head. For a split second, he thought about the three of them in bed last night, all joined together. 'What do you take me for? I never called the cops on nobody all of my natural existence.'

'So if I ask you to do something for me . . . you won't turn it down without at least thinking about it first?'

'Sure. Of course not.'

Robert held up his bandaged hand. 'I can't hold a rifle properly, until this heals. I was wondering if you could do it for me.'

'A rifle? Me? I don't know one end of a rifle from the other.'

'It's child's play. You hold it, you squint down the telescopic sight, you see your target in the crosshairs, and you squeeze the trigger.'

'I can't do that.'

'Of course you can. My grandmother could do it.'

'Then OK, maybe you should ask your grandmother.'

'I would, but unfortunately she's suffering from cremation. And besides, I'm asking *you* to do it. It's not like I'm asking you to kill anybody. I'm the one doing the killing. You're just holding the rifle for me.'

157

Feely felt a chilly ripple of dread; but exhilaration, too. Last night he had discovered the wonders of complicated sex. Today, he could find out what it was like to kill somebody. He had never expected his destiny to take him so far, and so fast.

'*Coffee!*' Serenity screamed. '*If you don't want it, I'll pour it down the sink!*'

'We're coming,' said Robert, so softly that only Feely could hear him. 'Don't worry, Serenity, we're coming.'

Trevor Puts His Foot Down

Sissy called Sam on the telephone a few minutes after 7:00 am.

'Sam? Sissy.'

'Morning, Sissy! Hope you slept good. I know I did. Three pages of Clive Cussler and I'm in dreamland.'

Sissy took out a cigarette, one-handed, and lit it. 'Sam, I read the cards again last night.'

'Oh, yes? I hope they told you that we're due for another blizzard.'

Sissy coughed. 'Something worse than that, Sam. Those three people—they're going to kill somebody else, and I think they're going to do it today. I have to go talk to the state police.'

'Phone them. Or send them an email.'

'I need to talk to them in person, Sam. They won't believe me, otherwise.'

'I'm sorry, Sissy. It's snowing, and I'm seventy-one years old.'

'But we might prevent an innocent person from being killed!'

'I don't think so, Sissy. I know you believe in what your cards have to say to you, but I don't.'

'Sam, the cards have given me a very clear and specific warning. Somebody in a vehicle is going to be killed, and the vehicle is going to carry on going, even though they're dead.'

'I'm sorry, Sissy. I really am.'

Sissy blew out smoke. 'No, you're not. You're all out of moxie, that's your trouble.'

'Sissy, don't you think that I feel useless, too?'

'What? What the hell are you talking about?'

When he spoke, Sissy could hear Sam's false teeth clicking.

'We're lonely, Sissy, you and me. Both of us lost the person we loved more than anybody else. Our children have all growed up, and we don't like to impose on them too much. So we sit alone, believing that we're no good to nobody.'

'*Sam*—I am not doing this because I feel sorry for myself, or because I feel redundant. I am doing this because I know that somebody is going to die. You can't deny that I heard voices yesterday! You can't deny that I was irresistibly drawn to go to Canaan, whether I wanted to go or not!'

'I never heard voices, Sissy; and the only place I felt irresistibly drawn to go was stone-nowhere.'

'Sam—'

'Sorry, Sissy. I'm staying inside today, close to the fire, and so should you.'

'You eunuch!' she snapped, but Sam had already put the phone down. She took a fierce drag at her cigarette and muttered, 'You *eunuch*.' But she knew that she didn't really mean it. If the situation had been reversed, and Sam had asked *her* to drive all the way to Canaan, in the snow, because of something that he felt in his water, she wouldn't have wanted to go, either.

She went into the kitchen to make herself a cup of tea. She felt hungry but she didn't really know what she felt like eating. A big fresh-cream cake, with a shortbread base, and heaps of strawberries on it, and strawberry syrup—that was what she really felt like. But all she had in the fridge was a slice of blueberry cheesecake that was three days past its sell-by date.

She was still waiting for the kettle to boil when there was a quick rap at the kitchen door. It opened almost immediately and Trevor came in, his shoulders and his balaclava sprinkled with very dry, granular snow.

'Trevor! I wasn't expecting to see you! Especially *this* early!'

Trevor shut the door. He took off his hat and his gloves and briskly chafed his hands together. 'I wasn't expecting to come here.'

'Look,' said Sissy, 'I'm so sorry that I didn't call you about going away to Florida, but I was so busy . . . I had to go up to Canaan to see about that poor woman who got shot.'

160

'I know,' said Trevor.

He took off his windbreaker and went through to the hall to hang it up. Sissy followed him to the doorway and said, 'What do you mean, you *know*? How do you know?'

'It's not very easy to explain.'

'All right.' Pause. 'But why don't you try me?'

Trevor cleared his throat. 'Last night I couldn't get to sleep.'

'You should try verbena. Verbena's very good for insomnia.'

'Momma, this wasn't insomnia. This was like—' Trevor hesitated, trying to find the exact word for it. 'This was like sleepwalking, only I wasn't asleep.'

'I don't understand.'

'I don't, either. I don't understand it at all. But I couldn't stop feeling this tremendous urge to get out of bed and get into my car and drive north.'

Sissy stared at him. She very much hoped that he wasn't telling her what she thought he was telling her. 'You've been working too hard, that's all. You wait till you get to Florida, you'll feel much better after a few days' rest.'

Trevor shook his head. 'What did you tell me? You said you could feel it in your bones. Well, that's exactly the way that I felt it. I felt I had to go to Canaan, to save more people from getting killed. And it wasn't like I had any choice in the matter. I was physically being *pulled*.'

'Really?'

'I kept tossing and turning and telling myself that it was ridiculous. I tried a sleeping pill, but that only made me hallucinate, on top of being awake. Jean woke up and asked me what was wrong, so in the end I told her.'

'And what did she say?'

'She said the same as you, that I was stressed. But I could *feel* it, Momma, I could feel it dragging me out of the house, and I can *still* feel it, just as strong.'

Sissy took hold of both of his hands. She looked into his eyes and for the first time she saw uncertainty, and magic.

'You may look exactly like your father, but inside you're just like me, aren't you?'

Trevor nodded. There were tears in his eyes, and Sissy suddenly realized how much this was affecting him.

'I didn't think—I never had any idea that I could feel this

161

way. It's like I'm needed, *urgently*. It's like I'm important to people that I don't even know.'

'Yes,' said Sissy. 'You are.'

'But how *can* I be? I just want to lead a normal life, you know, and take care of Jean and Jake, that's all.'

'Trevor—we're *all* important to people we don't know, but not many feel it as strongly as you and I do. It's like there's a whole pool of consciousness, which everybody's floating around in. For some reason, you and I can feel other people's love, and other people's distress, just as clearly as we can feel our own.'

Trevor sat down at the kitchen table. 'I don't know what to do about it. I can't just ignore it. But it's making me feel like an alcoholic who has to have another drink.'

Without a word, Sissy went through to the living room and came back with Le Cocher Sans Coeur. She laid the card on the table in front of him. 'I turned this up last night. A man being killed on a moving vehicle, which doesn't stop. With any luck, it hasn't happened yet, but I seriously think it will.'

Trevor wiped his tears away with his fingers. 'What are you going to do about it?'

'I think it's time to talk to the police. I didn't want to do it yesterday, in case they thought I was nothing but a silly old fool, but yesterday I think I found the people who shot that woman.'

'You *found* them? You're kidding me.'

'I don't have any proof . . . only the cards, and the same feeling that you have. They live in Canaan, on the north side, just across the railroad track.'

'Are you sure about this?'

'How can I be sure? I might be mad, for all I know, and the cards might all be nonsense. But if this prediction comes true, and I don't try to stop it, then I'll never forgive myself.'

'OK . . . let's call the police.'

Sissy said, 'No . . . I think we have to talk to them face-to-face. We have to show them this card, so that they can see it for themselves.'

Trevor looked up at her. 'Were you as old as me—you know—when you first had this feeling? Or did you always have it?'

'I guess I always had it, in a way. I can remember crying, when I was a small girl, because I knew that somebody was very sad, even though I didn't know who it was. And I could always sense when two people really loved each other, even when they were pretending not to. But—'

She took out another cigarette, and lit it, but Trevor didn't say anything, and did nothing to stop her.

'—I have to say that it wasn't until I met your father that I really began to develop any genuine talent for fortune-telling. It was your father who taught me not to be spoiled, and self-centered. He made me look at other people, and consider what *they* were feeling, instead of always thinking what was best for me.'

'I can't imagine you being self-centered.'

'Oh, believe it. I didn't give a hoot about anyone, so long as I was having a good time. I hurt a lot of people, along the way. But, well, most of them are dead now, and I don't suppose the others can even remember. That's one thing your father taught me: if you ever do anybody a bad turn, *they* might forget it, but *you* never will.'

Trevor stood up. 'Let's go, then. If this prediction is going to come true, then the sooner we tell the police, the better.'

'You'll drive me?'

'I told you, Momma. I *have* to.'

Sissy put on her mother's fur coat and her big furry hat and wound a long green angora scarf around her neck. Trevor helped her down the driveway to his Land Cruiser and then they set off down the steeply sloping road to Route 7. The morning was like a black-and-white photograph. The snow was fine and dry and it scuttled off the hood of the SUV in tiny pellets.

'Don't you think you ought to call Jean?' Sissy suggested.

'I'll call her later. She didn't really want me to come round to see you.'

'I see.' Sissy was silent for a while, until they reached the main road. Then she said, 'You're not nuts, you know, Trevor.'

Trevor looked at her and his face was very serious. 'I know, Momma. That's what I'm afraid of.'

Then he put his foot down and they headed north toward Canaan, on a highway so deserted that they felt as if they were the only people left in the world.

High Velocity

Feely was still in the bathroom when he heard the car horn tooting outside. He continued to sit there, frowning at the dog-eared copy of *The Book of Lists* that he had found on the windowsill, but then it tooted again, and he knew that it was Robert.

He fumbled to finish, and pulled up his pants. He made sure that he flushed the toilet. That was one of the things about Bruno that had always disgusted him: Bruno would always leave his turds for other people to discover.

'Feely!' called Serenity, from her bedroom. 'Touchy wants you!'

Feely hurried awkwardly downstairs, almost tripping on the cuffs of his borrowed chinos. He struggled into his shoes, and opened up the front door. Robert was standing in the driveway, next to his car, which had almost a foot of snow on the roof. The exhaust was smoking in the cold, so that Robert looked like a magician, surrounded by vapor.

'Where the hell were you?' Robert demanded. 'I'm doing my best to be unnoticeable here. A ghost, remember. Instead of that, I have to wake up the entire neighborhood.'

'You could have knocked on the door.'

'You think I'd ever touch that knocker? That knocker is bad luck. Or maybe you don't believe in bad luck.' He held up his heavily bandaged left hand. 'This is bad luck. I think it's turning septic, in which case I will probably wind up with blood poisoning and everybody will get what they want. To you, Feely, I leave my CD collection.'

'That's OK, I don't dig Bob Dylan too much.'

'That's because you were born at the wrong time. Not to mention the wrong place. That's the trouble with being a baby, you don't have any choice. You take your first look out of your mother's muff and even if you don't like what you see there's no turning back. Come here.'

He beckoned Feely round to the back of the car. With a sweep of his right elbow he cleared most of the snow off. Then he opened the trunk and said, 'There—what do you think of that?'

Inside, the trunk was lined with assorted cushions, some of them satin, some of them brocade, some of them plain chair-cushions filled with latex sponge. On one side of the trunk was a plaid traveling-blanket, carefully rolled up. Robert reached inside the trunk and unrolled it.

'There,' he said. 'What do you think of *this* baby?'

Lying on the blanket was a black rifle, with black telescopic sights and a matt black stock.

'You know how much this cost? Over ten thousand dollars. It's a Remington 700 Sniper Rifle, .308 caliber. Actually it belongs to a friend of mine who is not yet aware that he lent it to me. He's in Chile for nine months, on business.'

'I couldn't shoot that,' said Feely, brushing the snow from his eyes.

'Of course you can. It's a beauty. It takes five .308 rounds, in a flush internal magazine, and you load each round manually, using the bolt. It's very slow, but that's not the point. It has a bullet velocity of 2,650 feet per second and the great thing is that the .308 bullet retains a significant amount of energy after passing completely through the human body, so it keeps on going for several hundred yards after hitting its target which makes it much more difficult for crime scene investigators to find it. It also has a stop percentage of ninety-nine percent. You know what a stop is? A stop is when you hit somebody when they're trying to attack you, and they stop attacking you; or when you hit somebody when they're running away and they fall down after ten yards. That's the technical police definition of a stop.'

'I still couldn't shoot it.'

'No?'

'Categorically not.'

'Not just not, but categorically not?' Robert pulled a philo-sophical kind of face. 'Well, that's up to you. That's entirely up to you. *I* can't use it, even though I made myself the solemn promise that I would bring down one happy person every day seven days a week. With my hand all screwed up I couldn't hold it steady. But there you are. Different people have different values, don't they? I picked you up when I saw you thumbing for a ride in that blizzard because that's the kind of person I am. I feel that I was put on earth to help my fellow men. But if you don't want to help me, I can't argue with that. Like I say, it's entirely up to you.'

Feely said, 'Don't get me wrong, Robert. I really appreciated you picking me up. I can't tell you how much gratitude that filled me with. But you're asking me to foreshorten a person's life.'

'What are you talking about? You won't be doing anything. You're my *proxy*, that's all. You may be holding the actual physical rifle, but it's me who's doing the shooting. If a puppet hits you on the head, it's not the puppet's fault, is it? You don't punch the puppet, you punch the guy who's got his hand stuffed up the puppet's rear end.'

Feely looked dubious. He *felt* dubious. The snow fell on his black curly hair and on his eyelashes, and somehow he looked more Christlike than ever.

Robert said, 'The great thing is, nobody will see you doing it. This is the *pièce de resistance.*' There was a large *STP* sticker on the rear of the car, which he peeled back to reveal two circular holes drilled right through the metal.

'The back seats fold down, so that you can lie flat on your belly in the trunk. The muzzle protrudes about a half-inch through the lower hole and you can aim through the upper hole. You can take as long as you like to get a fix on your target, because nobody can see you, and when you've taken your shot, all you have to do is climb out of the trunk, push the back seat upright, and drive off, and nobody is any the wiser.'

'I don't know,' said Feely. All the same, he was very impressed by this mobile sniper's-nest. The idea of hitting back at the world which had treated you so badly, while comfortably lying on a pile of cushions, that appealed to him somehow.

Robert hung his left arm around Feely's shoulders. 'It's up to you, Feely. Like I say, different people have different values.

166

When I offered you that ride, I wasn't thinking to myself, what can this guy give me in return? It's like last night . . . I shared Serenity with you, didn't I? I actually shared her with you. But did I think, what's Feely going to do to repay me for being so generous? Of course not.'

'I'm sorry, Robert.'

'What's to be sorry for? She really goes, that Serenity, don't she? She really likes it. How do you say that in Cuban, she really likes it?'

'I don't know . . . *ella tiene furor uterino.*'

'Is that it? *Ella tiene furor uterino*? She has a furious uterus? That's terrific. That's amazing. So what are you going to do, Feely? Are you going to shoot this rifle for me or not?'

Feely looked at him and even though he didn't say anything Robert knew that he was going to do it. He winked, and gave him a giddyap click with his tongue, and then he slammed the trunk. 'Let's get some coffee with a slug of something in it, and then let's drive out someplace and find ourselves a happy person. How about that?'

Interview with the Suspect

Steve was staring out of the window in the interview room when they brought William Hain up from the cells. Snow was teeming into the parking lot, and the morning was so dark that it felt like the middle of the night.

William Hain was wearing a grubby green-and-white sweater with huge hexagonal patterns on it, and a worn-out pair of gray Levis. He hadn't shaved, and he smelled as if he hadn't washed for a while.

'Sit down,' said Steve.

William Hain sat down, and looked around the room, and coughed, and shuffled his feet.

'You're sure you don't want a lawyer present? It's your right.'

William Hain shook his head. 'What do I need a lawyer for? I took the van, that's all, and I already admitted to that. I didn't murder nobody.'

'Your van was seen opposite the Mitchelson house at the time that Ellen Mitchelson was shot dead. Directly opposite, parked in such a way that she was right in your line of fire.'

'I don't own no gun. You can't have a line of fire if you don't own no gun.'

'But you admit you were parked there.'

'I was only there for a couple of minutes. I needed a leak.'

'Can you remember what time that was?'

'I don't know. Eight fifteen or thereabouts.'

'So what did you do? You stopped, you relieved yourself, then what?'

'I drove down to Danbury. I was collecting some termites from Paulie's Aquarium.'

'Termites?'

'That's correct. Rick Bristow got me some supplementary reproductives from North Australia.'

'What the hell is a supplementary reproductive when it's at home?'

'If the king termite or the queen termite happens to die, they're like sitting in the dugout, waiting to take over.'

'I see. So what time did you get to Paulie's Aquarium?'

'Around, um, nine thirty I guess.'

'And this Rick Bristow . . . he can vouch that you were there?'

'Nope. The aquarium was closed. There was no notice or nothing in the window to say why. I hung around for a while and then I drove back home.'

'Did anybody see you outside Paulie's Aquarium?'

'I don't know. I just sat in the van hoping that Rick was going to show up, but when he didn't I drove back home. I stayed at home the rest of the day, finishing off my termite warren. Did you take a look at my termite warren, when you was looking around my house?'

Steve was doodling a laughing tree on the notepad in front of him. Loners and psychopaths, he hated them. They rarely had alibis, and they rarely had rational explanations for what they were doing. Yet he couldn't lock them up just because they liked spiders, or guns, or pornography, and nobody saw their comings and goings, and they smelled.

He was still trying to think of something else to ask William Hain when Jim Bangs knocked on the door and beckoned him outside. He went out into the corridor, leaving the door two or three inches ajar, so that he could keep his eye on William Hain's back.

'We finished checking over the van,' said Jim.

'Don't tell me. Nothing?'

'Nothing to indicate that a firearm was discharged inside it, or that a firearm was ever carried around in it.'

'Anything else suspicious?'

'Mice droppings, shredded-up newspaper, empty orange-juice cartons, two copies of *Jugs* and oceans of peanut shells.'

'*Jugs*? What's that? A pottery magazine?'

'There's no forensic evidence that William Hain is your shooter, Steve.'

Steve rubbed the back of his neck. 'It's beginning to look like our witness may have been mistaken, at least about the time-frame.'

'I'm sorry . . . but if there was only one single grain of gunpowder in that van, we would have found it.'

'Thanks, Jim.'

'What are you going to do? Let him go?'

'I guess I don't have very much choice. Besides, I wouldn't want his spiders to go hungry.'

Sissy's Warning

Doreen came into headquarters at 10:07, bringing a box of assorted donuts from the Litchfield Home Bakery.

'I'm trying to lose weight,' Steve told her, picking out a caramel-frosted donut with sprinkles.

'You should worry more.'

'You think I'm not worried? I've just had to release the only suspect we had for shooting Ellen Mitchelson, and Alan's still insisting that he's guilty of sexual assault.'

'You know he's not guilty. That boy couldn't sexually assault a fly.'

Steve pushed the rest of his donut into his mouth. 'Frankly, Doreen, I don't know what to do next.'

'Have one of those cinnamon ones. They're to die for.'

He was still clapping powdered sugar off his hands when Trooper Rudinstine came in. Trooper Rudinstine was tall, wide-shouldered, with scraped-back hair. Doreen always said that she really would have fancied her, if only she were a man.

'Sir? There's a woman downstairs who wants to see you. She says that she has some urgent information on the Mitchelson homicide.'

'Oh, really? Did you get her name?'

Trooper Rudinstine checked the piece of paper she was holding. 'Mrs Cecilia Sawyer.'

'OK . . . what are your impressions?'

'She's a senior, sir.'

'I see. And? You're trying very hard not to smile, Rudinstine. There's something else you're not telling me.'

'Nothing, sir. I guess you'd call her *individual*, that's all.'

Steve's head dropped forward onto his chest. 'Just what I need. An individual senior with urgent information on a random

171

homicide. They don't teach you about this at detective school, believe me.'

Trooper Rudinstine ushered Sissy and Trevor into Steve's office. She had been right about Sissy's appearance. Steve didn't know how many other sixtyish women were walking around Litchfield County in floor-length sable coats and hats that looked like upturned fire-buckets, but he guessed that they weren't exactly thick on the ground. He stood up and shook Sissy and Trevor by the hand and offered them a seat, while Doreen stood in the corner with her mouth full of donut, smirking at him.

Sissy opened her black crocodile purse and took out Le Cocher Sans Coeur. She laid it on Steve's desk, and said, 'There.'

'What's this?' said Steve, frowning at it but not picking it up.

'Le Cocher Sans Coeur. The Coachman Without a Heart. He comes from the DeVane deck of fortune-telling cards, first printed in France in 1763.'

'And this has exactly *what* to do with the Mitchelson homicide?'

'This has nothing to do with the Mitchelson homicide *per se*. This is warning you about the next homicide to be committed by the same person.'

'Oh, I see. The *next* homicide.' Behind Sissy's back, Doreen was almost choking.

Trevor leaned forward and said, 'My mother has a gift, Detective. To tell you the truth, I always used to think that it was hocus-pocus. But last night I felt it too, and how. My wife wasn't enthusiastic about me coming up here, she said I was suffering from displaced guilt because my mother doesn't want to come to Florida with us for a winter vacation. But the force was so strong that I couldn't resist it.'

'The force? As in, "May the force be with you"? That kind of force?'

'In a way, yes,' said Sissy. 'A collective unconscious, like Jung wrote about.'

'OK,' said Steve, cautiously. 'So what is the card warning me about?'

'It's quite explicit,' said Sissy. 'The DeVane cards always

172

are, if you know how to read them correctly. A man on a vehicle will be killed but the vehicle will keep on going, toward "Catastrophe."'

'And that's going to be the next homicide, by the same person who killed Ellen Mitchelson?'

Sissy nodded. 'I had to show you in person, because I don't think you would have believed me, otherwise.'

Doreen gave a suppressed snort and donut crumbs blew out of her nose. She had to leave the room, but even when she had closed the door behind her, Steve could hear her laughing in the corridor. He had to bite the inside of his cheek to stop himself from smiling—so hard that he could taste blood.

Steve said, 'I, ah—I think I can see what the card is telling me, but I'm not sure I understand where the force comes into it.'

Sissy made it obvious that she was trying her best to be patient. 'Detective Wintergreen, any strong emotion causes a ripple in the collective unconscious. Anger, especially, and love; and I am very sensitive to both.'

'So you felt—anger?'

'Exactly. Yesterday—after Ellen Mitchelson was killed—I felt an irresistible compulsion to drive up to Canaan. Somebody in Canaan is harboring such rage and frustration that they feel the need to shoot innocent people to get their revenge. It could be a man or a woman, but I have the feeling that it's probably a man.

'I saw Ellen Mitchelson's murder before it happened. This card, look, La Poupée Sans Tête. I've had several other warnings as well. I must beware a man locked in a chest. I must be careful of a trap.'

Steve looked at the cards and nodded and then he handed them back. 'Ms Sawyer, I know that you have the very best intentions, and that you're only trying to show how public-spirited you are, but you have to see this from my point of view.'

'Oh, I *do*,' said Sissy. 'Good heavens above, *I'd* be skeptical, if I were in your shoes. Here you sit, trying to solve a homicide using all the latest techniques and sophisticated police methods, and some batty old broad comes into your office with a dogeared deck of cards and tells you that she knows who did it, and what they're going to do next. I'm surprised you don't give me the bum's rush.'

Steve stared at Sissy, and Sissy stared back at him, and he saw something in her eyes that made him feel as if he had lost a minute of his life—as if the morning had subtly changed without him being aware of it.

'You know who did it?' he asked her.

'There are three people involved—two male and one female—but only one of them is the prime mover. See this card? Les Trois Araignées, the Three Spiders, two white and one black. I've seen them, and I'm sure that they're the right people. The force led me directly to the house where they live.

'See this card? I saw one of the men chopping wood, outside the house, and he accidentally chopped his fingers while the other one laughed at him. It was almost an exact re-enactment of what you see in the picture.'

'And this was yesterday, in Canaan?'

'That's right. They're living in a house on Orchard Street. I don't know what number it is, but it has an SUV outside, covered with a blue tarp.'

Trevor said, 'You can go check, if you don't believe her.'

Steve kept staring at her, turning his ballpen end-over-end. 'It's not really a question of not believing her, Mr Sawyer. It's a question of resources.'

Sissy smiled at him. 'It's nothing to do with resources. The real problem is, you can't think how to explain to your colleagues in Canaan that you've been given a hot tipoff by a fortune-teller. And suppose it turns out that the fortune-teller's wrong? They're still going to be jerking your chain about it at your retirement party, aren't they? They'll be calling you Gypsy Rose Wintergreen.'

'OK,' Steve admitted. 'But you can see my difficulty. I can't send troopers around to the house without reasonable cause.'

'I'll tell you what,' said Sissy. 'Let me tell your fortune. If it's one hundred percent accurate, you'll agree to send officers round to the house on Orchard Street. If it's wrong in any respect, Trevor and I won't say another word, and we'll go home.'

'I'm sorry, I can't do this.'

'What, you're frightened that I might be right?'

'No, Ms Sawyer, it's just that I'm very busy with this case and I can't justify spending any more time with you.'

Sissy shuffled the DeVane cards and held them out to him. 'Go on, tap them.'

'Ms Sawyer—'

'Tap them, what do you have to lose?'

Steve hesitated for a moment. He glanced toward the door to make sure that Doreen wasn't looking in, and then he reached over and gave the deck a sharp rap with his fingernails.

Sissy clasped the deck in both hands, and said, 'Pictures of the world to be . . . I beg you now to speak to me.'

Steve raised an eyebrow at Trevor, but Trevor simply shrugged, as if to say, this is my momma, you'll have to take her like she is.

Sissy immediately turned up a card showing a man in a dark tangly forest. He had reached a crossroads and there were at least a dozen direction signs, all pointing different ways. Each sign said 'La Sepulchre' but each sign had a different symbol on it. One, a fish. Another, a woman's hand. Yet another, a dagger. The card itself was titled L'Énigme de la Tuerie.

'This is your Ambience card,' said Sissy. 'This is you, trying to solve your homicide—"the Puzzle of the Killing." Each sign gives you a clue, but only one clue is the correct one. The trouble is, each sign points to the grave.'

She turned up another card, and another. One showed a man arguing with a young boy, L'Héritier Ingrat. Another showed two people beating with their fists at a man's front door while a young maiden with flowers in her hair was weeping next to a well. Les Parents en Colère, the Angry Parents.

The Predictor card showed a man pushing torn-off pieces of bread through the bars of a prison cell, although the convict inside the cell was making a show of ignoring him. La Nourriture Odieuse, the Hateful Food.

'There,' said Sissy.

Steve examined the cards closely. 'This is my future? I'm going to lose my job with the state police and wind up as a prison warder?'

'Of course not,' Sissy told him. 'The key to your future is this card, the Ungrateful Heir. This tells me that you and your son have been arguing, because you believe that he should show you respect, while he believes that you don't really love him. No matter what he does, he thinks that you're not interested in him, or that when you say you care about his feelings, you're only pretending.

'For some reason, he's upset the parents of a young girl. Here they are, beating at your door demanding justice. Maybe the parents are under the impression that he's taken advantage of her, or made her pregnant. But look at the girl, you can barely see it but there's a tiny frog jumping out of her mouth, which means she's lying.'

Steve leaned across his desk and picked up the Predictor card. 'So what does this mean?' he asked her, and he couldn't disguise the fact that his hand was shaking.

'It means your son will be punished, even if he was innocent. And no matter how much you try to give him material things to make up for the way that you've failed him, he will still despise you. He doesn't want *things*, he wants *you*. Look— the man has a key, dangling from his belt, and the key has a heart-shaped top to it. The man might be pushing bread through the bars, to say that he's sorry, but if only he realized it, he could unlock his son and let him out of prison in an instant.'

Sissy carefully took the card out of Steve's hands and pushed it back into the deck. 'This is what will happen to you, Detective Wintergreen, unless you make sure that it doesn't.'

Steve stood up, and went over to the window. It was still snowing outside, and he could see his reflection in the darkness, like a ghost. At last he turned around and said, 'I want to talk to some of my fellow officers about this. Maybe you could wait downstairs for me. Trooper Rudinstine will bring you some coffee, if you like.'

'Very well,' said Sissy. 'But don't leave it too long. The future always comes quicker than you expect.'

Dwarves and Pepper

Robert finished his scrambled eggs and took another bite of toast, and then another.

'Feely and me have to go out for a while.'

Serenity was lighting up her first joint of the day. She was still wearing only a large turquoise shirt and bright red ski-socks. Her hair was all messed up and there were dark maroon circles under her eyes.

'You're coming back?'

'Of course we're coming back. We have some business to take care of, that's all.'

Serenity was having trouble getting her joint to burn. 'What possible business could you and Feely have in Canaan?'

Robert looked across the table at Feely and gave him a collusive smile. 'We're very important persons, Feely and me. In fact you could say that we're cataclysmically important.'

'Apocalyptic,' said Feely.

'Whatever,' said Serenity. 'So long as you two don't run out on me without saying *hasta la vista*.'

'You think we'd do that? We'd never do that. Now—I'm just going to change these bandages. I think they're starting to stink.' Robert waved his left hand under Serenity's nose. 'What do you think? You think they're starting to stink?'

Robert went upstairs leaving Feely and Serenity sitting at the table together in front of the dirty egg-plates. Serenity smoked for a while, and then she said, 'I saw the drawings you did. The ones of me.'

Feely felt himself blushing. 'I'm sorry. They were only extemporaneous.'

She leaned forward, grinning, with smoke leaking out from between her teeth. 'I thought they were cool. I thought they were really amazing. Nobody ever did anything like that for me before. Nobody ever cared about me that much.'

'I can't believe that. I'm sure your parents care about you.'

'Are you shitting me? My parents never cared about anybody. They don't have any feelings. Like I told you before, they're empty. Pepperpots with no pepper in them. You can grind them all you like but you never get anything out of them.'

Feely said, 'That's very metaphorical.'

'Well, that's me. That's the way I am. Metaphorical. You know what T.S. Eliot said? *We had the experience but we missed the meaning.* My parents had me but they never understood what the hell I was.'

She paused, and then she said, '*You* know what I am, don't you, Feely, because you're the same as me. We're *generous*, that's us. We give our bodies and our souls to anybody who has need of them. If you don't share yourself with other people, you'll never grow. You'll be stunted, like a circus dwarf.'

Again she paused. Then she closed her eyes and said, 'Do you love me, Feely?'

He felt himself growing even hotter. 'Sure. You read my comic.'

'What about Touchy? Do you think that Touchy loves me?'

'I don't know. He's full of so much rancorousness, I think he finds it hard to focus on anything else.'

'So . . . what's this business that you and him are doing together?'

Feely shook his head. 'I can't tell you that, sorry.'

'Oh, I see! I'm allowed to have sex with you, but I'm not allowed to know what business you're doing?'

'It's Robert's business, really, not mine. I'm just doing him a favor because he's hurt his hand.'

'Go on.'

'I can't tell you, Serenity. He'll kill me, if I tell you.'

Serenity stood up and walked around the table. She sat on Feely's lap, hooked her arm around his neck and forcibly rubbed noses with him, so that it made his eyes water. 'We're *lovers*, Feely. You and me, we were joined together. Nobody can ever say that we weren't.'

'He'll kill me.'

'Don't be a wuss. He treats you like his own son. He treats you *better* than his own son.'

Feely looked over her shoulder toward the fireplace, where another huge log was slowly smoldering. He had never realized that life outside El Barrio could be so ambiguous. Maybe Serenity was part of the conspiracy, too. Maybe she was trying to trap him into denying Robert, as well as everybody else. He couldn't work out if she were angel or devil, or neither, or a little of both.

'Robert wants me to shoot somebody.'

'What?'

'He has a sniper rifle in the trunk of his car. He wants me to shoot somebody with it.'

'Who?'

'Nobody special. Anybody.'

Serenity stared into his eyes from only six inches away, so that he couldn't focus. Then she started laughing. She laughed so much that she fell off his lap onto the rug, with one leg caught beneath the coffee table.

'Can't breathe!' she gasped, her eyes filled with tears. 'Don't make me laugh any more!'

Feely didn't know what else to say. 'You won't tell him I said that?' he begged her. 'Please, you won't tell him I said that?'

At last Serenity sat up and wiped her eyes with her shirt-sleeves. 'I love you, Feely. You're amazing. I think you and I should get married. Can you imagine my parents' faces, if I introduced you as my fiancé? Mother . . . this is Feely. He's a walking dictionary, and he shoots people.'

Mad River

Robert drove out of Orchard Street with his tires snaking on the snowy road. Feely clung onto his seatbelt and said, 'Take it easy, Robert. We don't want anybody to notice us, do we?'

'You're right. We only want people to notice what we *do*.' Feely could tell that Robert had washed his teeth, because he smelled strongly of peppermint toothpaste, but it still wasn't strong enough to cover the whiskey.

'Where are we going?'

'South-east. The wind's blowing from the north-west, so we'll come out of the wind like avenging avengers.'

He took Route 44, toward Norfolk. There was hardly any traffic on the road, and they drove nearly all the way to East Canaan before they passed another car. Robert didn't talk very much. His fingers were probably throbbing, and his senses were dulled with Tylenol. Every now and then he muttered something under his breath, but Feely couldn't make out what he was saying. The only word he picked up was 'transparent.'

They passed slowly through the center of Norfolk the way that Robert wanted them to, like ghosts. The village green was blinded with snow; and the redbrick library looked like a building from a Victorian Christmas card.

'Ever had the feeling that you're dead already?' said Robert.

'I don't know what you mean.'

Robert grimaced at him, but didn't elaborate.

On the east side of town they passed the dim illuminated sign for the Big Bear Supermart, with hundreds of cars parked around it, hundreds of them, like a silent gathering of lemmings. Then they were out in the forests again, with snow-covered pine trees rising on either side of them in tiers.

Feely sang, 'We love the subs . . . 'cuz they are good to

180

us . . . the Quizno subs . . . they are tasty, they are warm because they toast them . . . they got a pepper bar!'

Robert said irritably, 'What's that?'

'It's a TV ad, that's all.' Feely was just about to start singing it again, but something stopped him. Robert looked unfocused, and perplexed, as if he couldn't quite remember what he was doing here.

'You OK?' Feely asked him.

Robert lifted up his bandaged left hand and pressed it against his chin, but said nothing.

They had almost reached the Mad River Reservoir when Robert spotted a side road with a sign saying 'Mad Falls, 2m'. He jammed his foot on the brake and the Chevrolet slewed sideways and ended up with its nearside front wheel right on the edge of the roadside drainage-ditch.

He backed up, with twin fountains of snow spraying high up in the air. 'Mad Falls, this is the place! If ever I saw a place that was crying out to have something cataclysmic done in it, Mad Falls is it!'

Feely said nothing. He had started to hope that Robert was feeling too tired and too drugged-up to think about shooting anybody. But Robert stamped on the gas and drove them up a sharp, icy incline, and Feely was thrown from side to side until his shoulder was bruised.

'Mad Falls, you couldn't invent it!'

'What if it's unpopulated?'

'We only need one! One happy person, per day!'

Feely was silent for a while. Then he said, 'What if they're not happy?'

'Stop splitting hairs, for Christ's sake! They must be happy, to live here. If you lived here and you weren't happy, you'd have strangled yourself years ago.'

They drove for over ten minutes, the Chevrolet jouncing and slithering and sliding on the ice. Every now and then they hit a bush, and snow exploded over the windshield. Feely was beginning to feel nauseous, and it didn't help that Robert had the heating turned up to maximum. At last, however, they topped a rise, and there below them lay a small green-painted farmhouse, with a barn, and a collection of outbuildings. Smoke was blowing out of the chimney, and the lights were on.

181

'Here we are,' said Robert. 'All you have to do is ask, and the Good Lord will give it to you, on a plate.'

He turned the car around, and then he steered it into the right-hand side of the track, so that it was half-hidden from the farmhouse by overhanging branches. Then he killed the engine and put on his wooly hat.

'What do we do now?' asked Feely.

'We wait.'

'How long for?'

'Jesus, Feely, we wait until an opportunity presents itself. That's what being a sniper is all about. Some snipers, they can wait for *days* until an opportunity presents itself.'

'OK. I get the picture.'

They sat and waited. Robert drummed his fingers on the steering wheel, and occasionally lifted his bandaged hand and turned it this way and that. Feely whistled the Quizno jingle between his teeth. 'We love the subs . . . 'cuz they are good to us . . .'

'Is that the only goddamned tune you know?' Robert demanded.

'No. I know *Amor De Loca Juventud.* "*Mueren ya las ilusiones del ayer . . . que saci con lujurioso amor . . .*"'

Robert looked as if he had just broken a tooth. 'Just shut up, OK. Silence is better. Silence is more professional. You don't get professional snipers singing TV jingles, OK?'

'OK,' said Feely.

Another half-hour went by. Feely said, 'I need a leak.'

'Can't you hold it? Professional snipers have to hold it.'

'No, I really have to go.'

'OK, then. But close the door quietly. And don't write your name in the snow.'

Speed the Plow

L izzie came into the kitchen to find her father sitting at the table, pulling on his boots.

'You're not going out?'

Thomas Carpenter looked up at her and nodded. 'Got to clear that driveway, Lizzie. We don't want to be snowed in for Christmas, do we?'

'Oh, come on, Dad, we won't get snowed in.'

'That's what your mother said, last Christmas, and we couldn't get out of the front door till the second week in January.'

'Well, at least wait until the snow eases off.'

'Forecast says it's going to go on snowing all day, and most of the night. If I don't do it now, it could be too late.'

Lizzie started to collect up the breakfast plates. 'Dad, you're like a big kid. You just can't wait to try out your new snow-plow, can you?'

'That's nothing to do with it. I don't want us marooned here, that's all, the way we were last year.'

Thomas Carpenter stood up, and zippered up his bright orange coat. He looked old for fifty-eight, with spiky gray hair and a bristly white beard, and deep creases around his eyes. He could have been Ernest Hemingway's twin brother, except that he was shorter, and squatter, and his nose was bigger.

Lizzie tugged up his hood for him, and laced it. 'I just don't want you getting bronchitis again.'

'I'll be fine. That's dry snow out there. Dry as a crow's bone.'

'Well, I'll have some hot tomato soup waiting for you when you come in.'

'You're an angel, Lizzie.'

He opened the kitchen door and went outside. Lizzie stood by the window watching him as he crossed the driveway toward the barn. He always looked lonely these days. Sometimes she would come into the living room and see him sitting by the stove with a book open on his lap, but she could see that he wasn't reading. His mind was back to last winter, when Lizzie's mother had still been here.

Lizzie finished clearing the kitchen table and stacked the plates and mugs into the dishwasher. She was a tall girl, with very long auburn hair tied in a ponytail. She had the bulbous blue eyes and the washed-out face of a pre-Raphaelite princess, as if she had spent her life moping in water-meadows or lying on ottomans suffering from pleurisy. In reality she wouldn't have known what a pre-Raphaelite princess was. She had been brought up on the farm with her father and her mother and her three brothers and she had left school when she was sixteen. Two-and-a-half years ago, she had married Ted, a widower fifteen years her senior who ran a machinery-hire business in Winsted. She never talked about Ted, or her wedding night, and she had never been back to Winsted since.

Thomas Carpenter opened the wide barn doors and there was his beloved yellow Club Cadet mini-tractor, covered with sacking. Along one side of the barn were shelves with every kind of fence paint or creosote or rust remover that you could think of; as well as scythe-blades and shears and complicated tractor attachments for sowing and edge-cutting and weeding.

His new yellow snowplow blades were already fitted. He had bought them this August from Ted, when he had gone to Winsted to talk about compensation for Lizzie's unconsummated marriage. Ted had insisted over and over that the marriage *had* been consummated 'even if Lizzie hadn't been one hundred percent *au fait* with what was supposed to fit where.' As a gesture of conciliation, however, he had offered Thomas the new rear-fitted Driveway Superplow at a seven percent discount.

Thomas had been secretly praying that it would snow hard enough for him to have to use it. If it hadn't, he would have felt that God was censuring him for betraying Lizzie's trust.

He threw off the sacking, climbed aboard the mini-tractor,

and started the engine. He waited for a few minutes while it warmed up, and then he eased it out of the barn and into the snow. Behind him, the plow blade scraped noisily along the concrete floor, and then made a sharp chuffing sound as it bit into the snow.

Thomas sat in the tractor saddle, twisted around sideways so that he could watch the blades clearing a path twenty feet wide behind him. Ted had been right. These new rear-fitted snowplows cleared the snow real effective, and because they were being pulled, instead of pushed, they were much less of a strain on the tractor's transmission.

He reached the roadway, and turned the tractor around in a wide circle. A flock of crows flapped up from the trees on the opposite side of the track, and circled around him, croaking in irritation. Crows, he hated their very souls. They had perched all along the razor-wire fence when Margaret was taken away to the nursing home, ten or eleven of them, enjoying his sorrow and preening their feathers like the tar-black devils they were.

Sitting sideways, of course, he presented a much wider target, and he was less than a third of the way back to the barn when a .308 bullet penetrated his back about three-and-a-half inches to the left of his spine, and blew a substantial part of his heart out. Blood sprayed across the freshly cleared driveway, as bright as Lizzie's tomato soup.

Thomas lurched sideways in the saddle, but he didn't fall off. The tractor continued to chug toward the barn, with the snowplow clanking behind it. It trundled right into the open doors, and only stopped when it hit the larger tractor that was parked at the very back. Its engine raced, and then it cut out.

Silence. But then the crows started to caw, as if they realized that they had finally gotten the better of him.

After a while the farmhouse door opened and Lizzie looked out. 'Dad?' she called. 'Dad, where are you?'

Feely Triumphant

Feely turned around to Robert and his eyes were wide with excitement.

'Did you see that, man? Did you see that?'

Robert had been kneeling behind him, watching through the Chevrolet's rear window. 'Great shot, Feely. Truly great shot.'

Feely pummeled his fists on the floor-cushions. 'He kept on going, man, even when he was dead! He kept on going! I mean unbelievable! "Got to finish clearing this snow, folks, even with this giant-sized hole in me!"'

'You got him, Feely, no doubt about it. There's one less happy man in the state of Connecticut this morning, and it's all down to you.'

Feely struggled out of the trunk-space. 'What an exponential experience, man! Did you see the way he kept on going! He drove right into that barn!'

Robert opened the door. 'Time for us to be going, too.'

'He just drove right into that barn . . . *put-put-put*, like nothing had happened! And the guy was *dead*!'

'Come on, Feely. We need to put the seats back and get the hell out of here.'

Feely climbed out of the car. 'Are you OK, man? Didn't you think that was funny?'

'Hilarious. Now give me a hand with this seat.'

They lifted the rear seats and forced them back into position. Feely said, 'You're not upset, are you, because you didn't do it?'

'Why should I be upset?'

Feely pulled on his flap-eared cap. 'It's just that I never understood what a blast it was. Like, expunging a person. You can't describe a blast like that in words. There's nothing in the dictionary that gets you even halfway prepared for it. Not the thesaurus, neither.'

He was panting, and flapping his arms up and down like a penguin. 'Father Arcimboldo . . . all that stuff he told me about words. "A drop of ink makes a million think." Well, granted, that's conceivably true, but the difference is you don't personally see it when somebody reads what you've written, do you? Like it might give them a cardiac arrest or something, but you're not there to experience it, are you? But *this*, man . . . wow!'

'Get in the car,' said Robert.

'I mean you tried to explain it to me, didn't you, but—'

'Feely,' Robert repeated, and this time he pointed a finger at him like a pistol, with his thumb cocked. 'Get in the car.'

Feely walked around the front of the Chevrolet and climbed in.

'You're upset,' he said, as Robert started the engine.

'Do I *look* upset?'

'Yes.'

'Maybe I'm beginning to realize that you were right and I was wrong.'

'I don't get it.'

It was snowing so thickly now that Robert could hardly see where he was going. 'It doesn't matter,' he told Feely. 'It's too late now, anyhow. Especially for that poor bastard, whoever he was.'

'You think he was happy?' asked Feely. 'Wooo! I bet he was happy. He was so happy that he didn't want to stop going, even when he was dead!'

Trevor Confesses

The clock in the reception area was creeping up to quarter of twelve, and still Detective Wintergreen hadn't come down to see them. Outside, the day had grown so gloomy that the sky was almost dark green, and the snow was falling so densely that Sissy could hardly see to the other side of the parking lot. Inside, the light was bright and flat, and the entrance hall smelled of Johnson's floor-wax and warm computers.

Trevor flicked through a copy of *Connecticut Realty* magazine and then reread it, more attentively. 'Look at the price of this saltbox. Seven hundred and fifty thousand and change. That's . . . legalized robbery!'

He kept glancing up at the clock and then checking it against his watch. After twenty-five minutes, he said, 'How much longer do you think he's going to keep us waiting?'

'It doesn't really matter,' said Sissy. 'So long as he believes us.'

'That card reading you did for him—what was that all about? That wasn't exactly guaranteed to get him on our side, was it?'

'I said it as I read it. If it was true, then he'll know that we're serious.'

Trevor checked his watch again. 'Jean's going to be wondering what's happened to me.'

'Then call her.'

'No, it's OK. It's just that we're supposed to be meeting Freddie and Susan at two. They're buying a new leather couch and they want some objective input.'

Sissy sat back in her chair and stared at him with creased-up eyes. 'You've been lying to me, haven't you?' she said.

'Lying to you? Of course not! Why should I lie to you? What about?'

'Oh, come on, Trevor! I may be batty but I'm not stupid! Look at the way you keep twitching and shuffling and looking at the clock! You didn't feel anything pulling you last night, did you, and you don't feel it now! If you did, you wouldn't be able to think about anything else, except where you're being pulled to! This is life and death, Trevor! This is destiny! "Freddie and Susan are buying a new leather couch and they want some objective input." Give me a break!'

Trevor tossed the magazine onto the table. 'All right, Momma, I admit it. I didn't feel anything. I wasn't pulled.'

'So why did you tell me that you were? What was the point?'

'Your friend Sam phoned me last night. He said he'd spent the whole afternoon with you, up in Canaan, and that you had some hare-brain idea that you'd tracked down some murderers. He said he was worried about you, and that maybe I could help.'

'Oh, well, so much for friends.'

'He *is* your friend, Momma! He really cares about you! I told him we'd invited you to come down to Florida, but that you'd dug your heels in. So he suggested that I went along with this pulling thing, and humor you, so that you'd get it out of your system.'

Sissy suddenly felt very weary, as if she were three hundred years old.

'So,' she said, 'you were *humoring* me.' She opened up her purse and took out her cigarettes. The trooper behind the reception desk immediately lifted his head, like a sniffer dog. He didn't say anything but the expression on his face was enough. She dropped the cigarettes back in her purse, and made a loud click closing the clasp.

Trevor said, 'I'm sorry, Momma, but we were all trying to do what was best.'

'You think that's best, making a mockery of me?'

'Momma . . . we believe that you believe in all of this fortune-telling stuff.'

'I see. But you don't believe it yourselves? You think that my brains are turning into soft-scrambled eggs.'

'We think you need looking after, that's all. You should be relaxing in the sun, not chasing around Connecticut in the middle of a snowstorm, looking for imaginary murderers.'

'Do you know something, Trevor?' said Sissy. 'The only time I'm going to let you look after me is when I die. When that happens, you can tuck me up in my casket, and tell me a bedtime story, and put a lily in my hands. But just remember that I'm your mother, and until that day comes, *I* do the looking after. OK?'

Trevor lowered his head. But just as he did so, the elevator doors opened on the other side of the reception area, and Steve Wintergreen appeared, with Doreen and two troopers. Steve was zipping up his black windbreaker and it was obvious that he was in a hurry.

'Ms Sawyer?' he said. 'I'm sorry that I kept you waiting so long.'

'What is it? What's wrong?'

'We've just had a 911 call from a small place near Winsted. A man's been shot dead, apparently by a sniper.'

'That's terrible.'

'He was shot through the heart, Ms Sawyer. He was shot through the heart while riding a tractor and after he was shot the tractor kept on going.'

'Oh my God. Le Cocher Sans Coeur.'

Steve hunkered down beside her chair. He kept his voice low, so that the others couldn't hear him. 'I don't know if your card really predicted this shooting, Ms Sawyer. More than likely, it's a coincidence. Or maybe you hired a shooter to do it, to prove how good you are at foreseeing the future.'

'Oh, for goodness' sake!' Sissy protested. 'Do I look like the kind of person who goes around hiring hit-persons?'

'Don't ask me, Ms Sawyer. I've seen serial killers who look like altar boys. But you read my cards earlier, and I have to admit that you were uncomfortably close to the truth.'

'So *you* believe in me,' said Sissy, turning toward Trevor. 'Even if there are some who don't?'

'It doesn't matter if I believe you or not, but I can't sensibly afford to ignore what you told me. So right now I'm going to ask you this: do you still have this "pulling" feeling? Do you still think that somehow you're being drawn toward these people?' He paused, and then he said, 'What I want to know is, do you think you can locate them for me?'

Sissy hesitated for a moment and then she nodded. She knew she could. She could feel them in her blood, and her muscles, and her bones. She could almost smell them.

'North,' she said. 'Almost due north. And not too far away, either.'

'We're going to Winsted now,' said Steve. 'Do you mind coming along with us?'

'Yes, I'll come. As a matter of fact, I don't think I have much choice.'

'Momma, you can't do this,' said Trevor. 'Look, Detective, I'm really sorry about this, but my mother is an elderly person, not a state trooper, and you can't expect her to help you hunt down dangerous criminals.'

'Trevor,' Sissy interrupted him, 'remember what I said. Now—don't you have an appointment with a new leather couch?'

Showdown At Big Bear

Robert drove north-west, back toward Norfolk, right into the face of the blizzard. He hardly spoke, but he took repeated pulls from the Jim Beam bottle that he had borrowed from Serenity's father's cocktail trolley.

Feely on the other hand couldn't stop jabbering. He felt as if he had suddenly come alive. The meaning of his existence had become sparkling clear, and he could even see colors brighter. The snow-covered fir trees on either side of Route 44 looked like glittering choirs of angels, and he felt that they were singing for him.

'Father Arcimboldo, he wasn't trying to deceive me. He was trying to *protect* me, is all. He didn't want me to get involved with any kind of bellicosity because he knew I wasn't mature enough to comprehend its implications. But now I comprehend. Now I really, really comprehend.'

They were less than eight miles shy of Norfolk when Robert leaned forward and squinted hard through the windshield ahead of them.

'What is it?' asked Feely.

'Police. And it looks like they've set up a roadblock.'

Feely looked, and Robert was right. About a mile up ahead of them, red and blue lights were flickering through the snow.

'Maybe they're not looking for us.'

'Sure,' said Robert. 'And maybe the sun's shining.'

'They won't suspect that we did it, will they? How will they know?'

'They'll stop the car and they'll take one look at a drunk white male with his hand wrapped up in bloody bandages and a Cuban kid in a stupid hat who won't shut up, and what do you think they'll do?'

'OK,' said Feely. He could see the logic in that. 'So what do we do now?'

Robert thought for a while, and then said, 'We hide.'

'We hide? Where? There's noplace to go.'

'Oh yes there is.' Robert pointed to the huge illuminated brown bear that was grinning on top of the Big Bear Supermart. 'All we have to do is park in the parking lot, and how are they going to find us then? There must be six hundred cars in there.'

They reached the entrance to the Big Bear Supermart and Robert turned into it. The parking lot surrounded the super-market building on three sides, its bays radiating like the spokes of a wheel. They drove slowly up and down the salt-gritted asphalt, looking for a free space, their windshield wipers flapping wildly from side to side.

'What if we can't find anyplace to park?' said Feely. He was beginning to feel panicky now. Maybe this was how the conspiracy worked. Maybe they made you feel dazzled, as if you had discovered the answer to everything that had ever gone wrong in your life, but all the time you were walking blindly into a trap. He twisted around in his seat and he could see that the red and blue police lights were flashing right across the highway, and that they were stopping everybody—cars, SUVs, and trucks.

'Here we go,' said Robert.

A huge Toyota full of fat, pale-faced people backed out of a space in front of them. Robert waited while the driver wres-tled to straighten his vehicle up.

'Look at them,' he said, taking another swig from his bottle. 'The lardasses shall inherit the earth.'

He pulled into the space and switched off the Chevrolet's engine. 'OK, Feely. Now we get into the trunk and we stay there until the heat's off. You don't need another leak, do you?'

'I can hold it.'

'Very good. Very professional.'

They opened the rear doors and pulled down the back seats. Then they climbed into the trunk space, hunching up their knees so that Robert could pull the seats back up behind them.

He switched on a small green plastic flashlight, and shone it into Feely's face.

'Pretty cozy in here, huh?'

'Yeah,' said Feely, although he was feeling claustrophobic already.

'We have water, we have Gatorade, we have chocolate chip cookies. We can hold out for as long as we need to.'

'What if they search every car?'

'Relax. How are they going to do that? Six hundred cars and everybody coming and going like ants. And it won't occur to them that we pulled in here, will it? They'll be thinking that we wanted to put the maximum distance between us and Mad Falls, won't they? They're transparent. I can see the way their minds work. Everything's transparent.'

By the time Steve reached the roadblock, the traffic was backing up three or four miles, and he had to drive in the middle of the road with his lights flashing and occasional yips of his siren.

'Do you still feel them?' Steve asked Sissy, who was sitting in the front passenger seat next to him.

'Oh, yes,' Sissy told him. 'They're very, very close.'

Doreen, in the back, said, 'Who needs bloodhounds?'

Sissy turned around and smiled at her. 'I really don't blame you for being skeptical, my dear. I find it very difficult to believe it myself. But it's far too strong a feeling for me to ignore. It's like wanting a cigarette, to the nth power.'

'I don't smoke,' said Doreen.

'You eat chocolate, don't you?'

Doreen didn't answer that. Instead, she leaned forward to Steve and said, 'What if they're not here?'

'Then we'll have to look someplace else, won't we?'

'I'm glad I don't have to explain this to Lieutenant-colonel Lynch.'

They reached the roadblock and Steve pulled the Tahoe into the side of the road. A trooper with a heavy gray mustache came forward and peered inside. 'Morning, folks. Nice day for a manhunt.'

'How's it going, Trooper?'

'Not much so far. Couple of kids with no insurance. A woman with a coat on and nothing else.'

Sissy looked across the highway toward the huge brown bear. The pull was even stronger now. It made her heart beat slower, and much more heavily, so that she could hear her blood throbbing through her inner ears, *squelch-squelch-squelch*, like two people walking in the snow.

'Detective Wintergreen, they're here.'

Steve said, '*Here?*'

'That's right. Somewhere in that supermarket.'

The trooper looked at Steve and raised one eyebrow. Steve said, 'I'm just going to take a look. I may need some backup, OK?'

'You're going to look *here?*'

'That's right. I'll give you a squawk if I need you.'

'You're the boss.'

They drove into the parking lot. Sissy hadn't felt like this since she took a ride on the centrifuge at the Danbury Fair, when she was fifteen years old. She could hardly breathe, and she felt as if she were pinned in her seat.

'Are you OK, Ms Sawyer?' Steve asked her.

Sissy nodded. 'They're here, I'm sure of it. Somewhere in this parking lot. Left, go left at the end here.'

Feely said, 'What time is it?'

Robert switched on his flashlight and checked his watch. 'Twelve noon, in a couple of minutes.'

'I just wanted to tell you how gratified I am that you picked me up. I mean, everything we've done together.'

Robert turned himself over, with a grunt. 'Well . . . I can't say it hasn't been instructive.'

'Are you going to go on shooting people?'

'I don't know, Feely. Sometimes things change, even when you're not expecting them to, and all of a sudden the things you used to believe in don't matter any more.'

'Robert?'

There was a very long silence. Robert switched the flashlight on again, and then off, and then—when Feely still hadn't said anything—he switched it back on.

'What is it, Feely?'

'I don't know how to say this without you misunderstanding me.'

'Well, why don't you say it anyhow? There isn't much room for misunderstanding, is there, not in here?'

'What I wanted to say was, I love you, man.'

Robert stared at him, puckering his mouth up and moving it around the way people do when they're seriously thinking about something. Then he said, 'I love you too, Feely. You *zurramato*.'

Sissy whipped up her right hand.

'*Stop!*' she said.

Steve abruptly stopped, and the SUV that was following too close behind almost rear-ended them.

Sissy squeezed her eyes tight shut.

'What is it?' said Doreen, impatiently.

'They're very close. I felt something—I felt—'

She slowly turned her head and looked at Steve in bewilderment. 'Good God,' she told him. 'I felt *love*.'

They drove at a snail's pace along Row 20G. Sissy kept her window wide open, even though the snow was blowing in her face.

'They're very close now. They're very, very close.'

Their headlights illuminated a dirty, dark-bronze Chevrolet Caprice Classic, late eighties model. Sissy touched the back of Steve's hand, and nodded at it.

'You're sure?'

'I can feel love through a cinderblock wall, Detective.'

'OK, then. Let's take a look.'

Steve drove past the Chevrolet and parked the Tahoe fifty yards further down. He said to Sissy, 'Stay right here, please, Ms Sawyer. Doreen and me will go check this out.'

Steve and Doreen took out their flashlights and unholstered their guns and walked back to the Chevrolet. Sissy could see their flashlight beams criss-crossing as they looked inside.

'Someone's looking in the car,' Feely whispered.

'Sssh,' said Robert, in the darkness. But Feely felt him

picking up the rifle, and then he heard him operate the bolt. Very slowly, very carefully, Robert chambered another round.

Steve stepped back from the Chevrolet. 'Connecticut license plate. Let's run it through traffic and see what we come up with.'

It was then that Doreen touched his sleeve, and pointed to the rear of the car, next to the offside tail-light. There were two circular holes drilled in it, one above the another, and vapor was blowing out of them. Doreen blew vapor from her own mouth, and pointed back at the car so that Steve would get the point. *Breath. They're hiding in the trunk.*

Steve pulled back the slide of his automatic and stepped right up to the side of the car. Then he slammed his hand on top of the trunk and shouted, 'State police! Come on out of there with your hands where we can see them!'

Immediately, there was a sharp crack, and Doreen was flung up into the air and over the hood of a Malibu parked opposite. Steve fired into the side of the Chevrolet's trunk, four rapid shots, and then he ducked down and crab-scuttled over to Doreen. She was lying on her side with her cheek in the snow, and there was blood running out of her mouth.

'Stomach,' she whispered.

Steve unhooked his r/t and said, 'Officer down! Big Bear parking lot, Row G! I need an ambulance and I need backup! Now!'

He kept his gun pointed at the Chevrolet, while at the same time cradling Doreen's head with his hand. 'You're going to be all right, OK? Just stay awake, and keep talking.'

Doreen nodded. 'You don't get rid of me that easy.' Then she coughed, and more blood poured out onto the snow. 'Tell that psychic . . . tell her she's really psychic.'

'Robert?' said Feely. The trunk was filled with the stench of cordite and gasoline, and his eyes were watering. 'Robert, can you hear me?'

He shook Robert's shoulder but Robert was heavy and floppy and unresponsive. 'Robert! Come on, man, I don't know what to do!'

He shook him and he shook him but still Robert didn't

answer. Feely lay there, coughing, lit only by the pencil-shafts of light that came from the bullet-holes, and the holes that Robert had drilled for his sniper rifle.

What would Captain Lingo do? Captain Lingo could talk his way out of anything. Captain Lingo would climb out of the car with his hands up and say, 'You've saved my life, officers, and I thank you. I was being forcibly abducted by this homicidal maniac and only your instantaneous responses spared me from a grisly demise.'

He had used the phrase 'grisly demise' in his comic strip, but he had never had the chance to say it in real life.

'Grisly demise,' he whispered. Then he pushed against the rear seats with his feet.

At that instant, the Chevrolet's gas tank blew up. The two-ton car was thrown up into the air, blazing, and a huge orange fireball rolled up into the snow. It dropped down again, with a thunderous crash, and it lay there burning while police officers and shoppers gathered around and watched it.

Steve, shielding his face with his upraised hand, said, '*Holy shit.*'

Steve stayed with Doreen until the paramedics arrived. Then he walked back to the Tahoe where Sissy was sitting, her hands clasped together as if she were praying.

'How is she?' Sissy asked him.

'Pretty badly hurt, but the paramedics think she's going to survive.'

'I'm so sorry, Detective. I really am.'

'No, no. If it was anybody's fault, it was mine. They had a weapon rigged up in the back of the car, so that they could shoot without opening the trunk. I should have been more careful.'

He took off his hat and wiped the snow away from his eyebrows with the back of his hand. 'I'll organize someone to take you home. Maybe I can call on you tomorrow, so that I can work out what we're going to say about this.'

'I'd rather you said nothing at all—at least as far as I'm concerned.'

'Well, we'll see,' said Steve. He looked at her for a while with the orange light from the burning Chevrolet dancing on the side of his face. Then he said, 'You felt *love*?'

Sissy nodded. 'People can hide hatred, you know, quite easily; and they can hide contempt. But it doesn't matter how hard they try, they can never hide love.'

The Snow Stops

The next morning, the snow stopped. Sissy went into the yard and stood listening to the silence. Mr Boots came out, too, and stood unusually close to her, his tongue hanging out, panting.

'What are we going to do, Mr Boots?' she asked him.

She was still standing there when she heard a vehicle outside, and then Steve appeared, wearing sunglasses with yellow lenses.

'How are you doing, Ms Sawyer?'

'Oh, I'm fine, Detective, thank you. How's your partner?'

'She's in pretty bad shape, I'm afraid. But she had surgery last night, and they're confident that she's going to pull through.'

'I never caught her name, poor woman.'

'Doreen. Doreen Rycerska. She always had a sharp tongue on her, but she's a good detective.'

'I'll send her some flowers. Would you like a cup of tea? I have some cherry cake, too. I didn't bake it myself. I can't bake cakes to save my life.'

They went inside, while Mr Boots stayed in the yard to roll around in the snow.

Steve saw the DeVane cards on Sissy's coffee table and picked them up. 'That was some reading you gave me.'

Sissy was setting out the tea-tray. 'Yes,' she said. 'They're unnervingly accurate, those cards. Sometimes I wonder if I ought to throw them away.'

'What you said about my son—'

'You don't have to tell me if you don't want to.'

'All I was going to say was, it was true. He was arrested for sexual assault, and when I talked to him about it, he said that he wanted to be found guilty, to get his revenge on me. Well—as you can imagine—that hurt.'

Sissy poured boiling water into the teapot and stirred it. Then she brought in the tray and set it down on the coffee table, next to the cards.

Steve said, 'Late last night, the girl he was supposed to have assaulted withdrew her complaint. Apparently she was terrified of what her parents were going to say, finding Alan creeping out of their house with no pants on.'

'Kids,' said Sissy.

'Yes,' said Steve. 'They let you down, they lie to you, they look you in the face and tell you that they hate you, but what can you do?'

The clock struck eleven, hesitant as usual, as if it didn't like to upset anybody by telling them that time was going by. Sissy said, 'Have you found out who they were, those two killers? I saw it on the news but they didn't say.'

'The older one came from New Milford. His name was Robert Touche and he was recently divorced. The other was a Cuban boy named Fidelio Valdes. He came from New York City. We've been talking to the girl they stayed with, in Canaan, but she doesn't know too much about them.

'How the two of them got together, and why they went around shooting people, we don't have any idea.'

'The cards warned me they were coming,' said Sissy. 'Two storms, both at once.'

'Maybe we ought to give you your own fortune-telling department, up at headquarters.'

Sissy passed him a slice of cherry cake. 'They warned me about a man in a chest, too. That's about as close as they could have come to a man in the trunk of a car. They told me about footprints, leading to a lake. That was the two of them, I suppose, making their way to the Mad River Reservoir. They told me about a bird, caught in a trap, but I still can't work out what that meant.'

Steve stayed for over an hour. He enjoyed talking to Sissy because she was so uncompromising, but he found her reassuring, too, as if she knew that he wasn't infallible, but forgave him for it. He was tempted to ask her for another card reading, but in the end he didn't have the nerve. Besides, her last reading had given him more than enough to think about.

201

Sissy stood by the side of the house watching him leave, and waved. As she turned back toward the house, she thought she glimpsed Gerry, going into the back door.

It made her feel heavy-hearted, leaving him alone here for Christmas, but she would write him a Christmas card, telling him how much she loved him, and that she would soon be coming back.